ADVANCE PRAISE

"Ramiza Shamoun Koya's *The Royal Abduls* is filled with wonderfully flawed, yet deeply sympathetic characters who occupy utterly convincing and beautifully drawn narrative and emotional situations. Is independence freedom or isolation? How can we balance our own needs with those of our loved ones? How can we both protect ourselves and connect with others? Koya's novel reminds us that the answers to these questions are, of course, both deeply personal and deeply political, and in answering them, Koya performs the marvelous alchemy of dropping us into a story world that dismantles and then reassembles our sense of who we are."

—Karen Shepard, author of *The Celestials*

"*The Royal Abduls* is a novel for our times. It is a novel of struggle and a reminder of the hope that we once felt and that, hopefully, we will feel again soon."

—Carol Zoref, author of *Barren Island*

"After reading Ramiza Shamoun Koya's warm and wise debut novel, you will not soon forget the Abdul family, especially the tenderness between Amina and her young nephew, Omar, as both struggle to find happiness amid family turmoil and hostility towards Muslims in post-9/11 America. Koya imbues each page of *The Royal Abduls* with lessons of the heart and what it means to save yourself while protecting the ones you love."

—Mo Daviau, author of *Ever* ?

"Koya has crafted a tender-hearted She's cut to the heart of the devastat white supremacy on multi-genera families."

—Jenny Forrester, author of *Narrow River, Wide Sky*

THE ROYAL ABDULS

RAMIZA SHAMOUN KOYA

FOREST AVENUE PRESS
PORTLAND, OREGON

THE ROYAL ABDULS

The author wishes to thank MacDowell Colony and the Blue Mountain Center for the space and time to work.

Library of Congress Control Number: 2020930040

ISBN: 9781942436416

Distributed by Publishers Group West

Published in the United States of America
by Forest Avenue Press LLC
Portland, Oregon

Printed in the United States

1 2 3 4 5 6 7 8 9

Forest Avenue Press LLC
P.O. Box 80134
Portland, OR 97280
forestavenuepress.com

In memory of my father,
AbuBakr Sadiq Koya,
and
for my daughter, O,
the light of my life

I. THE ROYAL ABDULS

1.

AMINA ABDUL'S NEPHEW HAD begun to speak with an
Indian accent. She'd learned this when she went to dinner at
her brother and sister-in-law's row house in Georgetown, a few
weeks after she and her belongings had arrived from across the
country. Though it was fall, the day was hazy and hot. Amina
was unused to the humidity; she felt swollen, pregnant with
moisture.

She drove to their house while pushing her hair up off her
neck with one hand and steering with the other. Since arriving
she had cut her hair—previously worn in a long braid of indifference—into a sharp bob. She was also trying to sever her
smoking habit, which was difficult to do while attempting to
forget her boyfriend of six years, whom she had left behind in
California. He wanted kids and she didn't; when he'd pushed
her to make a choice, she had taken the postdoc in DC, leaving
the dry air of the Sierra Nevada for this fetid republic.

Now, driving through a thicket of endless traffic, she
doubted herself. What was she, a woman known for her lack of
social graces, doing in the city of politicians? It was Matt who
had been the networker, Matt who could charm grantmakers
and lab managers and department chairs.

What was she doing in a city at all when what she loved most was the isolation of fieldwork? Even the vegetation felt claustrophobic here, dense layers of scrub and weed and bushy deciduous trees. She was used to occupying the arid space beneath evergreens that sat like giants, sucking at the sky like candy. She closed her eyes for half a second and imagined herself back in the Sierras, between dry pine needle paths and branches that spread like roofs; at a honk she opened her eyes to find herself veering out of her lane. She was almost at her brother's house.

Mo and Marcy lived in a narrow, three-story, white rowhouse, squeezed between larger houses, with a small, fenced-in backyard. Marcy greeted Amina at the door with a hug. Her auburn hair sprawled wild around her head, and her trim figure rested easily in a pair of crisp khakis, a silver cell phone held to her ear. She waved Amina in, pointing apologetically to the phone and holding up one finger to say she'd be off in a minute. As always, Amina felt the contrast between them, she in her loose jeans and Old Navy T-shirt, Marcy the picture of urban chic.

Amina hovered around the living room for a few minutes, eyeing the taupe furniture and striped walls that gave off a vague heritage air. She considered sitting down but instead decided to go upstairs to say hello to her nephew, Omar. For eleven years she had seen him only at occasional holidays and through the annual mailing of school photos. When she saw the posting for the postdoc in DC, she thought about being closer to Mo, with all that was continuing to happen in the country, four years after 9/11. Getting to know his son, though, wasn't something she had given much thought to until she arrived.

The stairway was lined with photos detailing the inevitable progression of Omar's life from infant to sixth grader. She paused to study them as she went up, still hearing Marcy's voice down below. The actual Omar was in his room with the door open, lying on his stomach on his bed, but he sat up straight when she walked in. He had nut-brown skin and black hair that was longer on top, and he was just a little bit chubby still, which gave him additional appeal. He was Mo's child, no doubt, but the shape of his face and eyebrows hinted at Marcy.

"Hi. What are you playing?" Amina asked, unsure what to say.

"I'm not playing anything. I'm doing research for my history project on Indian dynasties." He was very earnest, and there was something formal about his voice. He almost sounded like her father, that South Asian colonial accent.

Amina looked around his room, which was boy-messy, with dirty laundry strewn about and lots and lots of action figures. On the windowsill she caught sight of something unexpected: an intricately carved silver knife, with a sheath over its sharp edge and a handle in the shape of a lion. She had brought it back from India after a brief visit many years before and given it to her brother for his birthday.

"Did your dad give you this?" she asked Omar, holding it up.

He nodded with huge eyes. "He said it came from India."

"Yes. I bought it there."

"You went to India?" He looked awed, like she had said she'd been to outer space.

"Just once," she said.

"Aunt Amina?" He paused and looked down at his hands. "Will you come to my school?"

"To your school?" she repeated, confused.

He nodded his head like a large puppy. "My teacher says we should invite somebody we know who has an interesting job. I told her you were a scientist."

"You did?" Amina cast about for a better response, something to get her out of going.

The stairs squeaked and then Marcy poked her head in. "Want a drink, Amina? Omar, this mess! Clean it up before dinner, okay?"

"Okay," Amina said, unable to look at Omar's eager face. *Why not?* She put the knife down and followed Marcy out.

Among the things she disliked: school, children, and talking about herself. She asked Marcy to pour her whiskey over ice.

Marcy's family was originally from North Carolina, and she had first met and loved Amina's brother when her family moved to Ohio in the ninth grade. Marcy and Amina had always been friends, too, though it had been a long time since they lived near each other. Now Marcy was the co-manager of the day-care center near the Capitol, which meant that while technically she had reasonable hours, for the most part she was never off duty for even one second, because when the kid of some representative's aide didn't have a place to go, it was up to her to make sure they were taken care of. So thus far, Amina had seen a lot less of her brother's picture-perfect family than she had expected.

Marcy had made a real southern meal for dinner: pork spareribs with greens and sticky sweet potatoes. Amina's brother finally arrived at half past seven, and after he kissed Amina on the cheek and Marcy on the mouth, they all sat down to the dinner table.

Mohammed—Mo to his friends and colleagues—worked at the Smithsonian, where he was an accountant. From what Amina could gather so far, he spent most of every day at work and most of every weekend in his study. He had been exactly the same as a brother when they were growing up: vague, presumably sweet, absent at crucial moments. As a young girl, she had worshipped him. Everything came easy to Mo, whereas for her, childhood was series of awkward events and unsuitable feelings. She had hidden behind Marcy and Mo when she was a teenager, taking on a bit of their fun and popularity by osmosis, which had helped her to survive.

Marcy tucked a napkin into Mo's collar and poured Diet Coke for everyone with plenty of ice piled in acrylic tumblers, and they commenced eating. There was a long silence, until Marcy cleared her throat and, Amina suspected, kicked Mo under the table.

"Omar," Mo said, in an overt effort to keep abreast of his family, "how is school?"

The boy put down his soda and stared at his plate thoughtfully.

"I would like," he said, "to watch a cricket match."

The accent was gone—perhaps she had imagined it?—but his speech had a formal quality that seemed surprising for an eleven-year-old.

Mo lifted a rib to his lips and then stopped and looked at his son.

"Oh," he said. "Sure, we can do that."

"Really?" Marcy and Omar said this at the same time.

"Um." Mo looked at Amina. "Don't you have some British people in your lab? Wouldn't they know something about where to see cricket?"

"I guess they might," Amina said, hedging. "Omar, where did you get the idea that you wanted to see a cricket match?"

He hadn't started eating again, as if he had been waiting to be asked.

"I am wishing to see the game that my people in India play," he said.

This time Marcy looked worried, her forehead crinkled, hands twisted together.

"Honey," she said, "have you been talking to your grandfather on the phone?"

He nodded. "Grandpa says it is the highest quality game in the world."

Mo looked at Marcy with a relieved smile.

"Of course," he said. "He has an interest in world affairs. Amina, why don't you see what you can do?"

Amina nodded and tried to resume eating. This, she supposed, was what it meant to be part of a family: the unexpected onset of vaguely distasteful responsibility interspersed with very nice home cooking. She felt pleased and disgruntled at the same time.

"We were wondering, Amina," Marcy said after a pause, "if you might do us another favor?"

"Of course." Amina paused with a forkful of greens halfway to her mouth.

"Would you watch Omar for a few days, while we go to the Keys for a weekend? Our time-share's coming up soon. Maybe it could be the same week you visit Omar's school?"

"Sure." Amina swallowed hard and tried to smile. It was a triple hit: school visit, cricket match, and babysitting. "I guess I could do that."

"I'll arrange with a friend to take Omar during the days, on the weekend, if you could just pick him up and drop him off; you could stay here or at your place, whatever you want."

"It's fine, Marcy," Amina said. "Really. It'll be fun." She looked at Omar, who gave back enormous Bambi eyes and not even a hint of a smile.

DRIVING HOME IN HER decade-old Honda, Amina blamed her father. He was an English professor—not of post-colonialism or world literature or even any kind of Asian literature, but a real, old-fashioned scholar of eighteenth-century English poetry. For as long as Amina could remember, it had only been their accents and their color that gave away her parents as Indians. Her mother was a hostess, a kind of suburban social genius at the locus of endless card parties and lunches and cocktail nights with other university wives. That was her work, and it was the exact kind of work that Amina hoped to forever avoid.

Her father occupied another world the vast majority of the time, only emerging for the occasional family outing or dinner party. But now he was growing old, and he was changing. As Amina understood, people were supposed to harden into their own habits as they aged. But her father, ever contrary, had developed a new interest: India, the homeland he had discussed only on rare occasions during her childhood. He spoke in Hindi to her mother sometimes, a language that Amina could only remember hearing when she was very young, and then only when her parents thought they were alone. Now he spoke it at the dinner table, which was more often than not laden with Indian food, a rarity when Amina and Mo were kids, and he subscribed to an Indian newspaper. Amina's mother told her that he had been interviewed by a colleague who was studying Indian independence, and that this had gotten him started.

He was nostalgic for his pre-immigration past, reaching toward rather than away from the Abdul family name. And it was this nostalgia that he was passing on to his only grandchild, to Omar.

2.

AMINA HAD A DECENT apartment in Adams Morgan, and the lab she had joined was a preeminent one in her field. But so far life in the capital had been frustrating, especially work, where she was a new postdoc and the only woman on staff at a level higher than technician. Just like in California, she found herself feeling second fiddle to her male colleagues, and the more she felt that, the more she kept to herself.

She was willing to carry out her cricket assignment, as a favor to Omar and her brother, but it was not a task she liked. The thing was, the English person in her lab was her boss, Christopher Tallin, and they still had yet to forge any kind of comfortable relationship. She occasionally wished to say things like, *Do you know what happened to those gels I put in two hours ago?* or *Why have you taken my samples out of the main freezer and put them in the grad student project fridge?* or *Why isn't my name going to appear at the top of the paper we were supposed to work on together but which I am actually writing while you play chess on your computer?* He hadn't made any effort to get to know her, and she'd followed his lead.

It was apparent to her that he was sleeping with his new TA—or, in grad school parlance, T&A—who was not British and whose name was Anjali. She too was Indian. Amina had overheard gossip to the effect that this new assignation was to fill the void after Chris's last lover had graduated and gone on to enter a PhD program in Finland. Still, she decided that for once she would not hold this against him. For Omar's sake.

Later that week, after setting up the sequencer with the latest samples from the site in Europe, she went to Tallin's office. She leaned against the office door and tapped twice.

"Chris," she said, "you like cricket, don't you?"

His gray eyes rose from his papers, and he seemed to count to ten.

"I do not," he said.

"Ah."

She did not want to go away empty-handed, so she swallowed and tried again. She did, after all, have ninety minutes before the machine would spit out results.

"But do you know people who do? My nephew wants to see a match. I've no idea where to take him, and I thought maybe you would know because . . ."

"Because I'm British?" He finished the sentence for her. He let his eyes run down her body while he thought about it, and she thanked God for the long shirt that hid her breasts, which were just big enough to draw a gaze but disappointing when it came to fancy dress. Besides, she knew that Chris wasn't actually interested in her; it was just habit that he looked her over.

"I'll ask around," he said, with a nod that told her she was dismissed.

"Great!" She left and went to her office. Door closed, she lit a cigarette and smoked it straight through, trying at the same time to envision a happy place, a place without entitled scientists, a place where nephews did not suddenly and without warning acquire the accents of their forebears, a place where animals openly displayed their genetic eccentricities without the aid of machines. And then she coughed and put the cigarette out.

An annual evolutionary genetics conference was

approaching, and Chris had decided they should submit a report on the initial findings of the hybrid zone project. She had spent her first few weeks at the lab reading through past articles, trying to summon a love for grasshoppers and wishing the work contained fewer tables of genetic data and more observation of actual grasshopper behavior, whatever that was.

Chris had assigned the task of writing the report to Amina, though all their names would appear beneath his on the abstract. He said this would help to catch her up with the work that had gone on before her arrival.

The report, as it turned out, was to be submitted to the committee on the Monday just after her weekend with Omar. She needed to make progress before then.

She was staring at her computer in a state of paralysis-inducing anxiety when she heard a knock at her door. She almost jumped out of her skin; her office usually remained a sanctuary fit for a monk under a silence vow.

"Yeah?" she called.

"Hi, it's Anjali, Chris's assistant?"

"The door's open."

Anjali walked in. Amina hadn't spoken a word to her since her arrival in the department, but she knew that she hated her; Amina had spent her life losing to girls who looked like Anjali, even—especially—in science. She had long black hair that she wore in pigtails or on top of her head in a chic twist, long eyes, and full, pouty lips. Today she wore a thin tank top and low-rider jeans fitted over slim, perfect hips. Amina knew Anjali was smart enough to be here, but how could she be stupid enough to be sleeping with Chris? Or was that smart, too?

"What can I help you with?" Amina smiled brightly and tucked a strand of chin-length hair behind her ear. It immediately came loose and knocked against her cheek.

Anjali sat down at the chair in front of her desk without invitation. "Chris said you were asking about cricket games?"

"Yes?"

"Well, my brother plays. There's a test match going on in

a couple of weeks, if you'd like to come. I wrote all the info down here, okay?" Anjali placed a piece of paper on the top of Amina's desk, covering up the *Journal of Modern Zoology*.

"It's my nephew, actually, who wants to go. Not me."

"Does he know how it's played?"

"No. Neither do I, actually." Amina resented presenting a weakness, but it was true.

Anjali stood, pulling her jeans up to her hip bones as she rose. "It's pretty complicated, but I'll be there Sunday afternoon. Look for me, and I'll explain the basics."

"Thanks," Amina managed to say.

Anjali turned just as she reached the door. "I'm glad you're working here, by the way. It's good to have another desi around."

Anjali exited and Amina reached for her cigarettes. *The problem with you, pretty girl*, she lectured in her head, *is that when you use your looks to get what you want, you make it harder for all of us.* She'd seen it in college and then in graduate school, the lovelies like Anjali getting all the attention from their emotionally underdeveloped male professors. And then she'd had to leave her own advisor after he made a pass at her. She'd done so without hesitation and had paid the price in opportunity.

Solidarity with those who played the game was not something Amina was willing to give.

3.

A COUPLE OF WEEKS later, Amina arrived at Omar's private school a few minutes early for her presentation. She stood at the door in the back of the classroom, pushing her hair off the hot back of her neck while the teacher finished her lesson on democratic principles. Amina had first put on jeans, then traded them for khakis, but they were too loose to look actually professional, and she had already sweated through her button-up.

The school was a fairly exclusive one, the opposite of the scruffy public schools she and Omar's father had attended. Omar's classroom was bright and neat and new, and the students sat in groups rather than rows.

"Who exactly gets to vote in a democracy?" the teacher asked. Omar raised his hand from a front table, his eyes bigger than ever, his chin raised in eagerness. To Amina's astonishment, he answered using a heavily applied Indian accent.

"It is depending," he began, "on which period in history we are speaking of."

Amina peered at him. He was second generation, born in America with a white mother and a father who had never spoken with an ethnic inflection in his life. Omar was speaking like his grandparents, like Amina's parents, like a real, bona fide, not raised in the States or maybe even just recently arrived, Indian. Actually, it seemed a little exaggerated, like Apu from *The Simpsons*.

"At first, women," he continued, "were not being allowed to vote at all." Amina could barely keep her mouth from dropping open. When she had left the East Coast for graduate school, Omar had been a baby. She'd returned to find him turned into a husky, doe eyed, pre-adolescent, and now there was this.

Two boys in the back nudged each other and suppressed giggles—Amina heard one of them whisper to the other: "no towel-heads either." Amina gave them a dark look. School, apparently, hadn't changed much since she'd left it; only the epithets had been varied. She forced herself to wait in silence until the teacher had ended her lesson and called her to the front of the room.

"Well," Amina began, surveying her audience of eleven- and twelve-year-olds. Omar looked to be the only Indian kid and one of only a few nonwhite kids in a shiny, immaculate-looking group. No snotty noses here. She pulled a little at the hem of her stretchy T-shirt and wished she was somewhere else, or that at the very least she had inherited a fragment of her mother's innate poise. Instead she continued with forced charm.

"It's great to be here. Today I'm going to tell you about my work as an evolutionary biologist—"

"Excuse me," a blond girl in a sparkled butterfly shirt interrupted. "Why don't you talk like Omar?"

Amina paused. "The question is," she finally said, "why doesn't Omar talk like me?" She looked over at the teacher, who looked back at her with a nervous giggle; she would be no help.

"Anyway." Amina cleared her throat. "My dissertation was on a type of moth that lives in the Sierra Nevada Mountains in California. I spent two years studying them—"

Sparkle butterfly raised her hand again.

"Is it true," she asked, "that in India rubies are bigger than apples?"

This time Amina looked at Omar, who had the decency to look ashamed.

"I wouldn't know," she said. "And today we are going to talk about moths."

The girl batted her eyelashes at Omar, and the boys in the back of the class snickered again. Amina launched into an explanation of evolutionary biology and tried to ignore everything else. After all, she told herself, she was lucky not to live in Kansas, where evolution was considered a crackpot theory and rational inquiry a punishable heresy.

After her presentation, Amina waited around for the finish of the school day so she could take Omar home with her. As a first-year postdoc, she didn't yet feel like a proper representative of science, and she was pretty sure her presentation had been less than inspirational. She wandered the school halls with a mixture of nostalgia and nausea. She hadn't fared any better in public school in Ohio than Omar seemed to be faring as a privileged kid in cosmopolitan DC. The difference seemed to be that while she had always resented being the odd one out, the brown, brainy kid, Omar was exoticizing his own self, and this she did not like to see.

Looking around for distraction, Amina found a display of student-made posters: "My Family," they all sang at the top. Students had created portraits out of collage elements, cut-and-paste combined with drawings. She looked for Omar's and found it in the bottom right corner. His poster featured his father wearing a turban and loincloth—clearly Gandhi—and his mother as Princess Di in white salwar kameez. Omar had drawn himself wearing jodhpur pants and a tiger-striped T-shirt and carrying a knife that looked precisely like the one she had seen in his room, the one she'd originally given to Mo. "The Royal Abduls: An Indian Dynasty," it read along the bottom.

Oh dear, she thought. She wondered if Mo knew. He'd had his own Indian-royal-fantasy phase, mostly centered around building model palaces the likes of which their ancestors would never have come near. It had been his one acknowledgment that he was Indian, or at least the only one she could remember.

At 2:55, a bell rang, and Amina headed back to Omar's room with relief. The students came out all in a rush at first, in a steady line. When she didn't see Omar emerge, she pushed past the last of them and went into the room. He was there, with the blond butterfly girl, and he seemed to be promising her jewels from his ancient princedom in the far north of India. And his accent was on:

"The color is unbelievable, red as blood, and when you look at it really hard you can see the lives of the previous owners. It is cursed! All of the owners have come to terrible ends."

"Terrible?" Little Blondie breathed.

"Omar!" Amina said. "Time to go."

He followed her obediently as she led him out of the school at a double-quick pace. As they overtook some of his class-mates jostling each other in the hall, she noted that not one said hello to him, nor even took note of his presence. They didn't acknowledge their recently deposed guest speaker either, but it was Omar she felt for; she knew how to be an outsider, but clearly Omar did not.

When they got into the car, she waited a few seconds after putting on her seatbelt, trying to think of what to say.

"Why do you talk about India so much in school, Omar?" she finally said. She didn't even know how to begin with the accent.

He shrugged.

"Did you learn those things from your mom and dad?"

He finally looked up at her with beseeching eyes. "No, they never tell me anything." His accent was American again. "Maybe you could? Because you've been to India?"

She nodded, as if this made sense; she'd been to India once, after college, to the wedding of a former roommate that was held in Delhi. She had seen almost nothing outside of Tara's house and an endless mob of strangers; she had felt invisible, untethered and gilded stiff in her borrowed sari.

"We'll see," she said. "In the meantime, try not to make things up, okay?"

He nodded with downcast eyes, and she pulled out of the parking space and started for home.

The drive from the school to Amina's apartment was short and silent. When they arrived, she gave him a brief tour of her three rooms. She had cleaned the bathroom and hidden her cigarettes and ashtrays and tried to buy food he might like. She left her computer out in the living room because the grasshopper report for the annual meetings was due on Monday and she still hadn't finished it; she had spent the last days cursing her luck—or Chris's intent—and making little progress with the actual writing.

Why had she agreed to be entrusted with a child? Amina's work was with insects, and that was no coincidence. She hated the way adults became willfully naive around children—cooing and pampering, plying them with sugar and indulging them, in utter indifference to the obvious knowledge that the world was a feral, hostile place.

Still, though she wasn't becoming a nurturer overnight, Amina was trying. It was in a way too bad that she wouldn't be able to take him to the cricket game, because she knew that, at least, was something Omar really wanted. But Amina had to finish the report, which expanded in scope every time she gave a draft to Chris for feedback. She didn't want to see Anjali anyway, and Omar would be better off with a friend his own age.

Marcy called from the Keys just around the time Amina's house tour came to an anticlimactic end. Marcy talked to Omar for approximately two minutes, with Omar responding in monosyllables to her questions, and then he moved to the TV while Amina took the phone to her bedroom.

"So everything's going okay?" Marcy asked Amina again.

"Yep. So far nothing's broken and nobody's crying." When Marcy didn't say anything, she changed tack. "How is Florida?"

They chatted for a few minutes, and then Amina finally

decided to ask. "Have you noticed anything about Omar's, umm, speaking voice?"

"Oh my God! Is his voice changing? But he's so young—"

"No, no, Marcy. No. I mean, you've noticed the accent, right?"

"What do you mean, an accent? Like a northeastern accent? Like *cah* instead of *car*? Or southern?" Marcy sounded horrified; she herself had eradicated all traces of a southern accent in the first year her family had lived in Ohio.

"Never mind, I'm probably imagining it." Amina wondered if it was his school voice, and if so, how long that had been the case.

Amina hung up the phone and then she and Omar sat for a few minutes in silence. She'd hardly spent any time with children, ever, or at least not since she'd been one. In graduate school, those with and without kids achieved a natural separation, born out of different sleeping schedules and financial obligations and potential for emergency. The people with kids were strangers to her; she had not been able to imagine herself as one of them. Matt thought this a terrible fault. Unforgivable, actually. When he'd said he wouldn't move with her, she hadn't fought him. She had thought that she loved him, but some part of her must have wanted to be free.

And now what to do? A movie would be fine, but they only lasted two hours. She could take him out to eat, maybe for Mexican or Ethiopian or something. Or Indian!

She congratulated herself on the idea and phoned for reservations at the Cheetah and Monkey, a place she'd been to when she first arrived. She could explain to Omar to say *masala*, not *curry*, and how to pick up food with just naan and your hand, and how in India, a pickle wasn't made of cucumber; instead of talking nonsense, she would teach him something that his parents and grandparents hadn't bothered to.

Omar still hadn't said anything. There were two hours before dinner. She didn't have an extra room, just a futon in the living room, so she couldn't even send him away to read or do homework. Instead, she turned on the TV.

"Do you like CNN?" she asked, and he gave what seemed a genuine nod. They watched a program on terrorism in Indonesia and ate potato chips; she decided it was a success.

4.

AMINA'S FIRST EXPERIENCE AT the Cheetah and Monkey had not been a good one. It was her first week in DC, and she was far from adjusted to the weather, her apartment, or the myriad complexities of postdoc life. The lab received the first install-ment of the National Science Foundation grant award, some of the money for which had gone to hire Amina, and they all went out to dinner to celebrate. Amina accepted the invitation with a little distaste because she didn't like to be the only woman in a group.

The restaurant was dark and slightly overheated, filled with tchotchkes. Everyone ordered drinks, and she sipped at red wine cautiously. Her boss was seated on the other side of the large round table, where he held forth on the virtues of their lab, the righteousness of their award, and the surety of Nobel Prizes, chairmanships, and a permanent flow of generous grant money for them all.

Her work in graduate school, as she had explained to Omar's class, was on a moth hybrid zone, a geographical area where interspecies breeding took place, counteracting the general rule that separate species could not mate.

The lab she had now joined was a prestigious one, and she

had been gratified by the job offer when it came. Her dissertation had confirmed the fact—suspected since the discovery of the site a century before by pioneering scientist Walter Sweadner—that unusual social behavior by certain groups of moths was due not just to environmental conditions but also to the fact of cross-species mating. Hybrids, which her lab in California had proven to be so through exhaustive DNA testing, were displaying abnormal behavior; in other words, hybrid DNA led to hybrid social structures. In her research she had tried to establish that specific social patterns came as a result of the region being a long-standing, stable hybrid zone.

The lab in DC focused not on moths but on a species of grasshopper in a mountain range of western Europe. It was the perfect post for her, allowing her to demonstrate that her expertise was transferable across field sites, that there was work to do all over the world. But she had been sorry to leave her previous project and hand it over to the next generation of graduate students and postdocs; her new job focused more on indexing—on models and spreadsheets—than on actual behavior.

She had a decent living situation, her brother and his family nearby, and a lab full of colleagues with shared knowledge. But she couldn't get used to being around so many people after seven years tracking between a quiet state university and the mountain field site; in both places she was left very much to herself. In California, she'd had Matt and a few—well, two—good friends. But mostly she kept to herself, out of the fray of graduate school politics: identity politics, sexual politics, even political politics held no interest for her. She liked her work—indeed her mother, Matt, her advisors, and even Mo had at one time or another accused her of being a workaholic—and wanted to get it done with a minimal amount of schmoozing along the way.

She tried to prepare herself for the transition from the West Coast to DC by exchanging her flannel shirts and Timberlands for button-up shirts and canvas sneakers, by cutting her too-long hair. She vowed to quit smoking and swearing, and to learn to be nice, DC polite; she'd be a city girl and get along with people. So far she was smoking more than ever, and she hadn't made a single friend.

That first night at the Cheetah and Monkey, everyone drank too much, suggesting the anxiety that Amina would soon learn Chris nurtured in all his underlings. The food seemed all the same, variations on tandoori and greasy orange-colored sauce. A fat colleague with a pencil-thin mustache leaned too close to Amina after the rice pudding. He had been very nice to her in the first days, helping to set up her computer and showing her how the samples were organized, but now he was very drunk.

"What are you?" he asked.

"Excuse me?"

"Are you Arab or Pakistani or what?"

"I'm Indian." *I'm American* is what she should have said, but she couldn't stand going through that dance at the moment. First night out with your new coworkers, she reminded herself. Be DC polite.

"Oh! Like this restaurant!" He seemed pleased by this. "Are you married?"

"No."

He stared some more. "Are you a lesbian?"

"Not currently." She started to get to her feet, anxious to get away from the personal turn he had taken.

"Have I offended you in some way?" His words were slurred and he leaned into her chair, pinning her coat beneath his arm. His head hovered somewhere around the level of her chest.

She shook her head, standing and pulling her coat out without apology. Her head swam a little from all the wine. She felt lonely for Matt, for anyone friendly, for someone who knew her and didn't have to ask what she was as though she herself was some species of insect. To always be foreign to some seemed suddenly too cruel, and she was exhausted. And drunk, she reminded herself, as she waved a vague goodbye.

"Amina," Chris called out from across the table, noticing her for the first time all evening. He sat too close to Anjali, who had been in the thick of the conversation all night. "Welcome to Washington, DC. I hope you realize how lucky you are."

"Exactly what I was just thinking," she said.

ON HER SECOND VISIT to the Cheetah and Monkey, Amina and Omar were seated at a table for two under the canopy of a Rajasthani tent. She wore a sequined tunic that her mother had given her, and Omar wore his tiger T-shirt. It was very romantic, and her nephew looked thrilled.

Omar, it turned out, had been researching more than Indian royal families. Instead of Amina giving him handy tips on how to eat, the meal consisted of her saying "I don't know" in response to questions about what different Hindi words meant, and where exactly places like Mahabalapurim and Maharashtra were, and how many dishes you were supposed to order for a festive versus a family meal.

After they had finished struggling with the menu, he started pointing at things around the room and asking what they were. The Cheetah and Monkey, she then realized, was not really an Indian restaurant at all, but rather an imitation of a nineteenth-century colonial idea of what an Indian restaurant was. There were old, antique-y artifacts all over the place, and they all probably had a use at some point, but she didn't know what they were. They finally asked the waiter, who was about seventeen, sexy, and quite probably Pakistani.

"Can you tell me, what is that?" Omar asked, pointing. His accent was muted but still present. He was pointing at a wooden piece with lotus shapes cut out of it.

"Umm." The sexy waiter looked puzzled and sucked his teeth. "A mold?" he suggested. "For baking things?"

"I thought people didn't use ovens in India?" Omar asked. He had a real worried look on his face, like he'd gotten something wrong on a test.

"Yeah, that's actually sort of true." The waiter nodded, looking surprised to discover this fact in his head. "Don't know, kid. There's lots of stuff here, you know what I mean?"

Omar nodded like this was a great and portentous truth, and the waiter exited with a look of relief.

Amina and Omar both practiced eating with their hands, which made for some amusing moments. Amina gave up at the galub jamun, which was gooey with sugar syrup, but Omar picked those up too, and licked his fingers afterward. But the conversation lagged once Omar realized she didn't have all the answers to his Indian trivia questions. He even managed to discuss cricket with the waiter while Amina paid the bill, but the waiter didn't seem to know much more about the game than Amina did.

Back at her apartment, Omar was quiet. He spent a lot of time looking around at her things — which were few and vaguely ethnic in origin, relics and gifts culled from her time in graduate school alongside the decorative items that her mother insisted on periodically giving her in hopes that she would develop an interest in interior design. She hadn't. She had lived with Matt in California, when she wasn't at the field site, in his attic apartment close to the university. Most of their accumulated possessions had stayed with him.

She still had a couple of unpacked boxes but mostly, left on her own, she tended toward a minimalist ethos. She didn't have much that was really Indian, and that seemed to be a let-down, because Omar asked again if she had been to India. She said yes, but it was a long time ago, and he sat down to watch TV again in something like defeat.

Whatever Omar was looking for, his need was real. She felt a twinge of guilt about the cricket match, but then she told herself to forget it; he'd be happier anywhere than with her. In bed, she fretted for an hour or two, angry with herself for not showing him a better time. *Tomorrow*, she told herself, *tomorrow*; and finally, she slept.

5.

AMINA FORGOT TO SET her alarm, and the next morning she woke late to find Omar glued to the TV, watching *Johnny Quest* on the Cartoon Network in Spider-Man pajamas. Johnny's sidekick was an Indian boy with a ruby on his turban. She'd forgotten that detail, but now she remembered how Mo used to love the show when they were kids. Back then, Johnny's sidekick was the only Indian they saw besides themselves and their relentlessly assimilating parents.

She made coffee for herself and hot chocolate for Omar, and they sat on her sad futon to watch the thrilling conclusion. She noticed he was holding something silver in his lap and she leaned in to take a closer look.

He held it up helpfully. It was the knife from India.

"What are you doing with that?" She stopped herself from warning him that it wasn't a toy.

"I just like it," he said. "I like to have it with me."

She assumed this had something to do with his emperor-of-India familial fantasy and decided to change the subject.

"Are you excited to go over to Davy's?"

He shrugged his shoulders. "It's just something Mom set up."

"Oh. Does that mean you don't like to go over there?"

He shrugged again. He'd never mentioned any friends to her, and from what she'd seen in his classroom, he didn't have many. But she wasn't going to probe him on what was probably a sensitive subject.

After serving a pathetic breakfast of cold cereal and warm juice, she slipped into old jeans and a pair of sneakers and drove Omar over to Davy's house. This turned out to be a largish townhouse on the northern edge of Georgetown, painted in patriotic blue and red. Amina kept the car running and let Omar out. He walked slowly to the door like he was going to his execution, never once looking back to her. A woman answered the door, a sleek little creature in calf-colored pants and a soft sweater.

"Very nice to see you, Mrs. Madsen," she heard Omar say in a ringing Johnny Quest–sidekick accent. Amina felt like yelling at him to stop, and she hated herself for it. Mrs. Madsen waved to her with a shiny smile and she waved back. Poor Omar, she thought, but she drove away anyway.

THE AFTERNOON DRAGGED; SHE found it almost impossible to concentrate on grasshoppers. Instead, she spent two hours lying on her bed in a frozen state that resembled a coma, thinking of Matt.

He had written to her recently, telling her news of the department, the status of his thesis, the weather. It was sweet of him to send an actual letter in addition to the occasional emails they exchanged. They had met in her first week of graduate school; they had a class together, a core course that he had dropped the previous year. This, she would soon learn, was only the tiniest echo of a larger pattern: he had trouble finishing things. He had started out two years ahead of her, but was now three years behind, frozen in a thesis-writing stasis that showed no signs of abating.

He had chestnut hair and startlingly pale skin and large,

rough hands and a high, soft voice that soothed her and comple-
mented her own brusqueness. It seemed reasonable to him to
suggest that they marry and start having kids before there was
any sign that he was nearing the end of his study. When she
was applying for jobs, he'd encouraged her by promising he'd
be by her side. But when she was awarded the postdoc, he
balked, suggesting they marry first. They argued until Amina
finally admitted she wanted the postdoc more than she wanted
children. "Then how can I go with you?" he countered, and
she didn't know how to answer that.

After 9/11, when she had thought for hours that Mo might
be dead, and as the small towns around them raised their proud
American flags, she felt like her time in California was up. She
needed to return to the real world, to know her brother and be
with people who looked like her. She left for this new world
with no idea of how lonely it would be.

She reread Matt's letter, wondering for the thousandth time
if she'd made a mistake. She knew her parents were puzzled—
and her friends in California were amazed—that she'd left a
perfectly reasonable mate at her age. Her mother in particular
was filled with what seemed to be a personal sense of indigna-
tion, as though Amina had left *her* and not Matt. This seemed
a little rich to Amina, after all the years that her mother had
chided her for staying with a man who did not marry her. To
everyone, it looked like she had chosen her career over love,
when really it was so much more complicated than that.

At three-thirty, she roused herself and sat at the computer
again. The paper was due on Monday, and she needed to not
just finish it up, but smarten it up. Right now it read like a tax
document. There was no evidence of her own interest and
capability, or of Chris's vast experience, just a droning recita-
tion of facts.

This wasn't the kind of science she had wanted to do, not
the kind she had set off to grad school to do. The best days
had been in the field, away from people. Her earlier papers had

expressed the transfixion she had felt; they had a buoyancy that brought them attention. Now that she was stuck in a lab all the time, analyzing instead of finding, retrieving, discovering, the light had gone out in her work.

AMINA AND OMAR SURVIVED the second night watching old movies and eating popcorn, reclining together in their pajamas against all the pillows in the house on the folded-out futon. She asked him about his day at the Madsens', but he didn't say much. He'd appeared at the door instantly when she pulled the car up and honked, like he'd been waiting for her, which she supposed said everything she needed to know.

They watched *The Philadelphia Story*, which she owned because it was Matt's favorite movie and he'd given her the DVD when she left. Omar showed his good taste by laughing and seeming awestruck at the same time. His eyes were wide at the horseback riding in formal clothes and the swimming pool with dressing rooms, and Katharine Hepburn's sculpted Egyptian goddess dress at the ball the night before the wedding. Amina loved that Omar appreciated it, this relic of an old America, an America where quick wits were like money and even actors projected intelligence and learning. She wondered whether for him, as it did for her, such social accomplishment seemed more tantalizing than beauty. She let him stay up until midnight, and they found a Humphrey Bogart movie playing on Bravo.

Sunday morning she took him to brunch—that at least was a new word for him—at a restaurant near her apartment. He had pancakes and she ate a farmer's scramble that made her too full when combined with approximately six cups of black coffee. In spite of the agonized look on his face—which she chose not to interpret as pleading—she dropped him off at the Madsens' again around noon so she could get to work.

Back at home, she sat at her desk determined not to make a repeat of the waste of the day before. She juggled paragraphs, made notes for the introduction, and checked citations. Chris had done the early research, compiling DNA proof that suggested they had a bona fide stable hybrid zone on their hands. She planned to pick up the data analysis where he had left off, adding in some of the perspective she'd brought with her from California, to try to balance submission to his authority and precedence with her desire to put in more of her own ideas.

She thought he was wrong, for instance, about what kind of hybrid zone it was; he thought that the physical environment was the most important factor in how these insects behaved, while she found it more interesting to look at socially constrained tension zones. A paper had recently been published in one of the major journals about deviant female behavior in simians. Some hybrid female baboons seemed to lack the genetic predisposition to be herded in harems by nonhybrid hamadryas males. They had to be constantly reminded of their social duties, and the minute a male stopped being vigilant, they ceased appropriate behavior. The work moved on from the genetics results into much more interesting social inquiry about the implications of those results.

This was what intrigued her, the type of research that had set her mind afire in the field. It felt like cheating to ignore what was obviously the most interesting direction.

But this was not her job now. She needed to concentrate. She sat in her chair in a slouch and chewed on the remnants of her fingernails, trying not to smoke. The ends of her hair fell forward in her face and she brushed it away without bothering to do anything to fix it. She stared at the screen for forty minutes before she got up and took a shower. She considered plucking her eyebrows. She wondered if Anjali plucked hers. She made more coffee and sat down again.

Finally, she picked up the phone and called her father.

"Dad," she said, "it's Amina."

"I know it is you," he scolded her, in what she now thought of as Omar's accent.

"And I knew that you knew," she said to annoy him. "Dad, I want to talk to you about Omar."

"What about my grandchild? How is the boy?"

"Has he been asking you about India a lot?"

She could hear her father exhale. "Asking, I don't know."

"But you're telling, and he's listening?"

"Amina, I am telling him because he wants to know, even if he does not ask. What does Mohammed tell him? Nothing."

"You never told us much either. I'm just worried about him, that's all. He's making up stories about being from a royal family and talking like a cartoon."

"A cartoon?"

"I mean he's acting like he comes from an eighteenth-century Indian family, like something he read in a book."

"First you say cartoon, now you say something in history?"

"Dad," she said.

She could almost see him shrug. "The boy is curious; he finds what he can. You could help him."

"What do I know about India?"

"Don't be thick-headed. He wants more than facts."

She hung up the phone troubled. *I am not a people person,* she thought. She preferred animals, or insects, or just plain trees, any trees.

Except Omar. She liked Omar. And today she had abandoned him. Those hours when she hadn't known where Mo or Marcy or Omar were or if they had been where the plane had crashed or if she would ever know her nephew, the realization that she might have lost them had led her to leave Matt behind and move here. So what the fuck was she doing?

Amina saved her document and got up from the desk. She went to her closet and found a newer pair of jeans and a nice pair of loafers, and a clean, unwrinkled turquoise T-shirt and smoothed her damp hair with her fingers, praying it would stay flat. She examined herself in the mirror for an extra moment: her thick black hair, her average body, her medium-brown skin, never fair enough for her mother. Her chin was long, and the end of her nose tipped just slightly downward. She wondered what Mrs. Madsen saw when she looked at Amina, and she hated herself for wondering.

She left the paper as it was, turning off the computer. She got in her car and drove to Davy's house.

Mrs. Madsen answered the door, looking taken aback.

"I'm sorry to come by without calling," Amina said, "but I have to pick up Omar."

"Omar!" Mrs. Madsen called in one direction. She turned back to Amina with a perfect smile, showing her even white teeth. "Is there a problem?"

"No, not at all. I just realized there was someplace I have to take him."

The woman nodded, but looked like she was waiting for Amina to say something more. They stood uncomfortably for another minute. "Davy!" Mrs. Madsen called again. "Marcy's told me so much about you," she finally said to Amina.

"Really?" Amina said.

Mrs. Madsen smiled at her again, with an ingratiating tilt of her head. "We're so happy to have people like Omar in our life. And you. You're a scientist, Davy said?"

Amina nodded. From a doorway that was emitting loud TV noises, a boy emerged—a largish-for-twelve, sandy-haired boy who was, Amina realized, the *towel-head* culprit from science day. Omar followed, his head down, but his chin snapped up when he saw her standing there.

"It's very unusual, isn't it?" Mrs. Madsen continued. "I mean, for a woman of your faith." Amina gave her a blank stare, puzzled for a second. "I know how hard it is for Muslim women," Davy's mom added.

Ah. The narrative clicked in for Amina; she was the oppressed and Mrs. Madsen wanted to be the righteous sympathizer. This was what Mrs. Madsen saw when she looked at her.

"Our family is not exactly part of the Taliban." Amina said, guessing that Mrs. Madsen hadn't met Mo yet. "And Omar and I have to go."

Her nephew came and stood beside her with a confused look. She said, "We have to get to the cricket match!" and his face lit up.

"Cricket?" Mrs. Madsen said behind them.

Amina turned and said, not without sarcasm, "It's the game of our people." She marched Omar out to the car.

6.

By the time they arrived at the playing field, it was mid-afternoon. The field was out in Bethesda, reminding Amina yet again of the odd multiplicity of DC, the way it was no state and yet many states, one city connected without borders to many others.

The cricket pitch was surprisingly crowded. There were cars parked in the lot and up on the grass at odd angles, and as they got out of her Honda she could see a crowd in the bleachers, the occasional Sikh turban or embroidered skull cap floating on top like florid cake decorations.

They walked up to the sidelines, and she bought Cokes at the snack stand and then found seats, high up in a corner. She had done some research, and it turned out that cricket matches lasted forever. A test match, which this was, was an abbreviated version, narrowed down to three days. She thought she understood why it hadn't caught on in the US—what TV station would devote three entire days to one match?

Omar seemed bright and alert, so she started to tell him things without him asking. She defined *wicket, googly,* and *century*. She made fun of the white outfits. She picked people out of the crowd and made fun of the clothes they were wearing, too. Omar remained silent but attentive. Just as Amina had exhausted her store of information and insults, Anjali appeared.

"Hey!" Anjali said, smiling as she climbed the risers, heading straight for them. "I'm glad you made it."

She was showing less skin than usual, in a long tunic over jeans, with beaded, tasseled Moroccan slippers. Her hair was in two braids, and she had a jet bindi between her eyes. Omar sat up straight.

Amina was almost relieved to see her. "This is my nephew, Omar."

He held out a hand and Anjali shook it, laughing.

"So you're the cricket fan, huh?"

"Yes."

"Have you ever been to a match before?"

He wagged his head from side to side. Anjali laughed again.

"In India, did you know, moving your head like that can mean yes?" She was teasing him, and he was delighted.

"Is that really true?" He said this with just the hint of an accent, like her clothing had set a precedent.

"Yep. Hey, my brother is on the team—you want to meet him later?"

Omar nodded, this time smiling.

"Thanks," Amina said to Anjali over his head.

"No problem." Anjali flashed her fetching smile again and left.

The match went into the evening. Amina bought snacks from the kebab cart and extra coffee for herself. Anjali came and went. Omar brightened whenever she was near. It was a sunny, not-too-humid fall day—a perfect day—and Amina relaxed, enjoying the sun on her skin. She felt comfortable in the crowd, and this surprised and pleased her; she told herself it was the contrast with working at home alone all the time.

Omar spent a lot of time looking around him, being sure to clap his hands when others did. Anjali had pointed out which was her brother's team, and he rooted for them like a die-hard fan, jeering at the other side with utter loyalty. Anjali's brother

was tall and turbaned. Amina hadn't realized Anjali was Sikh—
why would she have?—and had a hard time imagining her in
her hipster jeans at a family dinner with the bearded man on
the field.

Around five o'clock, Anjali reappeared with ice cream bars.
They sat together and watched as a batsman headed toward
a century—a hundred runs—then cheered as Anjali's brother
caught him out just before he reached the mark. The next
batsman stepped to the plate, and Anjali turned and looked at
Amina over Omar's head.

"Amina," she asked, "where did you go to grad school?"

"California."

"Did you like it?"

Amina paused, considering how to answer. "Like it? No. I
did not like graduate school."

"Why not?"

She could tell Anjali that her first advisor had wanted her to
sleep with him and she'd had to change to another. She could
explain how the woman she'd called her best friend had begun
sleeping with Amina's ex-advisor. That no one would help
Amina at all, except Matt, and when it came time for grants
every year, she'd always had to apply on her own. That all in all
she'd just been relieved as hell that they conferred the degree on
her in the end, which they mostly had to do because against all
odds, she'd had her name on an article published in *Evolution*,
which had attracted some attention. But why go into it with
someone who had already gone over to the dark side?

"I didn't seem to fit in," she said in curt summary.

Anjali nodded. Amina noticed that the bindi was loose on
her forehead.

"Yeah," Anjali said, looking down, her voice almost shy, "I
don't feel like I fit in with our department, either."

"You seem to do okay," Amina said.

Anjali looked up at her and met her eyes, the edges of her
mouth turned down and vulnerable. "I do?" she said. "I didn't
think so."

Before Amina could say anything, Omar suddenly reached up to Anjali's face and pressed the bindi into her forehead.

"Your third eye was crooked," he said, in his finest Apu voice.

"Thanks, Omar," Anjali said, putting an arm around him and tickling his ribs. The batsman was called out, and the teams switched sides.

WHEN THE MATCH ENDED for the day, Anjali came to find them again.

"Let's go meet my brother!" she said to Omar. They led the way for Amina, hand in hand, toward where the players were milling about on the edge of the field, shaking hands with each other and greeting friends and family as they arrived from the stands.

Anjali walked right up and introduced them to Prakash as he loaded up a blue duffel bag. He had a stern mouth and dreamy eyes over a trim beard. He bent over to take Omar's compliments, a giant over a bean sprout, before Anjali hustled Omar off to meet some of the other players.

Prakash and Amina shook hands and he said hello in a deep, smooth voice that made the back of her neck tickle a little.

"What do you do when you're not playing cricket?" she asked.

"I run a bookstore," he said.

She wasn't sure what to say to that. "I'm a biologist."

"Then you must read a lot of books."

"Not really," Amina said, then regretted it. "I mean, not so much anymore, now that I'm out of grad school. I learned to hate them there."

He actually picked up on her ironic tone and answered back in kind. "You might learn to love them again in my bookstore." He produced a business card and she took it in silence.

Where was Omar?

"You can at least give it a try," Prakash said.

"What?" Amina asked.

"My store. It's near the Mall, easy to find."

"Oh. Thanks, but—"

Omar ran up to show her a ball he'd been given, his voice gushing with excitement. Prakash waved, his silver bracelet flashing in the late sun, and left before she could say anything else. Her hands were sweating and had a slight shake as she took Omar's ball in hand and admired it.

"Amina-Auntie, it was so much fun, don't you think?" His accent she was now used to, but where had he picked up the *auntie*?

"That's *chachi*, to you, Indian boy," she teased, giving him the Hindi term. He looked surprised.

7.

On Monday, Amina dropped Omar off at school before work. Marcy and Mo were due back in the afternoon, and he could take the school bus home as usual. He exited the car with his backpack, saying thank you and goodbye in one breath, and she felt pleased with herself for having survived it all unscathed.

At the lab, she handed in her draft, and everyone else contributed their sections, and then they all waited to see what Chris would demand in the way of revision. There was a kind of hush as the week began, a calm before the storm; no one expected that he would like the work they had done. She tried to concentrate on other things.

In the middle of the week she was called to the phone in the common space outside her office. She was puzzled about who it could be and more flabbergasted still to discover that it was Anjali's brother, Prakash. After a shocked silence she hoped had not lasted too long, she recovered.

"How did you get my number?" she asked.

"My sister works there, remember? The number is the same."

"Ah." Her cheeks were hot, and she let her hair fall forward and surround her face. She was not going to date him. She was not.

"So." He seemed very patient.

"So?" She glanced around to see if anyone was listening.

"Aren't you wondering why I've telephoned?"

"I am," she said. She looked down and noticed that the laces on one of her sneakers were untied.

"It's only that I was thinking," he began, his deep voice slowing down, "that Omar might like to learn how to play cricket. And I lead a kind of informal group of kids that gets together to practice on weekends. Maybe you'd like to bring him this Saturday."

"Oh," she said, surprised. "Omar's not mine. I mean, he's just my nephew."

There was a pause. "Scientists are funny people."

She giggled a little in spite of herself. "I guess I can bring him sometime. I'll call his parents and ask about this Saturday."

"Good," Prakash said.

"Thank you," she said.

"And then sometime maybe we can go to lunch," he said.

"Okay." The word just came out, before she could think.

"Really?"

"Yeah. But not this week, because I'm still working on—"

"The report, yes, I know. Anjali seems concerned about it as well."

"Scientists are funny people," she said. She hung up and then realized, mortified, that she had a date.

SHE PHONED TO ASK if she could take Omar to the cricket practice, and Marcy said that she'd ask Mo if he wanted to go too. After three emails and a series of voicemail messages, it was finally determined that Mo was, as always, too busy.

Mo was waiting with Omar at the door when she arrived at their house wearing sweatpants and Reeboks. He looked tired, and didn't invite Amina in.

Omar didn't seem to mind that his dad wasn't coming. He was wearing a very large Redskins jersey—typical of Mo not to point out the ironies therein—and new sneakers, and his feet hardly seemed to touch the ground.

"Thank your aunt Amina," Mo told him.

"Thank you for taking me to play cricket, Chachi," Omar said.

Mo looked sidelong at Amina, his eyes narrowed. Just when Amina thought he was going to ask where Omar had learned to call her that, he took a step back and put the door between himself and Omar. "What time will you be back?"

Amina shrugged. "A few hours? I'll call."

She worried about her brother; they were too much alike in their willingness to immerse themselves in work and forget about more human things. Their father was always working, with their mother's constant support, and they seemed to have absorbed his work ethic, each in their own way. Even during their trip to Florida, Marcy had confessed to Amina, Mo had kept in constant contact with the office. His only concession to leisure was to read the entire paper every morning on the beach while she swam.

At the field, Prakash was readily visible in a turban, black training pants with white stripes, and a fitted Real Madrid soccer jersey. Amina had to admit to herself that he looked pretty sexy. He took Omar and introduced him to the other kids—a racially mixed, unathletic-looking crew dressed in clothing from assorted sports other than cricket: football, basketball, baseball, dodgeball.

Amina stretched out on the grass with a genetics journal and a notebook. It was an unusually warm day, and the ground was dry and soft. The kids practiced throwing and batting in pairs, and then worked together as a group on some drills. Omar seemed to be doing fine, though he was, as usual, the embodiment of seriousness. There was something relaxing about listening to children play. She even closed her eyes, half listening as Prakash offered orders and explanations in a voice that somehow sounded familiar.

During the break, Prakash handed out drinks and oranges, and soon Omar trotted over to her.

"Don't you want some Gatorade?" she asked him.

He shook his head.

"How is it, the cricket?"

He smiled a little. "Did you see me pitch? Prakash said my googly has potential."

She laughed. "That sounds good."

"Amina," he asked, "I mean, Chachi?"

"Yes?"

"What does *desi* mean? All the boys were talking and they asked if I was sure I'm a desi. Am I?"

"Oh." Amina sat up. "Yep, kid, you are. It just means India: from India."

"Like born in India?"

"Not necessarily. I mean, I'm no authority. But I think it just means that you are of Indian heritage, and that we definitely are."

"Even though we aren't Hindi?"

"Hindu. And yes, no matter what religion we are, your grandparents still came from India, and so did their parents and so on from that."

Omar looked relieved. "That's what I thought."

When practice was over, she knew she should thank Prakash, as Omar's resident parent, but she was nervous that he would ask about lunch again. She ran her hands through her hair, pushing it back behind her ears, and walked over at what she hoped looked like a casual pace. She offered her appreciations, and he thanked her in return, his deep brown eyes meeting hers and holding there until she blushed and looked down.

"I would still like to get that lunch, Amina."

She hedged, aware that at that exact moment he was very

handsome. Very handsome, with a smile that flashed like a warning.

"I'm still working on that report," she said. "But maybe I'll see you at the next practice."

He looked skeptical, rightly so; she waved her journal and notebook in the air as if she was proffering evidence. She didn't want to seem rude, but how could she date this man? He was too sweet and normal; he was Sikh; he played cricket. And she was in no condition to be in a relationship; hadn't everything with Matt only proved that she was not the right lover for this kind of man?

In the car, Omar did seem happier than usual, bouncing in his seat as he chose the radio station he liked. She felt buoyant as well, her heart skipping a little as she went over the interaction with Prakash.

"Maybe your dad can take you next time," she said.

"Dad has a lot of work," he said in a matter-of-fact tone.

She nodded.

"So does Mom," he offered, in fairness.

"I'll take you when they can't, how about that?" she said. She tried to study him and drive at the same time, but every time she looked over at him, he was already looking directly at her with his air of expectation. Was there something more she should say?

Her own strategy, as a child, had been brute endurance. She had always done what everyone asked of her, but with her eyes fixed firmly on escape from her mother's antifeminist expectations. To her mother she was ever the disappointment, an average-looking girl who would not grow up to be a beauty and who was too smart for her own good. She had Mo as her companion—and then Marcy when they started, and along the way assorted geek friends whom she was bonded to more out of solidarity than affinity.

Some people looked back on childhood as a perfect time, the very locus of shelter and comfort and contentment. Amina remembered it now with an almost claustrophobic feeling, as a time of helplessness, a time when she had been without the power to change her own circumstance.

This was the feeling she thought she recognized in Omar. And she didn't know how to help him. Cricket was a start, but it wasn't enough.

8.

IN REALITY, THE REPORT had been revised in an end-of-week frenzy, and the lab was now focused on preparing a new proposal for a grant Chris had decided—unilaterally and with ten days to the deadline—they should apply for. The grant was not to fund a presence at the field site, but instead to hire more analysts to pore through genetic data. Amina could see the writing on the wall: more DNA sequencing, less real-world investigation.

Charts were being finalized and contributions sorted. Chris demanded her draft of a preliminary report on her progress even before she'd gotten into her office on Monday morning.

"Say please," she mumbled under her breath, shutting her door behind her.

She tried to settle in to work. She had come to hate his high-handed style, the way he expected she would always find the time to do extra work, even on weekends. Those with families, who were married and had children, said no to Chris all the time, with immunity. But in her case, Chris thought she had no reason not to work extra hours: no responsibilities that counted.

And really, if she was honest with herself, she always did have the time.

She scrolled through her emails. She was just about to open one from Matt when her phone started ringing. She picked up the receiver with relief.

"I'm trying to reach Amina Abdul, Omar's aunt?"

"Yes," she said, no longer relieved.

"This is the assistant principal at his school. We need a guardian down here immediately, and we've been unable to contact his parents."

"Is he okay?"

"He's in a great deal of trouble. His teacher found him threatening another student with a knife."

Amina put down the phone, grabbed her peacoat, and walked toward the door, trying not to make a scene by running. Chris tried to stop her as she left.

She barely paused. "I have a family emergency."

She drove hard but seemed to hit every light. She kept thinking how she should have told him not to bring it, that surely he hadn't threatened anyone, that he'd just accidentally been caught with the knife that she had known he was carrying around, and why oh why hadn't she remembered and stopped him?

She ran up the school steps two at a time, signed in, and raced to the principal's office. She slid to an abrupt halt when she saw two police officers in the room with Omar, a woman Amina assumed must be the principal, and Omar's teacher, Mrs. Pinkston, who looked close to tears.

"Omar!" Amina said.

"Amina, I didn't mean it." He sat on a low bench with the adults towering around him, and her heart shrank in fear at his vulnerability.

"Ms. Abdul." An African American woman in a neat red suit stepped forward. "I'm Principal Adama. We have quite a problem here."

"Can't I just take Omar home?" Amina asked.

Principal Adama shook her head. "I'm sorry. No one was hurt, but we are required to report these incidents to the police. I'm sure you understand."

"But he didn't mean anything, did you, Omar? The knife was mine. He just liked it; he didn't mean to threaten anybody."

One of the officers held up the lion-headed blade. "Is this the knife, ma'am?"

"Yes."

"It's a crime to bring a weapon into a school."

"Omar." She went and sat beside him. "Omar, you didn't want to hurt anyone, right?" She looked up as he squeezed tears out of his eyes, his head shaking vehemently. "Please. It was a mistake. Just let me take him home."

The principal looked genuinely uncomfortable, and the police officers made no move to leave. "Can I see you alone, Ms. Abdul?"

Amina, apprehensive, followed Principal Adama into the hallway.

"You have to understand how this looks. In these times, a Muslim child brings a knife into school—we can't just not report it."

Amina struggled to catch her breath, feeling like she had been punched in the gut. "What?"

"Now that the police are here, we have to file a report. This child needs counseling. He waved this knife at another boy, and Mrs. Pinkston said he has delusions of being some kind of Islamic ruler. He could be more troubled than you realize."

"That is fucking ridiculous," Amina said, and the principal stepped back. "The knife is decorative. He's interested in India. He made a mistake. So what? He's a child, he's eleven fucking years old."

"I'm sorry." The principal gestured back toward the door. "Let's see if we can get this over with quickly."

It took almost an hour to set up a room and interview Omar

and get him processed out of the school. He wept silently, giving short answers in his home voice to their accusatory questions. His Indian accent was gone, and Amina actually felt nostalgic for it. When they were done, Amina took him home. The principal said not to bring him back to school until she'd had a chance to consider the case.

She drove them back to his house, assuming he would like the comfort of his own room. He was quiet and so was she, wondering why neither of his parents had answered the phone messages left by the principal and then by Amina.

When they got inside, he went straight to his room.

"I'll make you something to eat," she called, but instead she sank down onto the couch. Where the hell were Marcy and Mo? What was she going to tell them? Why hadn't she taken the knife from Omar when she'd seen it? She shouldn't have been left with a child, and now what were Mo and Marcy going to think when she admitted that she'd known he was carrying the knife around?

After a few minutes of quiet agony, she heard cars driving up, and she braced herself to meet them. Marcy and Mo burst in at the same time.

"Amina!" Marcy said. "Where is Omar?"

"In his room." Amina began to explain as best as she could.

"Jesus," Marcy said. She turned and went up the stairs and straight into Omar's room without knocking. Mo shook his head and followed her up, but Amina could hear his footsteps take another flight and then the sound of their bedroom door closing. This left Amina to pace aimlessly around the living room, wondering if she should stay or go.

Marcy came back after about ten minutes, her face pale. She and Amina sat at the kitchen table and drank iced tea.

"I'm so sorry that you had to take that call."

"Where were you?" Amina asked.

"Mo doesn't want you to know. We just don't want you to worry." Marcy looked embarrassed and the rest came out in a rush. "We were at a marriage counselor. One of the conditions of the session—Mo's condition—is that I turn my cell off. And then we started talking afterward, and I didn't turn it back on right away." She gave a short cough that was meant to be a laugh. "I won't do that again."

They heard Mo coming down the stairs, and Marcy looked at Amina and put a finger to her lips. Amina nodded, and they waited in silence for Mo to join them. She felt off balance even though she was sitting still, as if the world was spinning at a slightly faster rate than she was.

"I'm sure the principal will come around," Marcy said as Mo took a seat. "She always seemed reasonable to me."

"These are not reasonable times," Amina said.

Marcy poured tea for Mo, but he left it in front of him untouched. They sat around the table in silence for a few more minutes. Then Mo stood up so suddenly that his chair fell over with a crash.

"It's bullshit," he said. "Pull him from the school." He left the room and went out the front door, slamming it behind him. Marcy got up and ran to open it again, as if to stop him, but then she stopped and just watched as he got into his car and sped off.

9.

THE SCHOOL EXPELLED OMAR. This fate was decided upon after only one meeting with his parents, during which the principal stressed that she would not press charges on behalf of the school. They enrolled him at the local public school, one that had a reputation for being decent, and Omar's private-school career ended in abrupt tragedy.

The next weekend Amina stopped in to talk to Marcy. Omar answered the door; if he had owned a pet, she would have guessed it had died.

"Hello," he said, his sad eyes unblinking.

"How goes it?"

He shrugged.

"Can I come in?" she suggested. "I was hoping to talk to your mom."

He led her to the living room. Marcy sat on the couch in front of the TV, her cell phone next to her like a faithful companion. Omar pounded up the stairs to his room. Marcy was wearing velour sweats, and she too looked depressed.

"I was in the neighborhood," Amina said, feeling awkward. She tucked her hair behind her ears.

Marcy put the TV on mute. "Did he let you in?"

Amina nodded and sat on the arm of the couch. "How's it going at the new school?"

Marcy tipped her head to one side and wrinkled her nose. "It's not the greatest school, Amina. But I've checked with his teacher and she seems enthusiastic enough. He's excited about some dinosaur project that goes through the whole year. I just worry."

"That he's still not happy?"

Marcy put her hands to her hair, pulled it into a ponytail, and then released it to spring back around her head, a series of exclamation points. "About what kind of friends he's going to make there."

Amina had been surprised when she arrived in the city to find Marcy and her brother stretching to pay the mortgage on a house in such an expensive neighborhood, straining to pay private-school bills that cost more than college. They were in middle-class professions. Amina could only think that it was Marcy's exposure to the congressmen and -women that had created this sudden class consciousness in her. If Marcy had been interested in social climbing, marrying Mo had not been the wisest choice; perhaps this hinted at the necessity of the marriage counselor.

"He's going to make friends with regular kids, which is what he is," Amina said.

"I know," she said. "I know, Amina. You're right."

Amina hesitated, and then dove in. "Can I ask what's happening with Mo? With you and Mo?"

"He's at work."

"That's not what I mean," Amina said. She could be patient.

Marcy sighed. "Mo is at work. Mo is always at work. Your brother is a workaholic."

And he's not alone, Amina thought, but she was resolved to be diplomatic. "But it's good you're seeing someone, that counselor."

"That," Marcy said, "did not work out."

"Oh," Amina said.

Marcy finally raised her eyes to meet Amina's, and then she looked guilty. "I'm sorry. This isn't your problem, is it? We're fine. We always have been." She laughed. "This is just what it looks like up close."

"I like to be close to you," Amina said, meaning it. "I'd like to help."

Marcy nodded, and then she nodded again, and then her cell phone rang. "It's Karen," she said. "Do you mind?"

"Sure," Amina said. Karen was Marcy's best friend from high school, an overachiever and class president who had become a cosmetician with five kids on the outskirts of Cleveland. Amina had always detested her, and the feeling had been mutual. Amina waved at Marcy and her phone and called a farewell up the stairs to Omar. He appeared at the top of them immediately.

"Goodbye," he said, waving his hand.

She resisted the urge to run up and kiss him.

10.

THE RUSHED GRANT APPLICATION went in, and Amina had a bit of breathing room to work on a paper of her own. The lab was running more smoothly now that the semester was in full gear, and she was able to spend less time on Chris's projects and more time on her own work. Chris undertook most of the committee work, which she was thankful for because it meant that she didn't have to do it and that he was often out of the lab at meetings.

Anjali invited her to lunch, and at first Amina said she was too busy. But she did owe Anjali a favor in return for the cricket connection, and so when Anjali approached her again about lunch, Amina suggested that they go to a French café nearby.

"I'll buy," she said.

They went early, because Anjali was auditing an archaeology class that started at two in a different section of the university. Anjali ordered salad niçoise and a cappuccino, and Amina had a heart-hardening brick of melted ham and Swiss and plain black coffee. They chatted about work and what it would mean to get this grant and about a new graduate student from Ecuador who seemed to know more than anyone at the lab, including Chris.

"My brother likes you," Anjali said, as the waitress took their plates and left them with their coffee. Amina nearly spit a mouthful out onto the table.

Anjali leaned toward her. "He's an excellent brother. I give him my highest recommendation."

"I'm not dating right now," Amina said. *Also,* she continued in her head, *don't you have enough relationships that mingle your personal and professional lives?* "And, it would be awkward."

"Not for me," Anjali said. "Feel free."

"But I don't," said Amina, without apology.

A dark look came onto Anjali's pretty face then, a look that reminded Amina of Omar and made Anjali seem very young. Her lower lip pouted out.

"Amina," she said. "I think I may have made a mistake."

"In recommending your brother?" Amina joked, hoping to head off the confession she felt coming. But Anjali just shook her head.

"I don't know what to do. I've crossed a line." She looked hard at Amina. "Do you know what I'm talking about?"

Amina felt like a panicked ungulate, a herd animal separated from its companions and desperate to escape.

"I think I might," Amina said.

"What would you do in my position?" Anjali asked.

Amina let out a long breath. "Anjali, maybe you should talk to your brother about this," she said. She reached for her bag and took out her wallet.

Anjali shook her head. "No. No way. Please," she said, leaning forward, "please, please promise me that you won't ever say anything to him about this."

"About what?" Amina said. She put down cash for the bill and stood. She couldn't do it. She couldn't help this girl sort out this kind of mess. Besides, the answer was clear: to stop sleeping with Chris. If Anjali couldn't see that, or didn't want to, then there was nothing Amina could do.

They walked back to the lab and returned to their separate corners. Chris had Anjali working closely with him. Amina hadn't noticed any tension between them, but then she had been trying not to look. She felt awful now, though. What exactly had Anjali been trying to say? That she was with Chris only because she felt coerced? That it had gotten too messy? Or that she hadn't slept with him yet but felt the pressure to do so?

That afternoon a job posting came over email, an announcement of a research position that would combine data collection in the field with focused genetic analysis. The job description fit Amina's qualifications, though it was a significantly senior position to the one she had now. It was in India, near the Himalayas.

She stared at it for a long time. So far, her experiment in urban living had been a failure. Her brother was distant and unapproachable, his wife too busy and distracted to be a reliable friend. Her brief influence on Omar had ended in disaster. She missed Matt without wanting him back. She disliked the head of her lab and most of her colleagues. And in spite of all these tangled lines of human communication, she felt alone.

Her short time in Washington, DC, had only confirmed what she suspected: she wasn't made for offices or fashionable research, interpersonal relations or chatting at office parties. Her mind was only engaged by the thought of being in the field again, in the silence where her only human company were workers paid to do her bidding.

And she had to admit that she, Amina Abdul, the woman without interest in race or identity or religion or nationality, was intrigued by the thought of returning to India. It was Omar's influence. All that talk and those questions and those large dark eyes had made her think about this country that had last preoccupied her in grade school. She had the odd idea that it would do her good to live in India; the idea seemed strange because she kept thinking of it as a return, like she was the immigrant, not her parents, like it was some kind of nest that she had been separated from.

She began to work on the application. She revised her CV

and cover letter, wrote notes to California requesting letters of recommendation, and began to compose a proposal for where she would take the research, trying to make the sentences just right. They needed to understand exactly how much she wanted the job.

11.

A COUPLE OF WEEKS later, Amina arranged to meet Marcy and Omar for an afternoon at the natural history museum. Her dinner invitation had not been repeated, and Marcy had been driving Omar to cricket. Amina had realized if she wanted to see them, it was up to her. She knew Omar was doing better at his new school. Marcy said he was newly fascinated by astronomy and by spelling; he had won a schoolwide spelling bee.

Amina was early and found herself walking around near the Mall. She went into the bookstore without thinking, and jumped a little in surprise when Prakash touched her arm.

"Amina Abdul, I'm happy to see you. How are you?"

"Hello. I'm fine, thank you. Just fine." She stopped herself from continuing in that idiotic vein. How many times did she need to say fine? She took a deep breath.

"Are you looking for something in particular?" Prakash asked. He was wearing a very crisp white shirt, and she tried not to stare.

"Maybe you can recommend something?" This wasn't a wise thing to say either, but her brain felt prickly and electric and not at all like her own.

"Sure." He led her over to a display table and picked up

several books with his large hands. The silver bracelet on his wrist flashed. He stopped after a moment and set the books down.

"My sister has been a bit distant lately. Has there been some trouble at the lab?"

"We've all been under a lot of pressure," Amina said; guilt washed over her as she lied. "To finish a grant with a tight deadline."

"I realize that work politics can be very difficult," he said. "But I wondered if perhaps you might be able to help her? She could use a mentor."

Amina cleared her throat softly and reached for the books. Their hands brushed together and she felt the warmth of his fingers. "I don't know," she said, shaking her head hard enough to clear it. "I don't see what I can do."

He nodded, his dark eyes on hers. "She trusts you. As one of us."

"I know," she said, looking away. "But I'm new, and I really don't have much say in what happens there."

He had disappointment all over his face. "Your nephew is well, I hope?"

"Omar's great."

"Good," he said. "Family is what matters."

"You know what?" she said. "I'm late. I'll come back for these." She set the books back on the counter and left the store.

As she walked toward the museum, a fall wind was knocking leaves from the trees. Amina wasn't finding the change in weather any more amenable than the sticky summer heat, and she shivered in the chill air. When she arrived in the lobby, Omar was sitting in silence on a bench while Marcy, looking frazzled, stood beside him talking into her cell phone. She put it aside when she saw Amina.

"Amina, I'm sorry, but there's an emergency with one of the kids at the center. Will you two be all right alone for a little while?"

"Sure," Amina said.

"I'll meet you back here for dino fries in a couple of hours, okay kiddo?" Marcy said to Omar. He nodded without looking up.

Amina wanted to take his hand as they went into the museum together. She wanted him to know that his mother loved him, that he always came first to his parents, no matter how it seemed.

The hall was crowded and hot, and they ducked in to look at rocks and gemstones for a while. But the sight of the large rubies unsettled her; she didn't want to remind him of the stories he had told. She steered him toward the dioramas of early mammals, thinking maybe she would recognize some of these monkey ancestors to tell him about.

It was a weekend, and the exhibit was crammed with people. Children shrieked and grasped at their parents and fought in mindless tantrum with each other, and she felt the familiar aversion to crowds, to families, to people. How heavenly it would be to walk the museum alone, her and Omar, to study exhibits at their leisure, and to try to get him to talk a little. Now conversation was impossible, and the noise level only increased the closer they got to the giant sloth.

"It's too loud," Omar suddenly said.

She felt relief. "You're right. Let's find something else to look at."

They walked out into the central, circular marble corridor and followed it, peeking into exhibit entrances. Three-quarters of the way around, the sound was reduced. She led him into a dark entry, only to realize that they'd entered a deserted exhibition of Islamic artifacts.

She paused, but then decided that the soothing quiet was worth almost any price.

"Let's see some of this stuff," she said to Omar, and he shrugged his passive assent.

They studied a number of objects in gold, and some porcelain with abstracted writing. She admired some beveled doors, and Omar's eyes seemed to fix on an enormous glass incense burner. Then they came to a display of weaponry.

Suddenly determined, Amina led him over to the case. They stared in somber silence at the case of engraved swords and ruby-encrusted hilts, at the animal-featured handles, and silver-threaded velvet scabbards. Amina's hair fell forward against her cheek, and she let it stay, shading her face.

"What happened to your knife?" she asked, trying to sound indifferent.

"The police took it," he said.

"I can get you another one," Amina offered.

He shook his head. "I'm not supposed to have knives now."

Amina looked around and saw a bench in the next room. She led him in, and they sat amid walls carpeted in red and amber textiles.

"What happened that day, Omar?"

"It was an accident." His lower lip puffed out in defiance.

"I won't tell your parents anything. I just want to hear your side."

Omar shook his head, but a single tear slid down his cheek.

"Did the boy say something to upset you?"

His dark head shook again, but this time it seemed more of a wag.

"What happened, then?"

Omar drew his lip in and bit it, tears running free down his face now. "I hate him. I hate him. I hate him."

She reached into her pocket for a tissue and gave it to him. "Who?"

"Davy Madsen." Omar pressed the tissue to his throat as if stopping a wound. "He said we were nothing. He said I wasn't even Indian because Indians were Hinduists and that I was a liar and that our family wasn't special. He said that Muslims will all die when the US has a chance. And then I showed him the knife and said I would kill him first." He sobbed and hiccupped, and snot ran down onto his upper lip.

"Okay. It's okay." She put an arm around him, and he leaned his hot face into her shoulder. Then he lifted his head and looked at her.

"I wanted to do it. I wanted to kill him with the knife. I would have."

She tried not to let the shock show on her face. She took out another tissue and tried to wipe his face clean.

"You wouldn't have, Omar," she told him. "Are you listening to me? You wouldn't have. Just because you wanted to doesn't mean that you would have done it."

He started to cry all over again. She searched her mind for the words that could soothe the hunger in his heart and the fear in hers. She understood his ache for reassurance that their family, history, the world made sense. But all she could think to tell him was that he should find a way to escape into an inner world, to fiercely guard his solitude. Because there were no guarantees, and there were always people who were disappointing and cruel, and you could go your whole life searching but never find a place where you belonged. But she couldn't say that, not to an eleven-year-old.

"How about some dino fries?" she said. "We'll get ice cream, too."

He nodded, reining in his sobs. "Chocolate sauce?"

"Extra hot fudge and sprinkles, too," she said. "And whipped cream!"

His face broke into a radiant smile, the smile of a child again. They left the carpeted room and followed the red signs to the exit.

In the corridor, pandemonium continued unabated. She took his hand to guide him through a class of kindergartners, but even after they had passed through the pack, she still kept a hold of his sweaty, soft paw. They descended the stairs together, past skeletons and models and squares of printed text: endless charts of the unfathomable past, none of which painted the route to a rational future.

When they reached the cafeteria, he shook his hand loose, running ahead to locate the ice cream. She pushed back her hair with a sigh, feeling their separation like a pain. She poured herself a cup of black coffee and took it on a tray to where he stood in front of a vast array of confections—conjured for the multitudes who visited this hallowed hall of science day after day—and she ordered him his sweet.

II. CITY OF PEARLS

12.

OMAR WAS HAPPY. HE was always happiest when he had work to do, and now that he was deep into his project, and a secret one at that, even being at the new school bothered him less. Today, a Saturday, he needed to go to the public library to do some research. Late in the morning he emerged from his bedroom and went to see which of his parents might be found.

He was writing the family history, or at least the history of his father's side of the family, who came from a place called Hyderabad in southern India. He wanted to prove that his family was really Indian, even though they were Muslim and other kids kept telling him he was an *A*-rab and a towel-head; and he really wanted to show his father that their family was important, so he wouldn't be mad at Omar anymore about being interested in India. After the time he had brought the dagger to school, his father had told him to forget about these things, but Omar knew that if he could show how cool their family history was, his father would be proud too. Omar planned to give the history to him, maybe the story with a family tree that he would draw, as a birthday present that summer.

The idea for the history had come out of an assignment at his last school. He'd hated that school—and he was glad to never go back to it even if he did feel ashamed that he had been kicked out—although it was also true that his teacher had been nice to him in her girl-colored sweater sets, her teeth as white as people in commercials. She had told them to make a picture of their families, and it was then that he knew—not for the first time, really, but for the first time all the way in his head, all the way understanding—that his family was different from other families.

There was his mother, who was a lot like other mothers. She was pretty, too, prettier than Mrs. Pinkston, and she had red hair. She was busy all the time, and he often felt a longing for her, a feeling that he told himself was babyish. When he wanted to be with her the most, he read a book, which gave him almost the same feeling.

His father, his dad, gave him a different feeling. Omar was a little frightened of him, not because he acted mean or intimidating but more because he never bothered to be either. Omar just never understood what his father wanted of him. They were at a standoff—not a bad one, but one that made Omar anxious pretty much all the time. His father was busy, too, but in a different way than his mother was. It was less about activity and more about the fact that his mind always seemed to be thinking about someone not in the room.

His father's name, Omar knew, even at eleven, was profoundly and painfully not a good thing. When people said "Mo and Marcy," that seemed natural, just like regular parents. But when people said "Marcy and Mohammed," he knew from their tone of voice that those names did not belong together. The same thing sometimes happened when his mom introduced him as "my son Omar." Once someone had asked her if he was adopted. She hadn't changed her last name when she'd married his dad, so her name was still Benoit, but he and his dad had the Abdul name from his grandfather.

Omar was close to his grandfather and grandmother, except that they lived far away, so he only saw them a few times a year. His grandma was indulgent with lipstick kisses, too-fancy

clothes, and candy. To him, she was as handsome and digni-
fied as a queen. His grandfather, on the other hand, seemed
quiet and wise and interested in Omar as a person. He was a
professor who read poetry, old poetry that Omar found hard to
understand but that he knew deserved his respect. His grandfather was the human being Omar admired the most in the world
and, he suspected, the person who loved him the most. Not
because his parents didn't love him, but because they didn't see
him, really see him, the way his grandpa did.

His mom's family lived mostly in North Carolina, and they
visited them a few times a year. Omar didn't like them all that
much. The cousins lived in the same place and knew each other
really well, and he always felt like the new kid around them,
like he did at school. He saw his mom's sister Missy the most;
she wore a lot of makeup and spoke to him in a too-nice voice
that he didn't like, but she was nicer to him than her husband,
Lyle, who barely said anything, just made things with his hands,
like the bench Omar's parents kept in their garden. He liked
his grandma Benoit, his mom's mom, except that she was very
slow moving and old and didn't do much of anything besides
cook. She called Omar her "little man" sometimes, usually at
night after she drank her amaretto, which smelled sweet but
tasted sharp, as Omar had discovered for himself last year.

And then there was Aunt Amina, who had just moved here.
He hadn't seen that much of her before, and he was happy that
she was in his life this year. She was the one who'd found the
cricket team for him. She was very smart and a scientist, and
he wanted to learn things from her but he didn't know how.
She always seemed to be holding something back from him,
even though she sometimes seemed like the only person who
actually wanted to spend time with him; maybe she didn't
know he was smart. Another point of his project was to show
Amina that he was a researcher too.

The path from his bedroom led him down a narrow flight of
stairs, past rows of pictures of himself at various ages, including
the much-hated close-up of himself at five missing two front

teeth, down through the empty living room with its cushy beige couches and red-striped wallpaper, and finally into the kitchen, where he found his father sitting on a barstool at the counter eating toast. Breakfast, which had once been a family meal, had disintegrated, so that everyone ate separately. Often, his dad forgot he was hungry at all, and now Omar felt a moment of relief to see him there, eating toast at a regular time.

"Dad," Omar said, "can you take me to the library?"

His father looked up, toast crumbs littering his lips. He looked confused. "I can't, Omar. I'm busy."

"Where's Mom?" Omar had known his father would say no, and didn't try to change his mind.

"She's . . ." His father took a bite of toast and thought. "She's grocery shopping. She can take you when she gets back."

Omar nodded and, after grabbing a grape soda from the fridge, taking advantage of the fact that his mother was not around to get mad at him for drinking sugar in the morning, went back to his room.

He closed the door after hanging his Keep Out sign on its nail, and went to his closet. On the right side, behind the suits and button-up shirts and cardigan sweaters given by his grandmother, he had a secret stash in a shoebox. Included were CDs of sitar music, a few books of Indian history, a wool shawl that he had nicked from his grandmother—he had never seen her wear it, and indeed it was light brown and not very pretty and yet still Indian—a copy of a black-and-white Bollywood, which meant Indian Hollywood, film from his grandfather that he had never watched, and an antique silver knife in an engraved hilt.

The knife was the biggest secret, because his mother had taken it away from him when it came back from the police station and told him the she would keep it for him until he was grown-up. He had found it easily enough in the bottom of her sweater drawer and stuffed it away with the other things.

After the incident of the knife—he heard his mother refer to it that way, whispering on the phone, and had himself taken to referring to it as such on the one or two occasions when he felt it useful to impress on his new classmates that he had a dark and thrilling past—he'd promised to everyone, to put them at ease, that he was no longer interested at all in India. He returned picture books to the library, replaced an ivory elephant of his mother's to its rightful place on a side table in the den, and took the family portrait down from his sky-blue walls, a picture of Shah Rukh Khan, and a copper Hand of Fatima on a leather string that he had bought at a street fair. His parents' relief was palpable, and he was proud that he had put their needs ahead of his own and that he was able to make them feel better after the incident, which was an incident that still made him feel a little sick inside when he thought of it.

For now, he took out only a book of photographs and one of the CDs, which his grandfather had given him for Christmas. He put the CD on his stereo, but plugged in headphones so no one would know what he was listening to. He longed for an iPod onto which he could download all his Indian music but with secret names so his parents wouldn't know what it was. But Christmas had already passed before he thought of this, so now he would have to wait and make appeals at his birthday. He sat on the bed with a notebook and purple-ink pen next to him, and leafed through the pages. He couldn't pronounce the photographer's name—it was long and strange with many consonants and syllables—but he liked the pictures.

The photographs were all of people in India. The colors were bright and cartoonish, and everyone was very poor, and the animals in the photos looked like they were starving. At first, Omar had felt disappointed when he looked at the pictures, because the book he'd had from the library before was all pictures of palaces and forts, and he had come to think of India like that. But now he liked these pictures, too, because the people all seemed so sad and serious and that made them seem real, almost like he knew them.

In his notebook was a family tree that, so far, only went back three generations. His plan was to look through the picture book to see if any of the people were from Hyderabad, or to see if any of the names of his family—Abdul and Nasir were the ones he knew of so far—appeared attached to any of the places or people.

He knew, of course, that this was not real research. This was why he had to go to the library. But he had asked his aunt once how she had come to know so much, and she'd said that she had spent a very long time learning about very small things, and that it wasn't until after many years that she felt that she knew anything at all. He wasn't sure how that could be true, because she was a scientist and that meant, as far as he knew, that she conducted experiments, which must mean that she was learning important new things all the time. But still he took the spirit of it to heart, and it suited the secrecy of the project, after all. He would accumulate knowledge slowly, patiently, and then when it was done, and only when it was done, would he show everyone what he had accomplished.

After half an hour, he heard his mother come in the front door. He ignored her call for help carrying in the groceries and waited a safe ten minutes before wandering into the kitchen, where she was putting food away. His father, as usual, was nowhere to be seen.

"Hi, Omar," she said, sliding boxes of cereal side by side in the cupboard. He looked in vain for the tiger on his favorite Frosted Flakes, but saw only muesli, Raisin Bran, and the dreaded Grape Nuts. Sometimes, if there was a sale, she would buy him the cereal he really wanted as a treat. His hopes rose a little, though, as she moved on to stack cans of soup and he saw SpaghettiOs and Chef Boyardee ravioli. If she was feeling flexible enough for those, who knew what else she might have bought for him?

"Mom," he said, "can you take me to the library? It's for school."

"I'm supposed to meet Jean for lunch, and the Johnsons are coming for dinner. But maybe your father can take you?"

"He's busy too." Omar was careful to keep any hint of whine out of his voice; being practical was the key to getting something he wanted from his parents. If he made them feel guilty, he would be doomed to accompany his mother on endless rounds of errands and chitchat. "Maybe you could drop me off before you go to lunch and pick me up after?"

His mother stopped with a head of lettuce in her hand, frozen for a moment like a statue of a garden goddess while she considered this. "Well, I guess you are old enough to be there alone. You wouldn't leave? You'd wait for me to come inside and find you?"

Omar nodded emphatically. "Yes, Mom. You don't have to worry."

"We have to leave in a few minutes. Why don't you take these cans down to the basement for me? Your father's nowhere to be seen."

He went to the paper bags of soda and lifted them out. "Isn't there any regular Coke?" That was what his father drank, and he hated it when there was only Diet in the house.

"No. There isn't," his mother said in a hard voice that he had heard more and more lately when she referred to Omar's father. "He'll drink what I buy, I guess."

Omar dutifully carried two cases of Diet Coke into the basement and then went to pack up his backpack. His parents seemed to be having more and more small wars. He worried because he thought he could trace the start of their problems back to the knife incident. Still, for now he was happy, because he would get to go to the library, and because he'd seen her stash a jumbo pack of Oreos on the top shelf.

13.

OMAR HAD STARTED PLAYING cricket the previous fall; the practices stopped over the winter, but now that March had arrived, they were resuming. It had been arranged that Omar would go to cricket practice every other weekend and that his aunt would take him. He liked his coach, Prakash, and he especially liked Prakash's sister, Anjali, who was also his aunt's friend, and who sometimes came to practice, and so, although he wasn't very athletic, he looked forward to going again. Anjali was the prettiest girl he had ever seen, and she was nice, too. She didn't treat him like he was eleven, but just like a grown-up. For that reason, and the fact that she seemed to be really, truly Indian—if not actually from India—he was thinking about asking her to help with his project. But he somehow thought that his aunt might not like it, so he hadn't said anything to Amina.

Amina picked him up for the first practice on the first Sunday of the month. His mother had bought him a pair of K-Swiss sneakers in white and blue, and he wore shorts even though it was still cold. He hadn't seen that much of Amina lately, not since she had celebrated Christmas with them for the first time. His mom told him Amina was busy with a project at work, so he had resisted the urge to call her and ask to spend another weekend with her like he had in the fall. That had been one of the best weekends of his life.

"Howdy, Omar," his aunt said.

"Howdy," he said back, giggling a little. His aunt was full of unexpected mannerisms; she wasn't like any other adult he knew.

"Howdy, Mo," she said to Omar's dad, who had wandered out from the kitchen.

"Cricket today?" he asked.

"Indeed," said Amina. "'Tis the season."

"Did Marcy invite you for dinner after?"

"No, she didn't."

There was a pause while Omar looked anxiously between them, waiting for his father to issue the invitation. Instead his father took a long sip of iced Diet Coke, grimacing as it went down.

"Mom wants you to come for dinner," Omar finally said.

"We'll see," Amina said. "I'll come in when I drop him off, okay, Mo? And I have my cell."

She took Omar's arm and they went out the door together. He shivered as the cold air hit his bare legs and she looked at him with mild concern.

"Warm enough?"

"Yeah," he said.

They got into the car, and she put on some of her weird, depressing guitar music that was louder than what he expected an adult to listen to. She drove fast—too fast, his mother said—but Omar liked it.

The cricket pitch was a baseball and soccer field in Bethesda, across the river from his house. He liked the drive there, through the old brick buildings of Georgetown, which seemed historical though no one had ever explained their exact significance to him, and then over the glittery wide water and into a different kind of city.

This part of the city had very large new buildings and lots

and lots of stores with names that he recognized from adver-
tisements. His mother shopped at small stores in their neighborhood, and except for her weekly visit to the supermarket
almost never went to big places, the places with names that
made his heart swoop and hope, places that, he suspected, if
he shopped at them, would make the kids at school like him.
After the stores, there was a long stretch of TV houses: two
story, wood-paneled, with yard on all sides. Finally there came
the field, which was long and green, with metal bleachers
along one side and a chain-link backstop fence behind home
plate.

At the field, Omar surveyed the group. Like last fall, there
were two girls, Indian sisters who were always dressed in
impeccable cricket whites. About half the remaining dozen kids
were also South Asian—his aunt had given him the term, which
means from India, Pakistan, or Bangladesh, which all used to
be one country. Or Sri Lanka, which was Ceylon in most of
his books. The rest were from all over: Zimbabwe, England,
and Australia, plus four from the US. He felt weird about this,
because most of the kids were immigrants or the children of
immigrants, and they assumed that he was too, but his parents
had both been born in America. He wanted to talk to his aunt
about this, to see if they were still immigrants even though they
had been born here, but he hadn't gotten around to it yet.

Amina walked him over to where Prakash was warming the
early arrivals up with simple stretches. She walked more and
more slowly as they approached, until Omar looked up at her
and gave her hand a little tug.

"Omar!" Prakash said, his entire face—beard, mustache,
turban, and all—seeming to curve into a smile. "Welcome
back. Why don't you work on your stretches while we wait for
everyone to arrive?"

Omar nodded and moved closer to the other kids, some of
whom smiled and greeted him. He was grateful to be remembered from the fall. He hated always being the new kid, like he
still was at the public school he had started at after the problem

at his old school. But he stayed near Prakash and his aunt so he could hear what they were saying.

"I was hoping we'd see you back this year. You didn't respond to the email."

"Was I supposed to?" Amina asked, a little rudely, Omar thought. Maybe she was sick or something. "I took it as more of an open announcement."

"Ah." Prakash paused and rubbed the back of his neck.

"Anjali's not here?" Omar heard Amina ask.

"Some other week. Is everything at the lab okay? I mean, her work? She mentioned something about a problem with her boss."

Amina moved her head somewhere between yes and no. "I'm not sure."

Prakash didn't seem to believe her because he kept on looking at her like he was waiting to learn more. Finally he leaned in a little closer to Amina and said something in a quieter voice. Omar strained forward in a low stretch with his head turned so that his left ear was as close as possible to them.

"I'd like to let you give me another chance," was what Omar thought he heard. But that couldn't be right, because what would his coach have to give Amina a chance for? They didn't really know each other, or at least he didn't think they did. This was one of the things that frustrated him about adults: they had a whole world to themselves that they kept from kids and that made them absolutely impossible to understand. He resolved, not for the first time, to hone his spy skills.

The practice went quickly, in a series of drills and trials. Amina sat on the sidelines reading and didn't seem to pay very close attention. Omar thought he saw Prakash look at her more than once, but she didn't look back at him.

When they got back to the house, Amina didn't come in. She said she had work to do. When he came in alone, his mother looked pissed.

"I told you, Mo," she said, turning her head toward the kitchen where Omar caught a glimpse of his dad, drinking Diet

Coke from the can. "Is it too much to ask you to make an effort with your own sister?"

"It's okay, Mom," Omar said. "She said she had to do work." Sometimes Amina reminded him a lot of his dad. He wondered what it would be like if he had a brother or sister—would they be exactly alike, too?

14.

AT SCHOOL THE NEXT Monday, Omar was surprised to see one of the other kids from cricket practice at his school. They looked at each other in the hallway and said an awkward hello, and then they spoke again at recess. It was Hari, who said he had just moved to the neighborhood and that his family was originally from Guyana.

"Where's that?" Omar asked. "Africa?"

"South America. Lots of Indians like us live there." A fleeting expression crossed Hari's face as he said this, an expression of anxiety mixed with weariness. Omar knew that expression. It meant he was tired of explaining this.

"Have you read this book?" Omar showed him a book he had found at the public library. It was called *Kim*, by someone named Rudyard Kipling.

The boy shrugged, but he took it from Omar and leafed through the pages with interest. "Where's Lahore?" he asked, and Omar shrugged. He wasn't sure where in India it was.

They talked through recess, mostly about cricket, which Hari knew a great deal about. His favorite player was Sachin Tendulkar, who did Pepsi commercials in India. He showed Omar a card with Tendulkar's photo. He had favorite teams even in the smaller leagues and knew all their colors and lots of technical words that Omar didn't know or even really care about. But it pleased Omar, because too often he found himself with kids his age who didn't know much about anything, and who either looked to him as the brainy one to tell them the answers or punished him for the exact same reason.

He told Hari about his secret project, and couldn't resist bragging that he had been doing some research on the internet. Hari told him to be careful.

"Why?" Omar asked, puzzled.

"My uncle was on the computer and he typed in some kind of words that the FBI didn't like, and they came to his house and arrested him."

"Why would they do that?"

"They thought he was a terrorist, man," Hari said, shaking his head wisely. "My dad says we all have to be careful. He was stopped at the airport and he said that if he hadn't had an ID from the newspaper they would have kept him in jail."

Omar thought this through for the rest of the day. His mother and father had never mentioned any danger to him, though he knew that the knife incident was—in a way that he did not fully understand—connected to the day that the planes crashed and he was pulled out of his second-grade class and taken home by his shaken mother. He knew that when the boys in his classes called him an *A*-rab, or a towel-head, or made ticking-bomb noises at him, this also somehow meant that they were calling him a terrorist. All of this also had something to do with the War on Terror, which was a war in Iraq and Afghanistan against people who covered their heads and had beards but otherwise looked a lot like him. He thought, not for the first time, that it would be better if he watched the TV news more.

That night he continued reading the book by Kipling. It was about a boy around his age, a boy who seemed to be both Indian and English, and he lived like a beggar and knew women Omar suspected were not good women and wore basically rags and had no family. At nine o'clock, his mother came in and told him to turn off the light, and he sighed and put it away. Some days he said yes and then read under the covers with a flashlight, but tonight he was wiped out.

HE WORKED ON THE family history project most days after school. His mom now dropped him at the public library whenever she had errands to run, and he had collected some histories of Hyderabad. To his disappointment, they largely consisted of tales regarding battles between local rulers and the British. In fact, most of what he was able to find out about India was about the British, except for a couple of books written in a language that he knew was English but was so full of large and unfamiliar words that they seemed foreign. And Omar knew that he was a good reader for his age, so the discovery that there were adult books he couldn't read, not because of bad words but because of the way the words were placed, entirely amazed him.

One weekend, he decided he had to do something different. He slipped downstairs to the family computer and typed in his password—Tiger679999—to go online. He searched his last name and first name, but came up with thousands of listings. He tried his grandfather's name, and some of the listings came up in a foreign language. This, he suspected, was Hindi. Or perhaps Urdi. He logged off, overwhelmed, and telephoned his grandpa in Ohio.

"Grandpa, can you teach me to speak Hindi?"

He heard his grandfather give a little sighing laugh. "Of course, boy. But if you are being like your father and aunt, you won't remember a great deal."

"But I want to learn."

"I believe you are serious. But it's difficult, you see, to do over the telephone. It's better if you had some classes."

There was a pause as they both considered this.

"They won't let me," Omar said.

"Omar," his grandfather said, "I think you are right. But soon you will be going to college and you can study these things there."

Omar's heart sank, because he saw college as impossibly far away, a star shining at a distance that he feared he would never cross. But then his grandpa continued.

"I will send you some tapes and study aids and such, and you can learn a little on your own. Acha?"

"What?"

"Acha," his grandfather said, "means 'okay.' That is your first lesson."

"Acha," Omar said.

The books came a few days later, three slim volumes. One was a workbook for practicing script, one was a dictionary, and one was a phrase book. The books were brand-new, and Omar's grandfather had even thought to send them by Priority Mail at the beginning of the week, so that Omar would certainly be the one to collect the mail. His secret was still safe.

He set to work on the script, thinking that if he could master it by the weekend, he would be able to go to the library again with better results. But less than an hour into the first day, there was a lump in his throat and he was fighting back tears. The script was more difficult, more impossible and bizarre and foreign, than anything he had imagined. The letters curved and swooped in ways his small hands just couldn't follow, and the shape of the letters changed according to what came before and after them, and each word that he copied out ended up hanging at a sharp angle. He didn't even have good handwriting in English, and this was hopeless. He finally threw his dulled pencil across the room in frustration.

It was clear that he was not meant to learn languages. His research was at an impasse, and he was going to need some help.

15.

HOPE CAME IN THE form of his chachi, Amina. His parents were planning another trip for spring break. It did not seem to be a trip either of them wanted to go on, but rather one they felt they had to go on. He caught bits of ominous phrases from his mother's mouth when she was talking to her friends on the phone, things like "this is my last try," and "we have to make this work." He kept extra quiet, but the silence in the house seemed louder and louder. His father had started to drink beer at night instead of Diet Coke, and sometimes skipped dinner and only came home after his mother went to bed. He told Omar this was because he was working. His mother kept up a steady stream of conversation into her silver phone, but she never looked cheerful the way she used to, the way it now seemed to Omar she had always been before the knife incident.

His parents' bedroom and bathroom was on the top floor. There was a floor below that, with Omar's room, and a guest room that was also his father's study. The bottom floor had a kitchen and dining room and a living room that faced the front of the house. The basement was half-finished, with his mother's exercise equipment and the computer. Omar had always liked the house, its skinny stairwells and small rooms, the hushed and private feel it had, each floor seeming shut off from those above and below. But now he felt that it was top-heavy somehow, as though all that was important was going on behind the closed door at the top of the final flight of stairs. The house began to feel claustrophobic. He longed for more space, for big windows that looked out on a view, for a window in his bedroom that wasn't blocked by the leaves of their dying dogwood tree, one that let in more sun.

Finally, a plan emerged. His parents were leaving to go to Greece for two weeks, coming home just in time to celebrate his twelfth birthday. His aunt Amina had agreed to stay at the house to oversee him, the mail, and plant watering. Omar, jealous though he was of Greece, which he knew was maybe older than India, was excited to think that Amina would be with him for so long, and in his own house.

He was nervous, too, about what she would think of him and his bedroom and stuff, and so he spent a long time rearranging his room, even considering reinstating the Bollywood poster or the ivory elephant, so she wouldn't think he had been entirely frightened off by the incident. Amina had been to India, and though she didn't talk about it much, he didn't sense any disapproval from her when he expressed his interest in the country. Best of all, he would have her to himself for two whole weeks, during which he was certain that she would be able to help him make progress on the family history.

Amina arrived the day before his parents were to leave, and they had a long dinner together. The adults drank wine, and Omar was given sparkling cherry-grape juice. His mother was back to her usual happy and affectionate self, and she kept leaning over to kiss Omar's head and tell him she would miss him. His father had roused himself to barbecue steaks outdoors, and this seemed to have instilled a temporary sense of place in him; he participated in the conversation, asking his sister about her work and teasing Omar's mother about how much she had packed. Amina, Omar noticed, was wearing lipstick.

• • •

THE PLAN WAS THAT Omar would spend most days in after-school programs, until Amina picked him up around five, and she also said she could work at home, so some days she would be able to pick him up right after school. He dreaded after-care, which, aside from an arts-and-crafts program, felt an awful lot like being babysat; he was always the oldest kid there.

And he worried, as he had worried most days since he'd heard of the trip, that one or maybe even both of his parents might not come back; he worried about this so much that he didn't dare remind them that he wanted the iPod for his birthday. Instead he asked his mom for all kinds of details about where they would be staying and what they would do every day, and he was confused because she said they would just lie on the beach, which is what they did in Florida, so why fly all the way to Greece to do it? They were, as usual, hiding something from him.

The first day Amina picked him up from after-care was the arts day, but it wasn't a good one: he was forced to draw fruit in charcoal and couldn't use any color at all. His initial response to this task was dejection, but he cheered up when he saw that Hari, too, had been left to suffer after-care. They worked side by side, and Omar developed a brief enthusiasm for shading until he was reprimanded by the aide, a plump college student with equal parts cheer and cruelty in her personality, for making his picture too dark. When Amina picked him up, Omar rolled up the drawing and put it in a cubby and then waved goodbye to Hari, who had charcoal on his cheek and, somehow, the back of his neck.

"Who was that?" Amina asked him as they walked to the car.

"Hari," he replied.

"He's on the cricket team, right?" she said. "I didn't know you went to school together."

"He's new," Omar said. "He just moved to a new house."

They got into the car after Amina had moved a stack of papers, fliers, and books from the passenger seat. He sat and buckled himself in.

"Hari is from Guyana," Omar said as they drove toward home. "Do you know where that is?"

"South America?" Amina said.

He hadn't thought she would know, and they sat in silence for a little longer.

"He's Indian, though, right?" Amina asked.

Omar nodded.

"I had a friend from Tobago once," she said.

He turned to look at her, not wanting to say anything that might stop her, but that seemed to be all. "Chachi?" he said. "Sometime do you think you can help me with a project? When you don't have too much work?"

"Is it your dinosaur project?" His mom had obviously relayed the cover story.

"Not exactly," he said. "I'll show you when we get home."

But it took a while, because first Amina concentrated on making him dinner. He said it didn't matter and suggested hopefully that a pizza would be easy, but she insisted that he needed real, home-cooked food even though she admitted she didn't really know how to cook. He decided that it was good for her to learn, and so didn't mention that most nights lately his mom was so tired she just heated up old leftovers from the freezer or made him pasta with butter, which he usually ate alone in front of the TV.

Amina pulled some things out of the cabinets and looked at various pots and pans, and opened and closed drawers with an air of purpose. He left her there and went to his room, closing the door but leaving the Keep Out sign unhung.

In his closet, he pulled out the CDs, the Hindi exercise books, and two of the more difficult histories he had checked out from the library. He put some music on low and started in on the script. If he showed her that he was really studying, there was a better chance she would help him.

When Amina knocked to tell him dinner was ready, the door pushed open a bit from the force of her hand, and she stuck her head in.

"Is that sitar music?" she asked.

He held his breath and nodded.

"Cool," she said. "Why don't you bring it down and play it on the stereo in the living room?"

She had made some sort of vegetable-and-nut stir-fry with soy sauce, over unintentionally sticky rice.

"It's good," he said, wanting to encourage her, though it was actually strange and too salty.

"I was thinking," she said, "that maybe we could do some cooking together."

"Okay," he said. His mother had often mentioned the same idea, but thus far he had escaped untaught. He felt there was something vaguely girlish about learning to cook, and so he avoided it, because he did not want to add one more thing to the list of things that made him not quite like other eleven-year-old boys.

"How about if we learn to make some Indian dishes together?" she asked him. "Maybe Grandma will send us some recipes."

"Can we do that?" Indian food was different. He wanted to learn this.

"Of course," she said.

At his grandma and grandpa's house in Ohio, they always served American food when his family was there to visit. Just in the last year or two, though, as he had been allowed to stay with them alone sometimes, his grandmother had taken to serving Indian food at every meal. He sometimes liked it and it sometimes made him feel a little queasy. It had never bothered him not to eat Indian food at home. His mother cooked what she called southern food on the weekends or if they had guests, and she never made him eat too much in the way of greens or spicy sauces. At his grandparents', however, he was expected to eat everything, no matter how murky the gravy or bony the meat or slimy the vegetable. What he liked best were his grandma's chapatis and rice pudding, and those were always in plentiful supply when he visited.

"Can we make rice pudding?" he asked.

"We can," Amina said. "I think even we can do that."

After dinner he helped her clean up, showing her where all the dishes belonged and refolding their cloth napkins. Then she told him she had some work to do, and he nodded. She had forgotten about his research. Adults were never finished with work, it seemed. He went to watch TV.

That night, as he got into bed, she came to his room again.

"I forgot, Omar," she said, "about your project. I'm sorry."

"It's okay," he said. "Maybe you can help me some other time."

"Is it due this week?"

"Just something I have to do before school is over. Maybe you can help me this weekend?"

"Sold," she said, and waved good night. Just as she was closing the door, he remembered.

"Chachi?" he called, and she stuck her head back in.

"Chachi, are we immigrants?"

She raised her eyebrows a little. "Are we immigrants? No. You and me and Mohammed were all born here. And your mom. Your grandparents, my mom and dad, are immigrants."

"But all those people on the cricket team? They're immigrants?"

"Well, it depends on where they were born. That's the definition. Prakash and Anjali were born here, like us. But to some people, I guess we all still seem like immigrants because people whose family originally came from South Asia are still new to them."

"But we are definitely American?"

"For better or for worse." This was the kind of answer his aunt often gave, where he couldn't tell if she was joking or serious.

He let his head sink back down to the pillow and said good

night. He was still a little confused, but comforted that his aunt was so firm. Why did people then keep asking him where he was from? There had been the time when he used the accent, but it still happened now that he spoke in perfectly normal English: people—teachers at school, boys on the cricket team, friends of his mother's—would ask where he came from. He was born in Massachusetts, when his father was working there. He had lived most of his life in Washington, DC. Did people ask Amina where she was from? He put that on his mental list of things to ask her and then finally went to sleep.

16.

As the first weekend approached, Amina proposed two things: a day of cooking—his grandma had emailed recipes for sambar, a foolproof biryani, and rice pudding—and a picnic.

"The picnic," Amina said, tucking some hair behind her ears, "is sort of a group thing. With Prakash."

"With the cricket team?" They were off this week, but he wasn't surprised. Prakash had made a promise to take them all out for ice cream sodas, and maybe this was a new version of that.

"Actually," Amina said, "no. Just us. And Anjali and some other people who work at Prakash's bookstore."

"Why are we going, then?" Omar asked. "We don't work at the bookstore."

"Because we were invited, and I thought you might like to go."

Omar had many more questions, but he could see that Amina didn't want to answer any more of them. "Okay," he said. "Acha."

She looked at him and laughed. "Tikka," she said. "And Sunday we can work on your research project."

In his room, he made a change while his parents were away:

over the course of the week, he had taken out all his Indian things from their hiding place in the far corner of his closet and placed them around the room. He only propped the pictures up, not bothering to pin them again, because he knew he would have to take them down before his parents came back. But for now he felt deliciously bad, having the whole of it to look at all the time, and he even kept the knife out, though it was behind a framed photograph of his parents, so Amina couldn't see it if she happened to walk in. He put his books in a stack by his bed.

Omar had always been smart, always been conscious of being smart. It was something that made his parents sometimes proud and sometimes worried. His mom was afraid she wouldn't know the answers to his many questions, especially questions about math or history. He had learned, now that he was older, not to ask her too many things, unless they were very simple or maybe about the South, where she grew up. His father worried, Omar suspected, because he thought that if Omar was smart, he would need to talk to him more, and Omar's father didn't like to have conversations too often.

And so for a long time now, he had disguised his real interests as school projects, his love of books as reading assignments, and his science experiments as craft projects. This kept everyone happy. But the truth was that for a while he had been reading grown-up novels and even some science and history books, and he was experiencing the curious sensation that the more he knew, the more he felt he didn't know, and the more he wanted to find out. He was hungry, for things as simple as knowledge about how snow formed to things as weird and mind-bendy as what truth was when everyone's stories contradicted each other's. Though he could call his grandfather and talk to him about the things he thought about, in DC he had often felt alone in his thinking; until, that is, his aunt came along.

He considered how best to present the project to her. It had a practical element, which was his intent to silence kids at school and prove that he was Indian and not a terrorist. But it also had a scientific side, he thought, by proving that the Abduls were a distinguished ancient clan to be proud of. He sought evidence, and it was these words that he intended to emphasize when he presented his work-in-progress to his aunt.

ON SATURDAY THEY DROVE to the picnic. It was being held to the north in a park in Maryland, so they started off before noon with bags of chips in a plastic bag and baseball caps and sweatshirts in case they got cold. His aunt's chin-length hair was still wet and a little messy, but she was wearing lipstick again and a very pretty greenish top that had beads along the cuffs. She looked nice.

"I'm going to take biology next year, when I go to seventh grade," he told her.

"Yeah? Will you like that?"

"I'm not sure." He thought for a second. "You liked it."

"Science was the hardest thing to take at school, and I liked challenge. But now I wish I had taken more literature courses, or art history or something. More like the stuff you're interested in."

"Me?" He wasn't totally prepared for the fact that she knew this about him. "I like history, mostly."

"Like about the dinosaurs?"

"Not really." He saw his chance and took a deep breath. "Chachi, my project isn't about dinosaurs, you know. I just told Mom that so she wouldn't worry. I'm researching about Hyderabad."

"In India? You mean where Grandma and Grandpa came from?" She turned her head to look at him with her foot still firmly on the gas pedal, and he nodded quickly so she would turn back to the road.

There were a few moments of silence.

"So what kind of help do you need?"

He breathed out slowly. "I don't know what books to get that will tell me my information."

"What do you need to know?"

"I'm trying to find out anything about the Abduls," he said, turning in his seat to look at her. "Like where Grandma and Grandpa's families lived and how many people there are and where they worked. It's not the same thing as before, anything about India. Now I'm writing out the Abdul family history, to make a book as a present for my dad."

She snorted a little, then looked at him quickly like she was checking to see if he had noticed. He looked down at his lap.

"Okay," she said. "For Mo. Well, I don't really know where to get that kind of stuff either, Omar. We can look, but you probably need to speak Hindi or Telugu. This is really advanced research."

"Well, what would a real researcher do?" he insisted.

"Probably go to Hyderabad," she said. "Look at old records, court documents, marriage certificates, property leases."

His heart sank. He had already asked his grandfather if they could go to Hyderabad. His grandfather sounded sorry and sad and certain when he said that he didn't think he would ever be returning to India again.

OMAR CHEERED UP A little bit when they got to the picnic grounds. It was more woodsy than he'd expected, but they walked through the tall trees to a big patch of green where a few people were playing soccer and throwing bright Frisbees. It was a warm day, in the low seventies and sunny except for under the trees, where he shivered a little in his blue alligator polo shirt. He saw Prakash with some other people, occupying two tables on the sunny side of the meadow. Omar wondered if he could get Prakash to show him how to tie a turban.

"Hello, Omar," Prakash said, and then, to Omar's shock, he kissed Amina lightly on the cheek. "Hi, Amina-Auntie. You look very pretty."

Omar looked between them with a feeling of panic. What was going on? Anjali was nowhere in sight, so he was forced to follow Amina and Prakash to one of the tables. There he met two of Prakash's shop assistants, Jake and Meera, and a very tall man named Sushil, who shook Omar's hand with gravity.

"Sushil is a writer," Prakash said. Omar nodded, suddenly overcome with shyness, and the tall man gave a short laugh.

"I haven't read your books," Omar managed to get out.

"We'll get one for you," Prakash said.

"Not *Fatherhood*," Sushil and Amina said at the same time, and they all laughed in an adult way, and Omar gave up. He was the only child here, and he was going to be excluded. He wandered over to watch the soccer players.

He perked up a few minutes later when he saw Anjali approaching with two friends. She had not been to cricket practice yet this season, and he was excited to see her again. She was wearing a silky fuchsia shirt with the kind of jeans his mom called "designer" and the same Moroccan slippers he had seen her wear before. He loved those slippers. Her hair was longer and wavier than he remembered it being, but she was still exactly as pretty. He trotted over to her as she and her two companions were introduced to the people at the picnic tables. He too was introduced to them—the freckled one was Greg, the dark-haired one Rafael—and then he received a full hug from Anjali, during which his face was pressed momentarily against her silken front. He felt weak with happiness.

"Omar!" she said. "How's the cricket game?"

"You're on the team?" Rafael said with interest. He was medium height and had very long-lashed eyes; Omar felt suspicious of him.

"It's not really a team," Omar hedged, fearing he was going to come off as athletic. "I'm just learning."

"They're so adorable," Anjali said to her friend, and Omar thought for a minute she, too, would be lost to the grown-up world of innuendo and insider knowledge. But then she turned back to him. "I'm starving. Let's get some samosas!"

There were indeed samosas, along with peppery fried chicken, chickpea salad, cucumber raita, and spinach in yogurt—kichadi, everyone called it. There were also the bags of chips he and Amina had contributed because they didn't yet know how to cook, a strange kind with blue ones and another bag of all different colors, and at the other table he thought he glimpsed brownies and some kind of carroty cake.

Omar sat with Anjali on the grass and dipped a samosa in tamarind chutney. He ate one, and then a little of everything else, and then two more samosas. Prakash had put coconut and guava sodas in a cooler, and Omar drank a coconut one slowly, savoring the strange taste. Prakash and Amina and Sushil, he saw, were drinking white wine at the picnic table, while Anjali and her friends had brought beer in green bottles. They were talking about school, about their professors and something called a colloquium, and he tuned them out as he studied everyone else.

It suddenly occurred to him, watching his aunt and his coach lean in toward each other, their hands side by side on the bench, that Amina was acting like Prakash's girlfriend. They weren't touching, but they were talking in the way that he had seen in movies, in a way that meant love. When had this happened, and why hadn't his aunt told him? He abruptly put his soda down on the grass. It tipped over and its remains trickled out onto the grass, but he didn't bother to right it. He had told her about his project, but she hadn't told him this. And it was his *coach*. What if they had a fight and he lost cricket because she wouldn't want to take him anymore and his parents were always too busy and then maybe Hari wouldn't want to be his friend anymore?

"Want to play soccer, Omar?"

He looked up to see Prakash standing over him. A barefoot Anjali, Greg, and Rafael were already working their way out to the center of the meadow, kicking the ball to where Meera waved in the center of the field. Jake sat with his aunt and Sushil, talking about books. Omar shook his head.

"Come on, man," Prakash said, "it won't be the same without your skills."

Omar knew that he was making fun of him, and he shook his head again, aware that what was on his face was the look that his mother called sullen, and his coach didn't seem to like it any more than his parents did. Prakash finally shrugged and jogged out to the others. Omar hated him, he hated his beard and his smile and his stupid turban, too.

He felt like he was going to cry, and so he got up and went into the woods, where he found a large stick to gouge the earth with. This was how he passed the rest of the picnic.

THEY DROVE HOME AT the end of the day; the city hovered on the horizon, and the dark feeling inside him only seemed to grow as they moved closer to it.

"Why don't you have any kids?" he asked Amina. He was aware that this question could hurt his aunt, because he'd heard his mother say to his father that women without children were lonely. But he wanted to hurt her, because she had lied to him, and he also wanted to know if she was going to marry Prakash and have a kid of her own, one who would replace him.

She looked surprised. "Because I don't want to," she said, separating the words with care, looking at him out of the corner of her eye.

"You don't like kids?" he asked.

"I do like them," she said, "but that's different from wanting to be a mother."

"Mom says it's lonely not to have kids," he offered, as advice.

She nodded and tucked her hair behind her ears with her free hand. "Grandma says the same thing," she finally said. "Lots of people think that. But all people get lonely sometimes. And I have enough in my life the way it is."

Omar looked away, out the window at the world rushing past. She was probably talking about Prakash, about being in love with Prakash. Why wouldn't she just say it out loud?

17.

THAT NIGHT HE AND Amina watched a documentary about slavery on PBS. They didn't have any dinner because they'd eaten so much at the picnic, but she let him have cookies while they watched the show. He felt her turn to look at him a few times, but he concentrated on the TV, refusing to be bribed by something so simple as Oreos.

He now regretted telling her his secret. He vowed that he would not discuss his project with her again until she told him the truth about Prakash. When he went to bed, he put away the Indian things, all except the knife. That he put under his pillow again.

The next morning Amina made pancakes. Some of the pancakes were burnt, and some were alarmingly thin, but she graciously ate those and gave him several that approximated circles. He was quiet, but he ate them, along with orange juice, an adult vitamin, and chocolate milk that he mixed himself from a tin.

Amina was reading the newspaper. Omar had brought his Kipling book to the table, and he opened that after a few minutes of silence.

"Omar," she said, looking up as soon as he had done so.

"How about some research on your project today? I asked Sushil and he gave me some ideas for websites to look at, and then maybe we could visit the library."

"I already went to the library," he said.

"But maybe we could go to a better one, at my university, or to one that specializes in South Asia or in colonialism."

Omar wanted to ask her what colonialism was, but he was still mad at her. "I can work on my own. I'm learning Hindi."

"Wow." She leaned her head on one hand and studied him in a way that he found uncomfortable. He felt defensive.

"Grandpa's helping me."

"I figured," she said. "Well then, how about we both do some work this morning and then you can go with me to the market this afternoon?"

"What market?" he asked.

"We have to go to an Indian market to get some spices."

"Oh" was all he said, but the idea excited him.

The store was in Adams Morgan, where Amina lived and where his parents sometimes took him for Ethiopian food. But he had never been into a store like this. It was long and dark and narrow and very cramped, and each shelf seemed to carry endless colors and shapes and sizes of a zillion different kinds of things, most of which he didn't recognize. There were only two other people in the store besides the people who worked there, an African couple speaking a foreign language and studying a rack of DVDs.

He walked among rows and rows of what looked like beans, except that they were small and came in a variety of hues: orange and golden and black and white and green. Near the front were sacks of rice, but that too came in colors, a red one that said it was from the mountains called the Himalayas, a burgundy-colored one from somewhere in southern India, a jade rice from China. He also saw a whole shelf of tinned fruits with funny names, one with spikes around it like a medieval weapon, and at the front counter he saw what looked like a dozen different kinds of chapattis and bread in a case.

He approached the refrigerated cabinet to look more closely at the breads, and the old man behind the counter asked him what he wanted.

"Paratha?" he asked in a reedy voice. "Puri?"

Omar shook his head and backed away. "I don't know what those are," he said, and went to find his aunt.

At the back, near the bins of seeds and nuts and powders, Amina was talking to a woman wearing a black headscarf over all her hair and a long robe that came down to her toes. This scared Omar a little. He had seen pictures of women wearing the scarf on the front page of the newspaper, and it seemed that it meant something bad. But this woman was friendly, and she and his aunt were discussing mustard seeds and whether something called curry leaves—which he guessed was what you used to make curry—should be bought fresh. He fought off the urge to take Amina's hand. The woman in the headscarf reached out and rested her hand briefly on the top of Omar's head, as if in recognition.

Amina selected a few spices and some nuts, which the woman put in small plastic bags and closed with twisty ties. Then his aunt collected basmati rice and a small bag of the Himalayan rice, a larger one of orange lentils, which were what the beans were called, shredded coconut, and rosewater, and added all of these to the bags of spices in her basket.

"Do you want anything else?" she asked Omar.

"Chapatis," he said firmly. "And . . ." His eyes slid over to the DVD rack.

"A movie?" she said, and walked with him over to the rack. On the covers were plump Indians cavorting in small, brightly-colored clothes in what often looked like cold places, or family groups covered in unbelievable amounts of gold and silk fabrics. He'd read a lot about how India was poor, but from what he could see people were a lot richer than they were in the US, or at least they owned a lot more jewelry. He recognized Shah Rukh Kahn from his poster, but that was all that looked familiar. He hesitated, and his aunt reached to pick one up.

"Maybe we should ask for a recommendation," she said, shaking her head after reading the back cover.

The woman in the headscarf chose the two that she thought "the young man might enjoy most," and Amina held them up to Omar to choose. He pointed to Shah Rukh Khan, and Amina added him to the basket. At the counter she picked out breads with spinach and cheese, and a large stack of plain chapatti. The man, who was wearing a skirt like those Omar had seen in his books of photographs, stared between them.

"Your son?" he finally asked in a thick accent, handing Amina back her change and nodding toward Omar.

"My nephew," she said.

He moved his head back and forth. "Very good," he said. He held out his hand to Omar, who reluctantly held out his own, and the old man dropped in a plastic-wrapped sweet.

Emerging back outside, he felt almost like years had passed. Inside that store was another world from his own, and although it was strange and a little bit frightening at first, he had liked it.

"Can we go back there sometime?" he asked Amina.

"Of course," she said, "whenever you like."

He decided that for today at least, he forgave her for what he now called in his mind "the incident with Prakash."

ON THE WAY HOME, Amina asked if he would mind if they stopped by her apartment so she could pick up her mail from the last few days. He agreed, hoping that they might go inside again, but she left the car running with the stereo still on and ran in, returning in a few seconds with a pile of envelopes and catalogs that she threw in the back seat.

At home, he helped his aunt unpack the groceries. They left everything on the counter except the Himalayan rice, which Amina put in the cupboard as a surprise for his mom. He wasn't so sure his mom would like it, but he didn't say anything.

"I think," Amina said, "that we'd better get the pudding on."

She consulted the emailed recipes, then took out a large

heavy pot and emptied a half gallon of whole milk into it. She instructed Omar to stir and then went to sort her mail.

He sat on a stool and made slow passes at the pot of milk, sugar, and rice with a wooden spoon, feeling content. There were green cardamoms that were going to go in, and raw pistachios, and some fat yellow raisins like his grandma always added. He peered at the recipe on the counter and blinked to be sure he was reading it right: it was going to take hours to make this pudding. He felt downcast by this, as his arm was already tired and he had been hoping to help with some of the other things, especially the sambar, which had a rich color that he loved even though, in truth, it was not his favorite of his grandmother's dishes.

He looked over at Amina to ask if she'd known how long the pudding took to make, but stopped before saying a word. She was staring at a piece of mail with a strange expression on her face. It was a typed letter, and he couldn't tell if it was good or bad. She looked up and saw him watching her, and quickly put the note down.

"How's it coming?"

Omar studied her; it sounded almost like there were tears in her voice. But her face looked normal by the time she reached the stove and took the spoon from his hand.

"Let me do this for a while," she said, and he hopped down from his perch.

Overall, the dinner was a success. Unfortunately the pudding burned on Amina's watch and had to be thrown out. But the sambar and biryani tasted good, and they shared a chocolate bar for dessert. It was past eight by the time they ate, so Amina suggested they watch the movie another night. Omar agreed.

"Thank you," he said as he went to brush his teeth. "I had a good time cooking Indian food."

"You're most welcome, chef. The dinner was good. And we'll get better at it with practice."

He nodded. He liked the way she always acted as though they would have more time together.

"Hey, Omar?" she asked as he started off toward the stairs again. "Want to invite Hari over one day after school, instead of doing that arts program?"

"Sure," he said. He knew that she was trying to make him be friends with someone because he didn't have any friends, and probably because his mom had told her to, but he didn't mind. He'd also thought of asking Hari over, but there was never a good time for his mom. "I'll ask him tomorrow."

"Excellent," she said.

He started to thank her again, but then remembered he was mad at her for keeping a secret. It was easy to hold on to other sorts of anger, like when he was angry at his dad for forgetting things, or angry at his mom for being busy, or like when he got angry at the kids at school for being mean to him. But with his aunt it was harder; he kept feeling other things instead of the thing he meant to feel. He guessed this was what it meant to really like someone, what it meant to have a friend.

18.

ON MONDAY HE GOT Hari's phone number, and that night
Amina called Hari's mother to ask if he could come over. She
was a little quiet afterward, but she said Hari's mom had given
permission.

"We'll get pizza for dinner, okay Omar?"

"Sure."

"Do you need any help with anything?"

He did want her help because he was planning to try some
internet research again, but he wasn't ready to trust her. He told
her he had math homework and, after seeing her sit down at
her own laptop in the living room, went down to the basement.
On the desk next to the computer he found that she had left a
list of websites, some of them with passwords also. He sat and
stared at the paper, half wanting to run back upstairs and hug
her. But one of the things he liked about his aunt was that he
knew she didn't need him to.

He typed in one of the addresses with two fingers. His
mom kept threatening to send him to typing class, but he kept
insisting that they had those classes in middle school which was
really only a rumor he had heard.

The first site was a history site, about Andhra Pradesh,

the state that Hyderabad was in. He read about the ancient kingdom of Golconda, and about how the city had been conquered by the Mughal Emperor Aurangzeb, and about how it had three languages: Hindi, Urdu—which was Hindi written in Arabic letters—and the Telegu language that he'd heard his aunt mention. Hyderabad itself had a lake, and a twin city called Secunderabad, and was basically four hundred years old. He learned that there had been a state of Hyderabad first, at independence, and then it merged with Andhra Pradesh in 1956.

Much of the information was too dense and confusing for him. Who were all these people, all these names? How could a city have a twin? It was bewildering to think that all this really important stuff had happened before there had even been a United States of America. And he was having a hard time figuring out why the English people were there in the first place, and why they had such a say in what happened in India's history.

Some details enchanted him immediately, though: the emperors and the diamonds, the outlandish tradition of covering food in silver and gold foil, and the city's nickname, the City of Pearls.

"Pearls," he said out loud, softly.

His mother had pearls, boring white things that she wore sometimes when she wanted to look nice. Once when he was little he'd asked her what they were, and she said that each pearl on the strand stood for one of the blessings in her life, and that the largest one was Omar's. Once he had seen Anjali wearing pearl earrings, small ones that made her face seem to glow a little with their reflected light. But the pearls in Hyderabad sounded like something different altogether, something grander and brighter and more expensive. And maybe they were, maybe in India pearls really were gems more precious than the glittering diamonds in the mines or the fiery, radiant rubies in the crown of Aurungzeb. Maybe pearls meant more than gold.

He started to close down the computer, but then stopped. He opened a new window and typed the words *India* and *terrorist* and then, after a moment, erased them. He paused again, thinking, then typed in *Al Qeda*. After correcting his spelling, an endless list of choices appeared, and he scrolled down, past dictionary and encyclopedia entries, past newspaper and magazine articles. There was too much to read. He stopped again and thought. Then he opened up YouTube and tried again. This time a list of videos came up, and he began to watch them, the sound turned down low, until his aunt called down that it was time for bed.

THE NEXT DAY, HE asked his teacher why their city was called Washington, DC, and not something nicer. He had been thinking overnight about the name, City of Pearls, wondering why he didn't live in a place where cities had names like that. She looked at him askance.

"Don't you know who George Washington is, Omar?" she asked. He nodded, embarrassed, and waited for her to walk away. Of course he knew who George Washington was. He knew more about history than any of the other kids in his class. He had been asking something else.

But it wasn't the first time that he had encountered this problem, this inability to translate between the places he read about and the world that he knew. Last night he had lain in bed brainstorming new names for his home: the Cherry City, the City of Senators, the City of the Country. There was nothing so romantic as pearls, just the flowers, and the people who worked in the government, and all the regular stuff of life like school and roads and stores. It was like India lived in a space just one shift over, where all kinds of things were possible that could never exist here, in the city where he lived.

19.

THE DAY THAT HARI was supposed to come over, Omar wore his favorite shirt, which was a black-and-white polo that Prakash had once said looked like a rugby shirt, and the K-Swiss shoes that his mother had told him to reserve for sports. Right away, at his locker in the morning, one of the kids who didn't like him, Terry Campbell, came by and stomped hard on his foot so that the perfect white of his sneakers was marred by an oily streak. Though the kids were different at this school than they had been at his last one—there were, in the first place, lots of African American kids and others that he guessed were immigrants—Omar was having no more luck than usual being accepted by his peers.

He squirmed in math class as they reviewed the homework he hadn't done over the weekend, an old assignment on his desk as a red herring, quickly doing sums in his head with every question the teacher asked in case she called on him. She didn't, but when she came to collect their papers and shook his head, she looked almost shocked. Omar always did his homework.

In English, to his relief, they were reading out loud. Omar took his turn near the end, reading easily through a couple of paragraphs, and then they were released to lunch. He found

Hari at a table after waiting in line for hot lunch. Ordinarily his mother packed him something, but while his parents were away, Amina had been instructed to give him money to eat at school. He had been excited at first, but now, into the second week, he was beginning to see the disadvantages of school food.

"You're still coming over, right?" Omar asked, picking at a tiny breaded cutlet in red sauce.

There was a pause. "I'm supposed to ask you if you're a Muslim," Hari blurted out.

"What?" Omar put his spork down.

"I told my mom your mom's American, but when your aunt called, she was wondering. Also, I'm a vegetarian." Hari looked pained at each element of this information.

"You are?" Omar had never really paid attention to what Hari ate.

There was a silence while neither boy returned to his food and the questions hung in the air between them.

"My mom says we don't have a religion," Omar finally volunteered, feeling that it was his duty as the potential host to be clear. "And we're just ordering pizza tonight. Do you eat pizza?"

Hari perked up. "I eat cheese pizza."

"That's my favorite," Omar said, which was the truth, and they both resumed eating their lunches.

After school Amina was waiting with her car out front like all the real parents, and she made a big show of making sure they were buckled in, both in the back seat. At home, she offered grape sodas and another bag of the strange chips she liked, which Hari refused, looking suspicious.

"Hari's a vegetarian," Omar told Amina. "But we both like cheese pizza."

"I used to be a vegetarian," Amina told Hari, "for health reasons. I really loved it. And I like cheese pizza too."

Hari only nodded, but Omar could see that he too had been won over by his aunt's straightforward manner.

They took their sodas into his room, and Hari pulled out some of his CDs. They were hip-hop, which Omar pretended to like, and they sat on the floor with their backs against the bed and listened to the music turned up loud. It was almost like being in Amina's car.

"Do you want to see some of my Indian stuff?" Omar asked after a while.

Hari shrugged in agreement, and Omar realized how stupid he must sound to someone who was really Indian, who probably had Indian stuff all over the house and who was a real Hindu after all, and a vegetarian too.

"I mean the stuff for my research project about my family," he modified, and Hari looked slightly more interested. Omar took out the books and pictures and the Hand of Fatima, which Hari fingered with interest for a moment and then dropped when Omar pulled out the knife. He had told himself he wasn't going to do it, that the knife was a secret and that it had to stay that way, but it was his ace, his trump card, the only really impressive thing he owned. And he was right to pull it out, because Hari loved it.

"This is seriously cool," he said.

They started a game of bandit, which was cops and robbers except that the bandit had a knife and the policeman carried the Hand of Fatima, like a ward against evil, along with Omar's cricket bat, which had been a Christmas gift that year from his grandparents. Hari, to Omar's disappointment, called the knife before he thought to. He was unsure whether he should warn Hari to hide the knife from his aunt, but they were playing on the top two floors anyway so they wouldn't disturb Amina working at the kitchen table. Omar gave Hari a countdown of a hundred before he came looking for him.

The game took them until dinnertime, which they ate at the kitchen table even though Omar had asked if they could watch the movie. Bollywood movies, Amina said again, were too long. Hari said it was okay because the movies had too much love stuff. They ate chocolate cookies and then they dropped Hari off at home. It wasn't until Omar went to bed and curved his hand under his pillow as he always did that he realized his knife was gone.

20.

ON FRIDAY HIS MOTHER was waiting to pick him up after school, standing outside of the car with a big smile on her face. Omar ran toward her and then stopped when he got close because she looked strange, maybe because she was tan. He saw that she was wearing her pearl necklace, and the gems looked very white against her throat. She laughed and pulled him toward her in a big hug, mussing the top of his hair.

"Omar, you've grown!" she said. "You've gotten taller in just two weeks."

"I haven't, Mom," he said. He was embarrassed to be seen like this by the other kids, but he was also pleased.

"Where's Dad?" he asked as they drove toward home.

"He just went to check in at work," she said, her voice neutral. "You'll see him at dinner."

"You liked Greece?" he asked. "I read about it in the encyclopedia, and my teacher gave me a book of Greek myths."

"I liked Greece," she said. "But I missed you."

At home, everything seemed back to normal. His mom cooked a big dinner of fried chicken and mashed potatoes with gravy, and he told them about the chicken-and-Indian-food picnic, and about Hari coming over to play, and about

Amina's attempts to cook, which made them laugh. He didn't mention the Indian spice store, or his suspicions about Prakash, but he saw a look pass between his parents when he said that his cricket coach had organized the picnic. Maybe they knew Amina loved him; maybe everybody knew but Omar. He tried not to get upset about this.

After dinner, his dad went to watch the news on TV while his mom did laundry from their trip. Omar told them he was going to do his homework, but he had another plan: he wanted to look at the stars. He snuck out the door in the kitchen and into the tiny backyard, which had a brick walkway and a single sick dogwood tree. Every year it had fewer flowers, and every year his mom told his dad that she was going to cut it down, and every year she said she couldn't bear to do it. Some of his mom's gardening tools were lying next to the tree, and his dad's gas barbecue was covered and tucked against the back of the house like it was sleeping.

At school they were studying the planets, the clusters and black holes and suns that made up the whole entire world outside of planet Earth. He sat on the wooden bench that Uncle Lyle had made; Omar craned his neck to look up and took long, slow, deep breaths. The sky was clear, but it wasn't dark enough to see very many stars. He waited and waited for his eyes to adjust and then he was able to pick out first one, then another, then a sprinkling of faded twinkles all over the top of the sky, starbursts his teacher said came from dead planets billions of miles away.

How could this be? It was frightening and sad, somehow, to think that there was so much more than his Earth out there, to think how small he and his family were. It made him feel alone, alone all the way deep inside, from the back of his throat and into his heart and down into his toes. How could there be so much in the universe, and who could have made it? His mom and dad said there wasn't a god, but if there wasn't a god then where did they come from? How had the universe been born?

Hari had gods; they were Hindu gods that came in many

colors with lots of arms and jewelry and bright clothes like the Bollywood actors. His teachers all believed in God; it seemed like everyone did at school, like they believed in the flag and the USA. Omar wasn't sure about Prakash because he had a turban and he wore a silver bracelet that Hari said meant he was a Sikh, which was both Hindu and Muslim, but Omar had never heard him talk about God. His aunt Amina never talked about God either.

His grandpa had told him once that God was inside you. But when he looked up at the stars, he was sure that God was up there in the sky, like the light coming from the dead planets was a language, and God was speaking to them in a kind of code he had made up out of light waves and dust and sparkle. He said a quick prayer to them, to the stars that were like gems in the night and to whatever gods that talked through them: *Thank you*, he said, *for bringing both of my parents home.*

SUNDAY WAS OMAR'S BIRTHDAY. Eleven had been tricky, but perhaps what followed would be better.

His mom had asked him a long time ago if he wanted to have a party, but he'd said no because he didn't know who he would invite. She'd looked disappointed. He knew she wished he had more friends and that she thought it wasn't normal that he didn't, and somehow that made her feel bad about herself. But she smiled and said they would have a special dinner together, just the family, and he could do whatever else he wanted. He decided it was too late about the iPod and resigned himself to getting whatever they had picked out for gifts.

There was another cricket practice that day. He didn't really want to go because it was his birthday and because of the Prakash/Amina situation, but on the other hand, Hari had promised to bring the knife to practice. He had sworn to Omar that he had taken it accidentally. At first he said he would bring it to school, but Omar quickly told him not to. For the first time, he told Hari about the knife incident, and Hari looked deeply impressed and said he understood that it was far too dangerous.

So he told his mom he'd like to go to cricket even though it was his birthday, instead of going to the aquarium or the Mall like she suggested. Amina called to see what they were up to, and his mom told her about cricket and she said she'd be happy to take him so his mom could stay home and cook his birthday dinner. Omar hoped this wasn't really about her seeing Prakash.

Amina was late picking him up. She said sorry and wished Omar a happy birthday right away, but he didn't feel it was very polite to be late on his birthday, and the team was already on the field by the time he arrived. He looked around for Hari, but he wasn't there. At first Omar didn't worry, but then they got past the first drills and into the scrimmage, and he started to wonder.

It was chilly, and Omar wished he had worn more clothes. He kept dropping the ball when it was thrown to him, unable to concentrate. Hari never showed up. He had the knife, and he had promised to bring it, and then he hadn't. This, Omar felt, was a birthday worse than shit. Maybe turning twelve wasn't going to be so great after all.

Fortunately his aunt didn't have a chance to talk to Prakash at all because the father of the Indian girls had come with a list of questions about coaching methods that he immediately began to discuss with Prakash when practice ended. Amina and Omar just waved goodbye and left the field. Omar looked between his aunt and his coach, trying to detect further signs of romance, but he didn't see anything.

Amina drove him back to the birthday dinner. He felt better when he got home because his Mom had cooked chili, which he loved. There was shredded cheese to put on top for Omar and onions and chilies for the adults, and skillet cornbread with honey and ham in it, and tortilla chips for Omar to scoop out his chili with. He was allowed two grape sodas, and his mom kept patting the top of his head, like he'd done a good job to turn twelve even though all he'd done was stay alive.

His parents talked to Amina, telling her all about the trip, mostly stuff that Omar had already heard. After the chili, his mom took out an ice cream cake decorated like a baseball—they didn't have a cricket ball, she said—and they ate that too after he had blown out the twelve blue-and-white candles.

For presents, he had a stack of books about dinosaurs from his parents, and a wooden model of a T. rex with metallic paints. Amina gave him a soccer shirt that she said came from Europe. There was no iPod, but his grandparents had sent him a check for fifty dollars inside his birthday card, so maybe he could buy one himself.

"It seems like you two had a great time together," his mom said.

"And Omar kept up with his homework?" his dad asked, although Omar had already told him that everything at school was fine.

"He was very responsible," Amina confirmed. "He's even working hard on some extra work on his own."

Omar looked at her in astonishment, his spoon halfway to his mouth.

"Oh yeah?" his mom said. "The dinosaur project?"

His aunt gave him a little kick under the table, which he thought was very bad behavior for an adult, and he closed his mouth. Both of his parents were looking at him.

He opened his mouth and closed it and then tried again. "I was doing some research into our family history." He couldn't believe he was saying it even as he said it, but the presence of Amina made him feel, in an overwhelming way, that he could not lie.

"Like what?" his mom said, in a very casual voice, but he saw her glance toward his father.

"Kind of like a family tree," Amina said.

"Yes," Omar said. "Exactly."

His mom smiled, looking relieved. "Well, I can help you with that, for my side. We can work on it together next weekend. Maybe we can call your grandma in North Carolina and see what she can tell us. I think Missy did something like this once; we can ask her if she calls tonight. Mo, you can help too, right?"

His dad shifted a little in his chair, and poured himself another glass of wine, filling it all the way to the top. Omar's mom gave him a look, which he ignored.

"Probably my dad would have the most information," he said. "Have you already talked to him?"

"A little," Omar admitted. "But maybe I'll call him again."

"We don't know that much family stuff, do we, Mo?" Amina said. "We never really had that much interest when we were growing up."

"I don't know about that," his dad said. "It's just that we never met our grandparents or anything, or anyone from the family in Hyderabad. We were a little bit isolated. But I was interested, once."

"You were?" Amina and Omar said this at the same time, while his mom simply stared, her eyes narrowed.

"Of course," he said, lifting his glass. "Don't you remember, Amina, when I built that palace?"

"Yeah," she said. "It was huge."

"It was a model of the Red Fort in New Delhi. I was planning to do a whole series of forts, but Dad said there was no room to keep all of them."

Omar stared at his dad as he drank. He had read about the Red Fort, he had seen pictures of it, and he knew it was real, yet it amazed him that his dad knew of its existence too.

"Really," Amina said, "it was Dad who didn't have any interest then. He was so busy enunciating British poetry. And now he's a sentimental fool for all things Indian."

"Well," Omar's mom said, clearing her throat. "I think probably Omar should check over his homework and get to bed, because there's school tomorrow."

Omar nodded. He could tell his mom didn't like where the conversation was going. As he left the room, he looked back at his dad another time, his dad who had once built the Red Fort, his dad who had never told him this.

A few minutes later he came back to get his book. Halfway

down the stairs he stopped and listened to the adults talking in the low voices that he knew to take as a warning.

"We just want to be happier, both of us. I think this is the best way," his mom was saying.

"What about the house?" he heard his aunt ask.

"Omar and I will stay here, for the time being. Mo will start looking for an apartment," his mom answered. She said it matter-of-factly, like it was no big deal.

Omar turned and ran back up the stairs as hard as he could, not caring if they heard him. He slammed his door and threw himself on his bed. They were going to do it, the thing he'd feared: they were going to get a divorce. It was his birthday, he was twelve, and he was supposed to be happy, and instead his parents were going to get a divorce and live in different houses and he would never, ever, be happy again. When his hand went under the pillow and the knife wasn't there, he was filled with rage, and he threw the pillow across the room.

He got up. He gathered up all his Indian stuff, all the research materials, even a library book. He dumped everything all together in his duffel bag and carried it down the stairs. In the living room, as his mother called out from the kitchen to ask him what he thought he was doing, he heaped it all into the brick fireplace, the posters and books and CDs and all his notes, crumpled into kindling, even the pages of curving Hindi script. Then he took a long wooden match from a tall red box, and he set his India on fire.

III. INCIDENTS WITH KNIVES

21.

SPRING WAS BEAUTIFUL IN Washington, DC. After the brief warm spell in March, the cold had descended again, but now it retreated quickly after a last deep frost, and the sky and ground seemed to lighten with relief. It rained enough to flood surrounding areas, and then buds began to appear on trees, and in the ground, hard green shoots forced themselves through the solvent earth, eager to find the sun.

Amina, who in California was often accused of insentience when it came to seasons, found herself a little in love with this one. She opened windows in her apartment, walked on the Mall to view the cherry blossoms, and found herself actually sniffing the air at particularly colorful spots. Perhaps she was beginning to relax and get used to the city. It was more likely, however, that she welcomed any distraction from the problems she had wrapped about herself like swaddling clothes.

Amina's life was growing complicated at a rate she was tempted to call exponential. She had received a letter granting her the research position in India she had applied for, at what was suspected to be a new hybrid zone, starting in September.

She had become involved with Prakash in spite of that, finding herself unable to resist his warm, intelligent charm, his persistent interest in her. The relationship had progressed beyond an easy exit strategy, and she had not yet managed to tell him about the new job.

Her brother was separating from Marcy. Marcy had her battle armor on, Mo looked more and more defeated, and Omar looked like he had been burned to the ground. Work at the lab had only grown more intolerable, Chris's militant method and dictatorial tendencies making her crazy. She wanted to support Omar, but as things had only disintegrated since her arrival in the capital, she was unsure how to proceed, how to offer her inadequate wisdoms. She didn't know how to help her nephew while at the same time contemplating departure.

Marcy called to say that she was thinking of sending Omar to a psychologist.

"Don't do it," Amina told her over the phone, speaking to her sister-in-law while wearing pajamas at two in the afternoon on a Saturday. Marcy had called her a lot lately, and Amina was getting used to long sessions on the weekends.

"But Amina, you've seen the issues he's had this year. And he absolutely refuses to talk to me about the divorce, and I think he should be speaking with someone, even if it's not me or Mo."

"I don't think he has issues. I think he has normal questions. I think he's growing up."

"Amina, don't take this the wrong way, but you don't have any kids, and I don't think you know what you're talking about."

Amina felt as though she'd been slapped. She waited a few seconds, past the moment when she wanted to tell her sister-in-law to go fuck herself—here, experience with Chris was helpful—and then took a deep breath, smoothed her hair behind her ears, and proceeded.

"I know him, Marcy. I've gotten to know him. And if you send him to a psychologist, he's going to think he's even more of a freak than he already does, and that's just going to do more damage."

"You mean he's already damaged?"

Amina could hear anger and tears in Marcy's voice.

"No, Marcy, I don't think he's damaged, at least no more than the rest of us." She sighed and tried to think of something consoling to say. "He's trying to work things out in his head, he has a lot to get used to, and yeah, he's probably really upset. Just give him a little more time to work this through. He loves you and he loves Mo, and he's going to adjust if you just allow him the space to do so."

Marcy let out a long, ragged breath. "I guess it won't hurt to think about it a little longer." She paused. "I'm sorry about what I said before."

"It's only the truth. And anyway, how are you? Have you and Mo been talking?" Amina stood and went to put on another pot of coffee.

"We talk. Well, I talk, and he listens, and we get nowhere. Have you seen his apartment?"

"Nope." Amina didn't mention that she had made lunch plans with Mo the next day, to see where he was living and whether he was eating anything other than fast food.

"I don't see how he can take care of himself, but I can't live with him either. And I've got nobody to talk to."

Amina didn't say *Hey, Marcy, you've got me*, because she didn't see how that would be helpful, and she also had enough tact not to mention that Marcy seemed almost constantly on the phone with one friend or another. She loved Marcy, and she made a last attempt at sympathetic noises before hanging up.

Amina spent a few minutes pacing around her apartment. It had grown over the last few months to look as though a human being, rather than a robot, lived in it. She had hung a Japanese print and a photo of a mountain in New Hampshire that Prakash had given to her because its multisyllabic Native American name was translated as "She Who Stands Alone." He also printed a photo of himself playing cricket, which she had not put in a frame but instead stuck to the refrigerator with a Smithsonian magnet. She had invested in lamps to assuage the effect of overhead lighting, and her last unpacked boxes had been hidden in her bedroom closet. It felt almost like home.

But what a mess—what a serious fucking travesty—this had all become. At work, she had just a few more weeks before she had to commit to a new line of research. She needed to tell them that she was leaving her postdoc mid-residency, that she was going to work on a new project, a rival project even, in India. But she also felt an almost deafening roar of obligation, her obligation to Omar, to Marcy and Mo, to a man she liked an awful lot and who in turn liked her enough to be hinting that she should come to meet his family at a reunion next month.

She poured some coffee and lit a cigarette. It was becoming a struggle to smoke as much as she did and hide it from Prakash, who occasionally sniffed at her in puzzlement. But then, that wasn't nearly as hard as hiding from him the fact that she was thinking of leaving the country at the end of the summer.

22.

THE NEXT DAY SHE drove out to Mo's new apartment in Virginia. It was in the kind of hideous apartment complex she despised, a concrete block with a hotel feel. *Make that a prison feel,* she thought, as she rode the elevator up past the endless rows of identical doors.

Her mother, Maya, had called to tell her that it was her duty to take care of Mo now that he was separated from his wife.

"Mom," Amina said. "Mo can take care of himself."

"But Amina," her mother argued, "you are unmarried."

Amina refused to take the bait. The phone line was silent. Amina imagined her mother sitting at her writing desk with her to-do list in front of her:

* buy cantaloupe
* have hair done
* order new stationery
* annoy Amina

"Marcy says you are seeing someone," her mother finally said, driven to direct attack by Amina's resistance.

"Marcy shouldn't be telling you that."

"Why not, when you tell me nothing?"

"Mom, I'm not having this conversation. I'll check up on Mo, but I'm sure he's fine."

"He is depressed."

Amina couldn't deny this. He *was* depressed, although it was hard to tell exactly how much because his normal state was so uncommunicative. But she did feel an obligation to make sure he was all right. Up until now she had focused on Marcy because it was so easy. There were no guarantees, however, that Mo would talk to her about the divorce at all.

She arrived at the appropriate number and rang his doorbell, which gave an obnoxious, short squawk. She imagined prison bars being slid aside. Mo opened the door and greeted her with something akin to enthusiasm. He showed her around the two rooms plus tiny kitchen in less than thirty seconds, and then they sat on the squeaking-new vinyl couch.

"So how are you?" she asked. He had elegant good looks, and a straight, slender physique that made him seem taller than his five feet ten inches. The only sign of disorder lay in his hair, which was longer than usual and looked unbrushed. Amina suspected that Marcy had been in charge of cutting it, perhaps dating back to high school.

"Fine. Good," he said. "Would you like some tea?"

She said yes more because she knew he wanted something to do than because she wanted the drink. She watched him putter in his kitchen space for a minute, and then let her eyes wander around the apartment. It was decorated with a large TV on a rolling cart, a black stereo on a short bookcase, and the couch. There was a barstool at a kitchen counter, which seemed to serve as his dining table, because the actual table was covered with mail, and a wilted plant in a basket had the look of a gift from their mother. It was not charming.

"How is your job?" he asked, returning with two mugs that she recognized as castoffs from the Georgetown house.

"Not too bad," she said. "I'm maybe looking at other options."

He nodded but didn't ask anything else, and she wished briefly that she could divorce him too.

"Marcy misses you," she said instead. "I think you could still repair this."

He nodded again, and she wondered if she should pinch him or punch him or tickle him, something, anything, to get a reaction. But then he responded.

"Marcy wants a different kind of husband than I'm able to be," he said.

"Or than you want to be?" Amina suggested.

His eyes met hers. "Amina, I am what I am. I haven't changed."

Is that a good thing? she wanted to ask. "Then maybe you can still work things out. You've loved each other for a long time."

He grimaced a little. "She thinks I don't love her anymore because I don't bring her flowers and take her out to dinner and talk to her about my feelings. I share every bit of my life with her, but she says I share nothing. I'm at a loss."

"You have a lot to lose," Amina said, thinking of Omar.

"You shouldn't have to worry about this," he said, standing, straightening his shirt with a downward pull. "These are my problems. How about some lunch?"

They went to a Chinese restaurant a couple of blocks away where they made their way through three courses without returning to the subject of the divorce. Afterward, she said goodbye at the door to his building and got straight into her car without returning to the dreary apartment. She wondered what he would do for the rest of his day, and then she realized that he would do what he always did: sit alone, read, make notes for work, and watch TV. Indeed, he hadn't changed.

23.

AT WORK, AMINA FRETTED. There was an article to revise, a graduate student to train, Chris to avoid, and a never-ending pile of technical work on her desk.

She sent an email to the research station in India. It was a site founded by a group at one of the Ivies and in more recent years taken over by an Indian team whose research had taken a similar track to her own after several seasons of preliminary analysis. *I have a family situation to resolve*, she wrote to someone named Dilpa Thakkur. *Could I possibly have a few more weeks to confirm?*

She wasn't sure why she asked for the time; she herself had made the application, in desperate certainty that lab life in DC was not what she wanted. She had chosen this from many options she might have taken, and at the time it had appealed to her that it was in India. The Thakkur Institute was in the foothills of the Himalayas, however, in a remote town far from Hyderabad or from any city of consequence. It was more isolated than the field site in the Sierras, certainly a far cry from the site in the Pyrenees that Chris supervised. Was she ready to remove herself so absolutely?

She sorted through the rest of her emails, a preposterously

long list of departmental announcements, miscellaneous news from an evolutionary-science email list and the headlines from the BBC. But then she saw that she had a message from Matt. He said that he would be in DC soon—for Memorial Day weekend.

She let the mouse hover over the Delete button. This was not what she needed right now. But instead of trashing it, she signed out and called Prakash. He had been away for a few days at a book fair.

"How about coming to my place for dinner?" he asked, speaking into his cell in a low voice that told her he was back at the bookstore.

"I'll bring the wine," she said, and they both laughed because she had once tried to contribute dinner, her mother's foolproof biryani, no less, and it had been burnt, without salt, and slightly underdone. Prakash, on the other hand, was a genius with food.

He lived on Capitol Hill, walking distance from his bookstore, in a neighborhood that was particularly charming at this time of year because of the many varieties of trees and the care that people seemed to take in nourishing the flowers and plants in their tiny front yards. Amina liked seeing the flowers, in a way that she didn't remember having felt before; she didn't know their names, but she liked the pink ones, the yellow ones, and the white ones equally. For a scientist, she had maintained a perversely underdeveloped sense of nature. Perhaps Prakash would know what they were called.

He greeted her in the way she liked, which was to say he took her into his arms, kissed her on the neck, and told her that she smelled good. She gave him a long kiss on the lips and let him pull her into the room with her arms still around his neck. He lifted her a little off the ground—he was so much taller—and squeezed until she laughed and told him she couldn't breathe.

"I missed you, Amina Abdul," he said. "Now where is my wine?"

He was in every way wrong for her. He had a life oriented around family and sport and his business, he was irritatingly formal at times, he adored children, and he was—though they'd avoided talking about it too much—undoubtedly somewhat religious. He was perfect, in other words, if what she had been looking for was a father, a caregiver, and a financial safety net. He was pretty damn good just to be sleeping with, she could not deny it, but she worried that it had gotten serious before she thought through what she was doing.

Of course she had never intended to be dating him at all. She had finally agreed to that long-promised lunch when the cricket practice had started again this year. Mo and Marcy had taken Omar to practices a few times in the fall. This spring, when they clearly had other negotiations on their minds, they'd asked Amina if she would mind taking him again. Because she had seen so little of Omar early in the year, she agreed. She'd almost dreaded seeing the bearded coach again, he of the sonorous voice and the bedroom eyes; and indeed, it had taken less than one complete conversation for her to agree to go to lunch, and only two lunches for her to agree to go to dinner, and only one of those for her to agree to go to bed with him. And so she had ended up exactly where she had never meant to go.

She had told him right from the start, at that first lunch, that she was no good as a romantic partner.

"Why don't you let me learn that for myself?" he said. He had leaned forward and put his hand on hers, and a surge of electricity went up and down her spine.

"One only learns by trying," she heard herself say. A part of her was outraged at the flirtiness he was eliciting from her, but she couldn't stop herself, not then at the lunch table when he leaned in to kiss her cheek, not two weeks later when he hovered at her doorstep until she invited him in.

Now, Prakash told her about the book fair in Seattle, and about his night out at a hotel bar called the Tiki Torch, and about talking to a man on the airplane about being Sikh and wearing a turban.

"I get tired of explaining," he said as he searched his cupboards for snacks. "I'm starting to wonder if it's worth it."

She looked at him, surprised.

"What do you mean, worth it?"

"I don't know. I guess sometimes I feel like I'm just blindly following these cultural rules out of familial duty rather than out of belief. What does it matter if I wear a turban and a bracelet? I gave up the knife easily enough. Why not the rest?"

She studied him and couldn't think what to say. She liked his long hair, tied up underneath his turban when they went out, long and loose when they were in bed. But she didn't know much about following traditions.

He gave her a basket of the taro chips she liked and a glass of the chardonnay she had brought, and told her to pick out some music. He had a lot of jazz, which is what she put on, and a huge collection of qawwali. He also had a lot of pop diva singers like Celine Dion, which is how she knew that he wasn't actually perfect.

She pressed Play, and Chet Baker's weird voice drifted through the living room and into the kitchen; she followed it and sat at the kitchen table to watch Prakash cook. He was now doing something violent to tiny chickens with butter and rosemary.

"How is the divorce coming?" he asked in an amiable tone.

"Oh, quite well," she said. "It's easy when everyone refuses to compromise."

"And Omar?"

"Marcy wants to send him to a shrink." She tried to keep the derision out of her voice, to see what he really thought.

"Maybe Marcy should be the one going?" he suggested.

Amina nodded. "I don't think Omar could take it."

He paused with his large hands wrapped around one of the small birds, like a man caught in an act of murder, and fixed his dreamy eyes on her with concern.

"You're smiling," he accused.

"At you," she said. "But about Omar, believe me, I'm cursing inside."

"Omar needs family," he said.

"Oh, I know," she said, tapping her fingers to rid them of

their desire to hold a cigarette. "Omar needs lots of love and attention, a mommy and a daddy who love each other, good friends to play with, and wholesome hobbies. But given that this is real life, what am I going to do?"

He set the baby birds on a roasting pan, put them in the oven, and then went to wash the evidence off his hands.

"You are his family, too," he said, drying his hands on a red kitchen towel. All his kitchen accessories matched in a way that was somehow still manly.

She felt the guilt rise like bile in her throat, and she drank down the last of her wine.

"More?" she said, holding it up, and he went to the refrigerator. He set the bottle on the table and sat across from her. He didn't say anything.

"My father has more or less said the same thing," she offered.

"And?"

"And, I guess I think I'm about ready for someone else to contribute. Like his father, for example."

"What about your parents? Couldn't they come for a visit, or invite him to come stay with them? I always forgot everything else when I was with my grandparents."

"That was in Delhi?"

"A few hours outside the city, on the road to Jaipur. We would go all together in one of those Ambassadors, with a driver, and there would be flowering mustard fields all the way, like we had landed in Oz. We used to go every year, during summer vacation, which is the worst time to visit India, when everything is enveloped in unbelievable heat. But I loved to be with my grandparents. It was like a separate world, completely without problems."

She looked at him with narrowed eyes. "It is difficult to imagine my mother and father offering such a paradise. But maybe you're right. I'll call them and see what they can do."

"Okay," he said. "Problem solved."

"Except," she said, "that Mo and Marcy are still going to

have this ugly divorce, and Marcy wants to sell the house, and Omar might have to go to a different school for the third time in under a year." *And I won't be around to help him,* she should have added, but she couldn't get the words out, couldn't bring herself to tell him.

"You can't fix everything, Amina," he said. "You especially can't fix your brother's marriage."

She nodded. "I just have this awful feeling that something's going to happen to Omar, like he's going to hurt himself. Maybe Marcy's right about the shrink."

Prakash gave a judicious shrug. "Your feelings of concern are justified, but Omar will be fine. Children are very adaptable."

He pulled assorted lettuces out of the fridge and washed them, looking like he had something else on his mind.

"You remember I mentioned the family dinner at my parents' house next month?" he asked, sorting through the leaves.

She put her glass down and it made a hard noise. "Yes." She on the other hand, was not so adaptable.

"Would you like to come with me?" He looked up from the lettuce and met her eyes. He must have seen the panic there, because he quickly added, "You can think about it and let me know next week."

"I'll think about it," she said. "Thank you." She realized how formal she sounded, how transparently awkward, but she didn't know what to say. She had to tell him she was moving. Why couldn't she do that simple thing?

24.

AMINA HAD AGREED TO give a paper at some end-of-the-school-year meetings in New York, and she planned to take the train up on a Thursday and return Sunday afternoon. She had not been looking forward to it, but after the conversation with Prakash she could hardly wait to get out of a city that suddenly didn't seem big enough; wherever she went she thought of him, of leaving him, and how very much she didn't want to.

Before she left, she called Marcy and asked if she and Omar wanted to go out to dinner. Marcy proposed instead that Amina take Omar out, as a favor, while Marcy went to talk to Mo. This was fine with Amina, who had been hoping for a chance to talk to Omar about his family history project. Mo had taken over cricket practice driving duty, and Amina's steady contact with her nephew had been broken.

That week it turned suddenly cool again. Amina wore a windbreaker over her T-shirt and stashed her umbrella in the car. At the Georgetown house, no one answered the door for a few minutes, and she wondered if she had misunderstood Marcy. Finally Omar came to the door looking unenthused, wearing oversize pants and a sweatshirt with the hood up.

"Mom's on the phone upstairs," he said. "We can go."

He had seemed to grow older just in the few weeks since his father had moved out. His head still only came up to her shoulder, and his cheeks were as round as ever, but his body was starting to change as hormones worked at his puppy fat. And if he had seemed sometimes sad to her before, his unhappiness now was much more marked.

She took him out to Chinatown, to a restaurant where she and Prakash had gone for Dim Sum on a couple of weekends. Amina tried not to think about telling Prakash; she tried just about all the time to put that out of her mind, to squash that feeling of guilt. She did the same with Omar. It was better to tell Marcy and Mo first, and then let them break it to Omar; they were professionals, after all. And he would understand, wouldn't he, maybe even be excited? She'd invite him to come for a visit, and he would have something to look forward to.

It took twenty minutes to find a parking space, and they arrived at the restaurant only to find a huge line streaming from the front door. She was worried at first that the whole thing had been a bad idea, but then Omar seemed to perk up as more and more people gathered around them, going in and out of the restaurant and crowding the sidewalks. He liked people, Amina realized. He was fascinated by them. For a time, she had assumed that his focus on her, his persistent questions and his quiet need, was unique. But now she thought that maybe he was just interested in human beings and didn't know enough of them; maybe he was just alone too much, without brothers or sisters, and now with only his mother and her cell phone.

"How's Hari?" she asked.

His face darkened at this, and he shrugged.

"You're not friends anymore?"

He shrugged again. "I guess so."

Okay, she told herself, *wrong topic*. Just then they were called into the restaurant. They were squeezed into a tiny table near the front window, a table already occupied by silverware, chopsticks, teacups, water glasses, wineglasses, soy sauce, chili paste, and a steaming pot of tea. Neon bounced off the glass and onto their faces.

"Can we order one of the fish out of the tank?" Omar asked, even before he picked up his menu.

She looked at him. "Can we order one and *eat* it, you mean?"

"Yes, please," he said.

ON THE TRAIN TO New York, she thought over the rest of the evening. They had chatted about nothing in particular over their dinner of fried rice, very fresh sea bass, and string beans. She told him all about her conference, and she asked for details about recent cricket practices. He clammed up whenever she touched on a subject that suggested the troubles at home.

In the packed restaurant it didn't seem appropriate to ask him about the project, so she mentioned it in the car on the way home. He told her he couldn't do the project anyway because it was too hard. He said that it was going to be a present for his father for his birthday but that he didn't want to give him a present now. And that was all. She offered to help him reconstruct the work he had done, and to order him more books from Prakash's bookstore, but he wouldn't say anything else except no. He had his sweatshirt hood up again, hiding his soft face from her.

The train rumbled into Penn Station through a dark tunnel. This was her first trip to New York since she'd moved back east, only the third time she'd been there in her life. She took a cab to her Gramercy Park hotel, and then went for a mid-afternoon walk.

It was markedly cooler than DC, and the trees that had lost their blossoms there a few weeks ago were in full bloom here. There was a dinner tonight that Chris expected her to be at, and her presentation was Saturday morning. She decided to aim herself downtown, and set off with her backpack over her shoulder and a cardigan under her windbreaker.

She was not a city girl. Though, to put it fairly, she was not really a country girl either. She had not liked growing up in a small-ish city in Ohio, she had not particularly loved the town in central California where she'd gone to grad school—though she'd been comfortable there—and she did not camp, bicycle, hike, or garden. She was attached to DC now, but not in a sentimental way. And New York always struck her as simply too much. She couldn't stand the crowds, the delirious quantity of everything: shops, restaurants, bars, theaters, small dogs. She sometimes felt the urge to ask city dwellers to exercise a little restraint.

She took Lexington downtown through a section of taller buildings and into an Indian neighborhood. She stopped at some windows to look at the trays of sweets in garish pinks and greens and oranges, topped with coconut or silver foil or pearly sugar drops. At a fast-food curry house, she picked up two samosas and carried them with her as she continued down the street. She paused again at a window that displayed mannequins in saris, salwar kameez, and lenghas, the fabrics silken and embroidered, the colors flashy and rich, as gaudy as the sweets she had just seen. Her mother wore sari only on rare occasions, and Amina had been forced to wear one only at that long-ago wedding of her friend in New Delhi. She had felt ridiculous then, and she concluded that she still would. She turned toward downtown and kept walking.

By THE TIME SHE reached the downtown buildings—City Hall, the courthouses—she was exhausted from walking so long on pavement. She was wearing sneakers, and all around her women were trotting around in heels, knee-high boots, platform shoes, and flip-flops, and none of them looked like they were bothered at all.

When she had talked to Sushil about coming to New York, where he had grown up, he told her to be patient, to look past the people in suits and to try to see the city of workers and immigrants that still thrived on the margins of the shiny business buildings and the Broadway theaters and the upscale restaurants. That had been what she was trying to do this day, and she had seen it a little, how people of so many races, ages, educational backgrounds, and aspirations lived next door to each other, each in their own small square of the hive, everything humming.

BACK AT HER HOTEL she changed into a gray suit and lipstick: a professional costume. She considered putting on a set of pearls her mother had given her for her thirtieth birthday, but then dismissed them as too fancy. She brushed her hair and sprayed it with gel and tried to smooth it behind her ears, aware that she was spending more time than usual on grooming herself. She hated dinners like this. They were little more than opportunities for mutual admiration or for competitive inquiry and boasting; sharing didn't so often seem a part of the process. Worst of all would be spending an evening with Chris, who always managed in some way to push her buttons.

The conference was in a midtown hotel a few blocks south of Central Park, a hotel that might have been anywhere on the planet. The lobby was graced by a large sign greeting evolutionary biologists (From Around the World!) and directing her to the tenth floor and a banquet room already crowded with scholars from universities and institutes, graduate students recognizable from their jeans and long hair, and a host of swirling waitstaff in white shirts and black vests.

She saw Chris and went to do her duty. He was trailed by two graduate students, both male. Amina had had a hand in selecting who'd come with them to the conference, and she had advocated for Xi and Joseph in part because she just couldn't bear to be at this conference with Chris and a young woman, whether it was Anjali or another. She was therefore guilty of gender discrimination, and thus the world went round.

Chris was standing to one side talking to a very thin man in German, but Xi and Joseph said hi to her. Joseph was in something like his twelfth year of study, which made him older than her, and he looked it with his paunch and squinty, eyeglassed eyes. Xi looked ten years younger than Amina, but there were probably only a few years' difference between them; he had come straight to grad school from Cal Tech, and he was one of her favorites because he had a sense of humor.

She set her bag down on a chair and responded to Chris's beckoning hand.

"This is Dr. Amina Abdul, who has been assisting me on the hybrid zone project," Chris said, and then he said the thin man's name and school, and he and Amina shook hands. Then the thin man asked where she was from, meaning why did she have brown skin, and then she answered Ohio and asked the same question back, so that they were confused and changed the subject to science. And then she and Chris did that about forty-five more times before they finally were allowed the mercy-slash-punishment of sitting down to listen to a guest speaker and eating a three-course dinner.

The food was overcooked, somehow preserved-tasting salmon with chewy pasta. In truth, Amina liked to eat. She had never bothered to learn to cook before this year, and she disliked grocery shopping, but one of the great benefits of the last year had been enjoying the food of Marcy and Prakash and the great variety of DC restaurants. She was a little disconcerted to discover this love; it was the psychological equivalent of fat. There was the bodily equivalent too; she had put on weight, mostly around her belly. She was going soft, becoming too fond of good wine and thoughtful food and men with beards. Except Joseph, she thought, bringing herself back to reality.

Xi leaned over to say something to her and she leaned over in turn. "This is very boring," he said. "But the food is divine." His food was untouched.

"More?" she said, offering her plate. "I filled up on the melba toast."

She saw Chris watching, and she straightened up. One of her duties at her job was to keep Chris from knowing what she was really like as a human being. She figured that if he knew, he would like her even less and consequently be more interested in sleeping with her. They had, in fact, found a kind of rapprochement in the last few months. He delegated to her from his side of the table at faculty meetings, she stayed in her office as much as possible, they each had favored graduate students, and work proceeded. It also helped that she could think about leaving, and so she didn't let him get under her skin as much.

Of course the main problem she had with him, that she still had with him, was Anjali. Anjali had been scarce around the lab this semester; she'd gone to Peru with friends over the winter break, and then she was recruited for a cataloging project. This involved going back through over thirty years' worth of samples, and Anjali and Melinda, a second-year grad, had drawn the task. It was not the sort of thing Amina liked to see female students doing—it was, essentially, administrative—but still she was relieved that Anjali was no longer Chris's direct aide.

Xi leaned over again. "Will there be dancing after dinner?" he asked, and she gave a little snort of laughter. Joseph looked at them disapprovingly. She adored Joseph. He reminded her of Matt, plus forty pounds and five years, minus charm and eyesight.

With dessert came the guest speaker, who was from Brazil. He talked generally about advances in comparative genetics research, about new avenues for funding, and about their duty to continue with their Very Important Role in a post-9/11 world. And then they were free to talk to each other some more.

As soon as he finished, Amina rose from her seat and excused herself, counting the steps between her and the door like a prisoner with escape in sight. As she did, a fiftyish woman with neat, graying hair and small rectangular glasses touched her arm.

"Excuse me," she said in a husky Indian accent, "are you Dr. Amina Abdul?"

"Yes," Amina said.

"I'm Dilpa Thakkur. I head the Thakkur Institute in India."

"Oh, wow," Amina said, taking her hand and shaking it. "I didn't know you were going to be here."

"We should have written to say so. But your email said you had some personal difficulties, and so I thought perhaps you might not be attending. I myself only decided to come last minute."

"That's great, though," Amina said. "I'm so happy to meet you in person."

"Is there somewhere we can talk for a few minutes?" Dilpa asked.

"Do you mind if it's not here?" Amina asked, feeling Chris's curious eyes on her.

"A cocktail, perhaps?" Dilpa said. "I'm staying at the St. Regis and the bar is worth seeing. We can just have tea if you like."

"I like cocktails," Amina said, "and that sounds great."

The bar at the St. Regis was not a bar; it was a movie set, or a dream. Amina was grateful for her suit and the lipstick she had retouched in the bathroom, though she had a bad moment of actual longing for an embroidered pashmina shawl like Dilpa Thakkur's. Dilpa, round-faced and a little plump, beautifully dressed, was not what Amina had expected. If Amina surprised her in turn, Dilpa gave no indication that was so. They ordered wine, which came in glasses roughly the size of hot-air balloons, and sat back in plush leather chairs.

Dilpa had been raised in Bombay, and received her PhD from Harvard. She'd met her husband ten years ago, when he returned to India to invest some of the money he'd made in Silicon Valley. She had given a report on a small amount of capital Dev had invested in the institute, he had been impressed in more than one way, and they had begun seeing each other. After two years of a long-distance relationship, he relocated to India and they were married. Together they had built the institute to put India on the map for research outside of the pharmaceutical, which was what it was chiefly known for.

All of which explained a few things: how a scientist from

India had flown to the States "last minute" wearing an exquisite shawl and booked a room at the St. Regis, for example. In spite of these facts, Amina liked her.

"I read your paper on the wild silk moth years ago and admired it. We're so eager to have you come to work with us," Dilpa told her. "We'd love to have somebody head this project who has done previous hybrid zone work. But it's been difficult. As I'm sure you're aware, we are not in the most desirable location, particularly for westerners."

"I like that it's remote," Amina said. "I don't mind."

Dilpa looked pleased. She said they could give Amina a few more weeks to make her decision, if she needed it. Amina immediately felt the absurdity of asking that. How could she say no? It was what she wanted, what she had been looking for, what she—not Prakash, not her mother, not Mo, not Omar— what *she* needed.

"We'd like you to start in September; we'll be finishing up the prelimary lab results, and it would be a perfect time for a new scientist to arrive and take over the next stage."

Amina thought. September still seemed far away, a future that she could not quite see. India in the fall sounded perfect.

"I like everything you've said," Amina said, hearing the words rather than feeling her mouth form them, "and I'd like to accept your offer."

"I'm so happy," Dilpa said, leaning forward to squeeze her hand. And Amina said that she was too.

They finished their drinks, and then a man in a monkey suit whistled for a cab for her, and she was whisked back to reality and her suddenly claustrophobic-feeling room at the hotel downtown. She was happy, wasn't she? This was what she wanted. It was perfect for her. She would have her better job, she would be able explore India, she would get away from all the people she had not been able to help. Would anyone truly suffer without her? She doubted it. People were better off without her. She kept saying that to herself throughout the night as she tossed in her bed, unable to sleep.

• • •

FRIDAY SHE ATTENDED PANELS for most of the morning, stopping for lunch with Xi and Joseph, and then she hit a few more along with a guest lecture by a recent—and rare—female inductee into the National Academy of Sciences. After a quick falafel dinner with Xi, she crashed in her room and watched TV, sick of scientists. The next morning was her turn.

Amina's panel was about interrogating different perspectives on the outcome of hybrid zone interbreeding. Chris allocated himself the more glamorous side of things, their conclusions about the stability of the tension zone they had identified and their suggestions on a formula for the naming of hybrid species. He was a discussant with two National Academy of Sciences members while she was stuck in a room full of also-rans and up-and-comers. She could only hope that she still qualified as the latter.

She was the only woman on the panel, though there were plenty in the audience. She had met two of the other participants before; one was an ancient Russian whose work she had admired at the onset of her graduate study, and the other a researcher from Kyoto University whom she had met in the field when he did a summer internship at the field site in the Sierras.

The transitional area in the Sierra Nevadas had been studied for many years; the technology that enabled DNA sequencing had really opened the field up, from observation of phonotypical characteristics in the zone to more precise measurement, based on a hybrid index score that graded the degree of hybridization and presented them with a map of increasing and decreasing hybridity within the zone.

This allowed her to engage with an old argument: some thought that interspecies mating led to decreased fitness, while the site that Amina now worked on suggested—as had her graduate work—that hybrids sometimes had an increased adaptability to their ecological surroundings. That hybridization, the creation of beings without a species category, could make for success was still an alarming idea to some.

The new job in India would take her away from this, or rather, would put her on the other side of it. Instead of merely analyzing the data already collected, she would be in charge of a group that would strategically trap and observe, collecting periodic data—targeted in any manner Amina deemed fit— to be analyzed at the Thakkur Institute's own up-to-date genetics lab. She could tailor her observational work, guided by continuing analyses of the samples by Dilpa and her team in the lab. It was exactly what she wanted and a dream job for a scientist in the early stages of their career.

From her panel seat at the front of the room, Amina searched the seats for Dilpa Thakkur but didn't see her. When it came time for her presentation, Amina enunciated carefully, using a PowerPoint presentation that Anjali had constructed under her supervision. She got through her comments just fine, and the questions afterward showed that in this space at least, her point of view was gaining favor.

Coming out of the room, she felt good. Her career was finally headed in the right direction, she told herself. She had made the right decision.

25.

AS SHE RETURNED TO DC on the train, Amina began to feel melancholy. She kept thinking of Prakash and his family dinner. It was like she could see a whole future with him, as if it already existed. Amina Abdul: Prakash's wife, cricket mom, Sikh daughter-in-law. It would be a good life—for someone else.

She sighed. She was pathetic and foolish and sentimental. The car was nearly empty, so she used her cell phone to call Matt.

"Amina?" He sounded surprised. "Why didn't you return my email?"

She explained how busy she had been; he sounded understanding when she told him about Marcy and Mo's divorce, and impressed when she said that she was calling him on her way back from giving a presentation at the conference in New York.

"How are you?" she asked.

"I'm dropping out of graduate school," he told her. "And I'm getting married. So I'm great."

"Oh." She felt stupid, in a literal way, as though someone had borrowed her brain for a few seconds. "Congratulations," she managed to say.

"I'm going to go work for my dad." His father worked as a textile designer in Milwaukee.

"That's great," she said, trying to perk up her voice. "Really. I'm happy for you." He was getting what he wanted. Just not with her.

"Natalie's parents live in DC, which is why we're coming. Can you meet us for a drink one night? I'd like you to meet her."

"She's heard a lot about me, I take it." Amina could only imagine.

He laughed. "Some. But really it's just something I would like."

And that, she thought, was that. Some roads closed, while others opened up. When she and Matt first met, she had been so eager, so utterly involved by their work. It had seemed a straight path she was traveling, one that led directly from her first science classes to her graduate studies.

She fell in love with biology early, the way that other young girls fell for horses or dolls. In seventh grade, Darwin's theory of natural selection was first explained to her. She could still remember the thrumming of recognition inside her as she thought it through. She had gone to the library alone and leafed through books, studying the pictures of nature's sensible mutations: the long tongues of hummingbirds, the brilliant colors of tiny frogs, the stretched necks of puzzle-patterned giraffes. It was as though everything fell into place, then, as though she had found the words that explained everything, including her own befuddled self. Evolution felt like a rescue. When her parents showed their exasperation, asking her how she could be so careless, so quiet, so unheeding of their social rules, she had an answer in her mind: it was survival of the fittest. When her teachers praised her for her perfect scores, she thought: adaptation. She was different, she thought, because she had to change from what her parents were to survive; she was a mutation in progress, a halfway spot down the evolutionary road.

Of course she hadn't known as a girl what she knew all too well now, that survival of the fittest was an unfitting and misleading summation of Darwin's ideas. Now she knew how fragile even the most ingenious innovation might be, how overcompensation for one context made a species vulnerable to disaster. If you put all your evolutionary effort toward fitting into one situation, and the situation changed, you were doomed.

AT HOME, THERE WERE two messages: one from Prakash, saying that he really hoped that she would come to the family dinner with him, and another from Omar, saying he needed a ride to cricket practice. It was too late for the practice, and she didn't know what to do about Prakash, so instead of going to the phone she located her cigarettes, lit one, and sat on the couch with her feet on the coffee table.

She exhaled a long plume. For so long she had been out of the fray of these kinds of complicated relationships; grad school provided a stasis pervaded by anxiety and unrealistic focus, but it sheltered her from so many responsibilities. It surprised her, she had to admit, that Matt had shaken it free. It was sad that he would leave without his doctorate, but then it had been a long time since he had cared about it. Now he would enter a new kind of comfort zone, a conventional one of marriage and children and a solid profession free from the vagaries of tenure.

And she, would she never enter into that kind of security? If Amina had been able to foresee how painful it would be to move on, would she have kept her distance from Omar, refused to have lunch with Prakash, ignored Marcy's babysitting requests? Because if any part of her could look back and say that she wouldn't change those things, then she had to admit that she wanted those connections, that she had, in her own bumbling way, forged them. Stupidly, she told herself.

She decided to call her parents. Her dad, as usual, picked up the phone.

"How is your brother?" he asked right away.

"How do you think? He's getting a divorce," she said.

"Is this certain? Have you talked to Marcy?"

"Yeah, I've talked to them both, Dad. Marcy's talking about selling the house." It seemed she could hear her father shaking his head over the telephone.

"This is a great tragedy for Omar," he said.

"He'll survive. But actually that's why I'm calling."

"Did something happen?"

"No, no. I just wondered if maybe you and Mom could make it for a visit soon. Or maybe have Omar out there once school's out. I don't think it's so good for him to be in the thick of all this."

"I too have thought the same thing. But his school year is not yet over and then your mother had arranged for the tickets to that ship scenario." He was referring to a cruise in the Mediterranean. "Of course, we have been thinking of canceling the voyage what with the problems there. But can you not spare some time to spend with the boy?"

"Dad, I *do* spend time with him," she said, in the petulant voice of his daughter. "But he needs more."

"Like these Indian things?"

"Yeah, like these Indian things. He needs to spend time with somebody who can talk to him at length and answer his questions and put an end to all this searching."

"He will spend his whole life searching."

"Dad, this is not a philosophical condition. Don't pretend that it is."

"Of course it is a philosophical condition! He's searching for a truth, for a belonging, for the meaning of his life. What is more philosophic than that?"

"He's twelve years old and he also wants real information. He needs you to tell him about our family in India. He needs to feel like he's a part of something larger."

"You and Mohammed never had such needs."

"How do you know?" she said. "Mo did, he says, and I think feeling connected to you and Mom's past, to your families in India, maybe it would have helped me to not feel so cut off from everything—" She stopped because her voice cracked. She was surprised she had just said that.

"I know what you told us at the time," he said. "I tried to teach you Hindi when you were young, do you remember that? You and your brother were embarrassed by us, you said you didn't care about such things. You wanted to be like the other kids, you didn't want to know about our pasts. You didn't want curry, you wanted hamburger and french fry. We only wanted to make you happy."

There was a long silence.

"Daughter," he said. "We as parents have made many mistakes. It would be better if you and Mo did not repeat them, though perhaps it is inevitable. But still I think that for Omar it is not too late."

"Talk to him some more about Hyderabad," she said. "Tell him about my grandparents, and the house you grew up in and your brothers and sisters. Tell him what it was like to go to the masjid on Friday and what your mother cooked for dinner and how it felt when the monsoon struck."

"I won't," he said. "I can't anymore."

She waited for him to say something more, but he withheld whatever his reasoning was.

"There's a possibility of a job in India for me," she said.

"What?" he said. "You, Amina? You would go to India?"

"I might," she said, feeling defensive.

"And what about Omar?" he asked.

"That's what I'm asking," she answered. "I'm asking you to help me."

ON TV THAT NIGHT she watched a report about two sixteen-year-old girls who had been taken into detention and denied legal representation because the FBI suspected that they were planning to become suicide bombers. Amina did not often watch the news anymore. In California she had, because it all seemed so far away. Now, in the political capital of the nation, the news was alive; it was being made and debated and fought over. It was an oppressive environment.

Did studying insects count for anything in such a world? She doubted it and yet she had no choice; this was what she loved to do, it absorbed her. She had fought for this career, and she didn't want it cheapened by the fact that she was a passive political bystander in a world that demanded impassioned activism. If she were a better person, she would be protesting and supporting legal action and spending her money on campaigns. Or fighting for the freedom of women, Muslim women like her mother's mother and sisters and cousins, in Afghanistan or Saudi Arabia or Nigeria. Or working for Greenpeace or Doctors Without Borders or the Red Cross. But instead she would go to the Himalayas to stalk wild things and pray not to be disturbed.

She went and retrieved a book of photographs from the back of her closet. In it were only a few old pictures, small square depictions of her parents' first house, closer to the university, where they had lived until she was in fifth grade, and then the new, larger house—a prelude to the current golf-course horror—that they had bought when her father received tenure. Amina was very thin and never smiling in the pictures. Mo always had the insouciant grin that had been a hallmark of his childhood, one that said he could enjoy all of this because he didn't care.

That look was gone in him, she thought. He never seemed to enjoy himself anymore. Maybe he would be happier without Marcy.

She noticed that her mother was wearing salwar kameez in the very early photographs, and that she even had red powder on her scalp and between her eyes to indicate her married status. She had forgotten that her mother, whom she thought of as fiercely suburban—track-suit wearing, pilates-class attending, ladies-luncheon organizing—had once been this other woman, an immigrant, an Indian with braided hair and gold bangles. Her father looked younger, with a full head of hair and, in a few shots, very large lapels. But by the time Amina had reached the age of eight, her parents had morphed into the people she recognized: her father with his receding hairline and air of abstraction, her mother with the permanently stiff helmet of beauty-salon hair.

Was it true that she had been embarrassed by her parents' difference? Probably so. But she still blamed them for erasing themselves so willingly.

On a whim, she called Mo. He didn't pick up the phone, but she left a message: Would he like to meet her next weekend for a walk or a visit to the botanical garden or a laser light show? She grinned at the last and hung up. Laser Floyd had been his favorite thing at the age of fourteen. It was strange how well she remembered that, but not the powder dot on her mother's forehead, or her father talking to her in Hindi, trying to impress on his child the language of his home.

You, Amina? her father had asked. As if somewhere along the way she had forfeited the right to his past.

26.

AMINA DECIDED TO HUNKER down, finish the project she was working on, and begin preparations for India. She had wasted enough time thinking; it was time to be doing. She had some photos taken, ugly ones that would probably serve to confirm terrorist status rather than citizenship claim, and then she dropped off her expired passport to be renewed.

She sent an email—an email that took over forty-five minutes to compose—to Prakash saying that she was really busy this week and that she wasn't sure the dinner with his family was a good idea. He wrote back to suggest they talk about it next weekend; she left off replying until she could think of an answer. She left a voice message with Marcy, asking how Omar was doing; when Marcy didn't call back, she decided to assume that everything was fine.

The week passed easily, as she focused on her work. But when she got home on Friday, she found a letter from her father among the catalogs and bills. She poured a glass of wine and sat down to read it.

Dear Amina,

Please forgive me for this outdated mode of communication. I have been thinking quite a lot of our phone conversation, during which I did not express myself clearly.

When I was born in Hyderabad, it had only just become a state. I was the third son, and the seventh of nine children. Indian independence had been some years before, but Hyderabad wanted to retain its own independence. There were armed struggles, and my father was killed resisting the incorporation into India. I never told you that, I have told you only that my parents had died before I came to the States, but I think it was this that made me turn from politics, toward literature. Only two of my siblings are now living, but they are the youngest of my brothers and sisters, and I left for college and then to the States without knowing them very well.

Such is my story, you see. What can I offer Omar? I don't want you to think that I do not remember the breaking of the rain over our roof or the taste of my mother's coconut chutney or the morning call to prayer. I don't want you to think that I am ashamed. It is simply the past; India is the past. Omar has your guidance and I trust you. Don't ask me to do more than I am doing, daughter. I am an old man, and it pains me to think of all this.

We have decided to continue on the cruise ship, and to have Omar to visit when we return. I am having some difficulty in my lungs, but the doctor says not to worry. Your mother sends her loving regards.

How typical, Amina thought, how typical of her father to be lyrical while he distanced himself. He was trying to force her hand, to tell her to step in and take care of Omar herself, to be the caretaker Mo had just lost, to give Omar a heritage she herself did not possess. Her father was asking, without saying it straight out, that she not move to India.

That Omar was desperately unhappy was clear. His grades had dropped steadily throughout the year; he was still isolated; his mother didn't work less for being separated from Mo. What could Amina do? He had two parents, after all.

But she had a bad feeling in her stomach. It was the letter; she balled it up and threw it across the room. She was her father's daughter, after all. She would leave. And someday when she was old would she say, *I had a brother, once, I had a nephew that I adored, but that is the past*?

The phone rang, startling her. It was Matt. He and Natalie had arrived in town, and could Amina meet them for drinks Sunday evening at a Greek place downtown? She said she could, because she was caught off guard, and then she regretted it.

She poured some more wine, and then some more, and then she went to bed without eating.

THE NEXT MORNING, AS Amina was drinking her third cup of coffee and considering for the thousandth time, fruitlessly and painfully, how to tell Prakash her news, Mo finally returned her call.

"I'm sorry not to call sooner." He didn't offer a reason why he hadn't.

"No big deal."

"Thanks," he said, "for your offer, but I'm fairly busy with work these days. I'm applying for a promotion."

"And this weekend?" she asked.

He hesitated. "I was supposed to have Omar all weekend, but Marcy has him; she's taking him to dinner with Missy. She and Lyle are in town from Charlotte."

"Then we'll go out this afternoon," she said, and when he started to say something she continued, "whether you like it or not."

She suggested a picnic at the park where she had once taken Omar to meet Prakash and Anjali. Mo offered to drive, and she said she would bring the food. She went to Whole Foods and bought ham-and-brie sandwiches on baguettes, ripe Anjou pears, and a plastic container of bulgur salad. She also bought a small bar of dark chocolate for herself; Mo never ate sweets.

She was weirdly nervous. They had spent time alone together so rarely since he'd left for college. Since high school, there had always been Marcy, who was talkative and fun and bossy. She had taken over all social obligations from Mo, who had relinquished them, no doubt, with relief.

At the picnic site Amina spread a flannel blanket, a leftover from California. They sat and ate in the sun, while a soccer game unfolded in the center of the grass and families barbecued at tables decorated with balloons. She felt a little silly, bringing him here, just the two of them alone. Her brother was as stiff as ever, wearing black chinos and sneakers and a shirt that was buttoned too high up his neck.

After they ate, they walked in the woods. The forest floor was squishy, but their feet scratched against fallen leaves. New ferns were out, and the foliage overhead was thick enough to block out the heat of the late spring sun and mitigate the bit of humidity that had arrived that week.

"I think I'm going to take a job in India," she told him.

He actually stopped walking. "You're what?"

"I've been offered a position with a research institute in India, at a new hybrid zone that's been discovered in the foothills of the Himalayas. I think I'm going to take it."

He nodded and continued walking, his back straight.

"That's it?" she said. "That's your response?"

"It's like you," he said.

"What does that mean?"

"It's like you to leave. You're always leaving."

Now she stopped to stare at him, flabbergasted. "Me?"

"You always do whatever you want," he said, enunciating

each word with care. "You are always free, while other people have responsibilities."

They began to walk again.

"You have responsibilities," she said after a minute, "and yet you manage to avoid them."

He looked at her. "I work; I support my family; I do my duty."

"You avoid asking your wife to come back. You avoid Omar. You avoid me, Mo. Have you ever once asked to spend time with me since I moved here?"

He looked pissed. "I do not avoid my responsibilities. Marcy made this choice."

"You should try making some of your own," she said.

"Like you?" he asked. "Choices like yours?"

They turned back at the next fork in the trail and, back at the grass, gathered their belongings from the picnic site. It had always been like this, between them. Their mother said they fought because they were so much alike. And they were; she could see it now, how they both concentrated on work, how they shut themselves off from family. In that they were most like their father.

"What are you doing for your birthday?" she asked as he pulled up in front of her apartment.

Their birthdays were only three weeks apart, and, as children, they had always celebrated together. Maybe this had more to do with the fact that it wasn't until high school that either of them had many friends, or maybe it was some kind of tradition of her parents, or maybe they had just liked it that way. She had felt that their birthdays connected them, that the dates affirmed her bond with her somewhat aloof older brother.

"I haven't given it any thought," he said.

"I'll call you," she said. "Maybe we can go out to dinner."

He gave a noncommittal shrug and waved farewell. She walked away with a heavy heart and he drove away to let himself back into his prison.

27.

PRAKASH WAS DOING INVENTORY at the bookstore on Sunday, but he called again and asked if Amina could come by one day for lunch next week. She gave a rambling speech about her backlog at work, knowing that it all sounded like an excuse, but unable to stop herself. He sounded puzzled, but he agreed.

She had to meet Matt and his new love downtown that night, so late in the afternoon she abandoned her computer and changed into dark pants and a green sleeveless shirt, slipping leather sandals on her feet. She stared at herself in the mirror; she had changed since he had last seen her. It wasn't just her hair, either. Maybe it was the absence of flannel shirts and boots and the air of concentration she had always worn while working on her dissertation. She was somehow sharper. But then perhaps Matt wouldn't notice.

The Greek restaurant was crowded and dark and loud. She found Matt and Natalie at the bar. Natalie was tiny and plump, a blond with short hair, dimples, and the skin of a baby. Matt looked older, more substantial. Happier.

They were drinking wine, and Amina ordered a pinot grigio that cost fourteen dollars a glass. She needed to keep reminding herself not to drink it all at once.

She heard about their wedding plans, and she told them about the lab and her apartment. Natalie was nice, so damn nice that Amina felt like pinching her to see if she could feel pain.

"I'm moving to India," she told them. "I've got a position at the Thakkur Institute."

"Where in India?" Natalie asked.

"The north," Amina said. "The foothills of the Himalayas. Nowhere in particular."

Natalie had spent a year abroad in India her junior year of college. She had been to the Himalayas, too, on a two-month trek through Nepal. Amina felt suitably humbled.

"It'll be great," Natalie said.

"Fieldwork?" Matt guessed, and Amina nodded.

She made it through another forty minutes before excusing herself. The couple had dinner plans with Natalie's parents, and they all walked out together. The night was warm and overcast, and the sky was glowing with refracted city light. They said goodnight. Matt gave her a big hug.

"You look really great," she told him.

"So do you," he said, and she knew from the way his eyes slid to the side that he was lying.

She went home and lay on her couch, a cigarette dangling from one hand, the smoke swirling in the breeze from an open window. Maybe she should try harder to stay with Prakash. Maybe Matt had the right idea; maybe it didn't matter what her work was or where she did it; maybe she should stay and raise turbaned sons and learn the rules of cricket. It wasn't too late; she hadn't told Chris that she was leaving. She hadn't told Prakash yet. She hadn't told Omar.

She changed into her pajamas and prepared to watch *It Happened One Night* on the classics channel. But then her nephew called in tears.

"Chachi?" he said. "Can you come and pick me up?" His throat was choked with snot and he was hiccupping small sobs that made it difficult to understand him.

She sat up straight. "Did something happen?"

"I'm at Dad's," he said. "Mommy is out with one of her friends. I want to go home."

"Why don't you ask your father to take you home?"

"Because he's asleep."

This was getting weird. "Omar, I'll come over, but only if you promise to wake him up."

Omar didn't say anything.

"Omar?" she said. "Have you already tried to wake him?"

Still silence.

"Omar?" she said.

"I think he's drunk," Omar whispered.

She drove over. She didn't wait for the elevator but took the stairs two at a time, her chest heaving by the time she reached the ninth floor.

Omar answered the door. He was fully dressed and so composed it was eerie.

"Hey, kiddo," she said, stepping inside. "Where's your dad?"

Omar nodded toward the kitchen but didn't move from his position by the door. She saw that he had his bag packed and waiting by his side.

She went into the kitchen and saw Mo slumped over the table. At first her heart stopped because she thought maybe Omar had it wrong, maybe Mo had had a heart attack or a stroke, but then as she got closer she could smell the alcohol. She saw beer bottles on the counter and on the floor. She went and pulled his head up, and saw that he had vomited a little down the front of his shirt. She shook him.

"Mo, you fucker," she said. "Wake up."

His eyes flickered and then opened. He moved his mouth from side to side, as if tasting to see if he could speak, and then he shook his head and closed his eyes again.

"Mo," Amina said. "Wake up right now or I'll call the police and report you."

His head tilted to one side and words came out in a slow, wavering slur, his eyes half open. "For what?"

"For abandoning your responsibilities as a caregiver." When

he didn't show any reaction, she said, "Omar's here, you shit!" and his eyes opened wider.

"Don't call the police, chachi," Omar said behind her.

She looked back. Omar was now in the kitchen doorway, composure gone, tears streaking his cheeks.

"Don't send my dad to jail," he said.

Amina released her grip on the collar of Mo's shirt. "I'm just trying to scare him, Omar. I won't call anyone."

Omar nodded, the tears still flowing.

Amina turned to Mo. "You: get up. Now." And then she guided Omar away from the door and into the living room. There was a video still playing, what looked like a horror movie, and the remains of Chinese takeout side by side with three cans of root beer. It was amazing that Omar himself had not entered into a state of sugar shock. She sat him on the couch and patted his knee.

"Do you want to go to my house?" she asked.

He waited a minute and then shrugged. Then he said, "I want to go home."

She really didn't want to have a scene with Marcy at this hour, especially before Mo was sober and able to provide a defense, if he had any.

"How about you come with me and then I'll take you home first thing in the morning?" she said. "Your mom's probably still out."

He nodded. "She'll be mad."

"Yeah," Amina said. "She'll be mad."

She picked up some of the cartons and cans and carried them into the kitchen, where Mo was leaning over the sink, splashing water on his face. She dumped the stuff down on the table, noticing with surprise that there was a book of poetry by Keats on the table. She filed that away for future conversation.

"I'm taking Omar. I'll drop him at Marcy's tomorrow morning."

Mo turned to look at her, his face dripping, the vomit on his shirt newly dampened. He looked pathetic. But he only nodded.

"Thanks."

"Do not," she said, trying not to raise her voice for Omar's sake, "thank me."

At home she put her nephew on the couch with a cup of tea and her softest blanket. She put her hand to his hot face, sticky with dried tears, and then she went to bed, too. She didn't sleep for a long time.

THE NEXT MORNING SHE intended to get Omar home early, before Marcy could track him down at Mo's, but she'd forgotten to set an alarm. She hadn't gotten to sleep until about five, so she slept until almost nine. It was Memorial Day, a no-school day, but Omar said that he and his mom had plans for the afternoon. She was supposed to pick him up that morning. By the time Amina had given Omar some cereal and poured three cups of coffee into her own stomach, it was past ten. Amina knew Marcy wasn't going to be happy.

When she pulled the Honda up to the house, Marcy came right out the front door and waited on the porch for them to get out of the car.

She managed to offer a reasonably calm, "Hi, baby. Why don't you put your stuff in your room?" to Omar, but her eyes on Amina were fierce. When Omar was inside, she started up immediately.

"Why do you have Omar?"

"I picked him up from Mo's, Marcy. That's all." Amina tried to make her voice soothing.

"And why did no one call me? Why did I have to go all the way over to Mo's fucking apartment?"

"Marcy," Amina said, "calm down."

"I will not fucking calm down," Marcy said. "I have a right to know if my husband is planning to farm out his parental duties to his sister. The next time he asks, I want you to call me. I will take care of Omar when he can't. If he wants to share custody, he has to learn to do it himself."

"And when you share custody, does that mean Omar is no

longer allowed stay with me?" Amina asked. It was one thing to let Marcy take out her anger at Mo on Amina, but she wouldn't accept being shut out of her nephew's life.

"What does it matter?" Marcy asked. "I heard from Mo about India. You're moving. End of story."

"Marcy," Amina said. She paused, but couldn't think of a justification for her behavior. Finally she simply said, "I love you both. I don't want it to be this way."

"Spoken like a true Abdul," Marcy said. "If you don't want it to be this way, then how come it is?"

AMINA DRAGGED HERSELF INTO the office later that morning to get some work done while the office was quiet. She made a stop at a Dunkin' Donuts for a muffin and a long sit in the parking lot, fighting off tears of anger in her car. On her voice-mail was a message from Prakash.

"I don't care about the dinner, Amina," his voice said to her, as she pulled down her blinds and lit a cigarette. "Just talk to me."

Fuck. Fuck fuck fuck. Did she deserve all this? When had everything gotten so out of control?

She called Mo three times, but he didn't answer the phone. Late in the afternoon she decided to go and check on him. He had been alive this morning, at least alive enough to tell Marcy about her move to India, but she supposed it was her responsibility to make sure he was recovering.

She rang the bell twice before he answered. He was wearing shorts and a sweatshirt, and with his long hair and unshaven beard he looked as down and out as she'd ever seen him.

He didn't say anything, just opened the door. She followed him to the couch and sat next to him, reaching herself for the remote to turn the TV off.

"Last night," she said, "was bad."

He didn't say anything, didn't look at her.

"Why did you do that?" she said. "How could you do that with Omar here? How could you let him see that?"

He still didn't speak, only put his head in his hands.

"Mo," she said, "I'm trying to help you."

He lifted his head then and looked at her. "Piss off," he said.

She stood up, her head strangely clear. "I only came to see that you're all right. Clearly you're back to normal."

"You're moving," he said. "You're going away. You can't help me."

"Then help yourself," she said in disgust, and she left him on his cheap couch, only pausing on her way out to turn the TV back on. *Let the asshole rot,* she thought to herself, but somehow she felt guilty even thinking it.

28.

WORK IN THE LAB slowed down as people transitioned to summer projects. A cadre of students and professors was going to the field site in Europe, several students had grants to conduct research elsewhere, and Chris was returning to England for two months. It made him seem almost human, that he would spend his time off visiting his family. But then Amina spoke to a group of students, who mentioned they were visiting London to do some research over the summer. Anjali was with them. It was all Amina could do to restrain herself from taking the girl by the shoulders and shaking her.

Instead, she went home and pouted around her apartment with a cigarette, her mind careening between Omar, Mo, and Prakash. She had spent two nights at Prakash's house, trying not to act distant, trying to act normal, even as she could see he knew something was up. She was trying to think if she was wrong to leave. But every session of soul-searching turned up the same answer: she should go; it would be better for everyone if she left. Because what would she do when Prakash asked her about children? What would she do if Mo kept drinking and lost the right to custody? What could she do if Marcy thought she was on the wrong side?

Just after she finished dinner, Marcy called. Amina hadn't spoken to her or Mo since Mo's experiment in self-destruction.

"I'm sorry I haven't been in touch," Marcy said. Her voice was neutral and pleasant, but Amina felt she was being spoken to like a stranger.

"I'm sorry about what happened," Amina said. "I should have called you and told you I had Omar with me."

"I just," Marcy said, "am so mad at Mo, and I took it out on you."

"I know," Amina said. It was probably more than that, but this was a good fiction.

"Omar is very excited about the game," Marcy said. "It would mean a lot to him if you would be there to watch."

"Of course I'll be there," she said. "Is Mo coming?"

"Omar asked first about you." Marcy's voice took on an edge at this.

"I'll call to invite Mo myself," Amina offered. "He should be there."

It took her another day and a half to work up the courage to call him again. And Mo said he would be out of town. Amina was astonished.

"Where?"

"I promised to visit Mom and Dad before they go on their cruise," he said, as if he took independent trips to visit people all the time.

"Brilliant," Amina said.

"It's just one game," he said. "And I'm having Omar out to stay with me on the weekends over the summer. Marcy and I talked about it and decided it's better to have him on a schedule."

"You did?" Clearly not a word had been peeped to Marcy about the cause of Amina's impromptu caretaking over Memorial Day weekend. Amina had no idea if she should tell Marcy, if Marcy had a right to know.

"It is. And Amina," he said, his voice becoming deeper, "what happened the other night won't happen again."

"Maybe I'll stick around just in case," she retorted.

"Then *you* should go to the game."

Amina hung up, frustrated. She wondered how their parents had gotten him to agree to the visit. His mother had done it, no doubt. She was an expert at manipulation. Anyway, it was probably a good thing. She distracted herself by starting to look through the paperwork Dilpa Thakkur had sent from India. There were guidelines for submitting the request for a work visa, annual reports from the last few years, copies of recent grant proposals, and statements of incoming funding. Dilpa and her husband ran a tight ship.

What really interested her were a couple of papers reporting preliminary findings about the hybrid zone. The early work by the group from the US consisted mostly of counting and group identification and behavioral observation. There was a wide range of phenotypes living in the zone, and the peripheral areas had also been monitored for most of the last decade. The latter stuff looked good to her, like research she could build on. The staff was not large, but she would be allowed to hire field workers and participate in the search for staff qualified to do basic genetic analysis.

She could really go, she could really do this, and to convince herself that this was true, she made a list of tasks. At the end of it she put "Tell Prakash." Then she scratched it out, chastising herself; he wasn't something for a list. He deserved better.

She started sorting through papers in her office, piling things in stacks that she mentally marked *essential, storage,* and *trash.* Soon she would have to tell Chris; she didn't want to rush it, because he wouldn't let her do anything interesting once she announced she was leaving.

On Tuesday, Prakash called.

"Amina," he said. "I really need to talk. Something is going on with you and I want you to tell me."

"It's just work, and I—"

"I just want to talk to you," he interrupted. "I want to know what you're thinking."

She felt awful. "I'm coming to the cricket game."

"That's not what I had in mind," he said, sounding frustrated. "Amina. Help me out here."

What choice did she have? "Okay," she agreed. "Let's talk this weekend."

She hung up and went to Chris's office. She asked for a meeting. He looked surprised but he told her to stay after the staff meeting on Friday and they could talk then.

29.

FRIDAY MORNING AMINA AND Chris sat at opposite ends of the conference room as people filed out and grad students stopped to ask Chris questions about project deadlines and vacation schedules and machines they didn't understand or that others were monopolizing. Anjali came over to Amina and asked how she was.

"Great," she said.

"I was just worried," Anjali said, "because Prakash said Omar's parents are getting a divorce?"

Amina could feel Chris looking at them; Anjali had a real talent for merging the personal and professional. "That's true," she said, "but Omar's doing fine. How is the cataloging going?"

Anjali accepted the change of topic and left the room after another minute. When Amina and Chris were alone, he asked what he could do for her.

"The Thakkur Institute has offered me a management position in the Himalayas, in a post that I think I might be better suited for."

He looked completely taken by surprise, and then almost immediately angry.

"You committed to three years when we interviewed," he

said, his mouth twisted in displeasure. "I've invested a lot in training you. A lot of candidates applied for your postdoc, you know."

"I appreciate all that you've done," Amina said, "I'm just not sure that I fit in here."

He shook his head. "I know the site. I don't even think it's a real hybrid zone. You'll be making a mistake."

"I would be able to get back in the field," she persisted.

"And your lab skills?" he asked. "You'll lose those. This is the type of work that gets funding, what we do here. You'll find yourself without any support, collecting data and unable to make anything out of it in a way that your fellow scientists can use, and to top it off you'll be in the middle of nowhere in a third-world country."

He seemed to calm down as he spoke, as if his anger was diminishing. She almost thought she detected a gleam in his eye when he said "the middle of nowhere." Probably he relished the thought as much as she.

"Let me know as soon as you decide. I'll have to ask you to train a replacement," he said, standing up as if to dismiss her.

"Fine," she said. "Thanks for the consult."

She was a little shaky when she got back to her office. She opened a window and lit a cigarette, blowing the smoke out as she puffed. Chris was right, in a way; it could be career suicide if the Thakkurs didn't know what they were doing. But then he couldn't know how stifling she found his tight little office with its ranked minions and minute measurements. He couldn't know how much she needed to get away, how much she looked forward to wearing jeans and hiking boots and living in a tent and waiting for hours in heat and sun. Alone, all alone. He couldn't know about all the things she had broken before she broke with him.

THAT EVENING, AS AMINA was preparing to leave for the weekend, a visibly upset Anjali came into her office without knocking.

"Anjali! What happened?" She pulled up a chair for the girl, then retreated behind her desk.

Anjali wiped at her cheeks, shaking her head. She started to laugh. "I've been fired, Amina."

"Fired? But you're a TA. Don't you just . . . fail or something?"

"No, I'm fired. I can't come back into the lab. Chris said I messed up the DNA sequencing, and that the NSF work is all wrong because of it."

"Fuck, are you kidding?" Amina said it without thinking, her professional demeanor forgotten.

"But I didn't, Amina, it wasn't me. He was—well, with—you know, right? With Trina. And he told me to finish the project, and I didn't know what I was doing, and I should have said no but I didn't."

With Trina? She was a first-year grad student who had flown completely under Amina's radar. "Okay," Amina said, trying to think what to do. "If he's responsible, I'm sure he'll come around. I can rewrite that part for you; it's not the end of the world."

"No, it's worse. He's pissed because I won't sleep with him. We did—I mean, there was a time when it seemed like I would, and now he says I'm some kind of tease, that I don't deserve my place here. Oh shit, Amina, what will I tell my family?"

"Hey," Amina put a hand out then retracted it, not sure what to do. "We'll think of something."

She let Anjali stay in her office, trying to be soothing as they talked it through. Then, before she knew it, Amina had offered to take Anjali back home with her for a drink and takeout. She felt maternal and consoling as she did so, but in the car on the way home she realized, uncomfortably, that she was acting not like a mentor but like a friend.

Anjali seemed to calm down as they drove. "Thanks, Amina, for distracting me. I can't believe what a mess I've made."

Amina looked at her out of the corner of her eyes and almost missed a red light. The words could have come out of her own mouth.

At Amina's apartment, Anjali pronounced her liquor cabinet—which consisted of Peach Schnapps, four beers from Pennsylvania, and an unopened bottle of expensive Scotch—woefully inadequate. They went out again, to the liquor store, where Anjali bought three bottles that she insisted would all end up in one drink.

"Ladies," the mustachioed clerk said approvingly, "it's good to see beautiful women who know how to drink." *Welcome*, Amina thought, *to the world of Anjali.*

At home, they talked about the lab, about the latest hire who would arrive in the fall, and about the unlikelihood of an end-of-the-year party including more than wine left over from the year's visiting lecturer receptions. Anjali told a story about how one visiting professor kept asking her for coffee, certain that she was Chris's secretary.

"People look at me and think I'm not smart," Anjali complained. "Because I like clothes? Because I outline my eyes? I don't get it."

She was mixing drinks as she said this, and for a moment Amina felt herself utterly seduced. Here was this smart girl, wearing high boots and a short skirt, a turtleneck sweater that outlined her breasts perfectly, her eyes still thick with kohl in spite of her tears, and her full lips glossy. Amina had never looked so good in her life.

Anjali brought over their drinks, which were a surprising shade of purple, and they toasted. The drink was a swirl of sweet black currant and gin and something bitter. For a moment Amina let herself get lost in it, but then she looked up to see Anjali looking at her expectantly. She put the drink down.

"The thing is," Amina said, "we don't live in a vacuum. We can't just do whatever we want, wear whatever we want, and let other people figure it out, because other people can misinterpret. They can, and they will. In your case, Anjali, they do. And no matter how much confidence you have about your actions, you can't control the repercussions."

Anjali rested her lips on the rim of her glass and focused her brown eyes on Amina. "That's what happened at the lab?"

"It's easy to lose control when sex gets into the picture."

"You assume I've been sleeping with Chris." Anjali said this like she expected it.

"No. I don't think that."

"Then what *do* you think, Amina?"

Amina tried to be clear about this at least. "He should know better than to make obvious sexual overtures to his subordinates. I think you made a mistake to trust him, to let the whole lab see him show you so much favor."

"Like an idiot."

"No," Amina said. "It could happen to anyone. It happened to me."

"To you?" Anjali put down her lipstick-rimmed glass, her eyes wide. "You had an affair with one of your professors?"

Amina shook her head. "He tried. I didn't."

"Well, you're better than me," Anjali said, and took a gulp of her purple drink.

"I was in love with him," Amina said, and then stopped, surprised at her admission. She put her drink down. "It killed me to say no. I couldn't believe he'd put me in that position. And then he went to my friend."

"But you did the right thing!"

Amina shrugged. "It didn't feel right. None of it. I was young," Amina said. "With not enough experience of power and how pervasive it is in human relationships."

Anjali studied her. "You talk like Foucault."

"Uh-oh."

"I'll make more drinks."

They had three more, only remembering to order food after the second, which was a mistake. Amina was far drunker than she should be with a graduate student from her own lab, let alone the baby sister of the man she was planning to break up with. But it was too late to send Anjali home, and too late to un-drink the cocktails. She resigned herself to having made, as Anjali phrased it, another mess.

Anjali stayed the night on the couch, in a T-shirt of Amina's that read "I Love Wild Silk Moths," a present from Matt. It was nearly noon when Amina woke with a headache and the vague feeling that she had forgotten something.

She went to make coffee, trying to make as little noise as possible for her own sake as well as the sleeping Anjali's.

"Crap!" she said out loud, suddenly remembering.

"Huh?" Anjali said sleepily, sitting up with kohl still smeared prettily around her eyes.

"I said I'd go and see Omar—cricket—Prakash," she said. She stopped herself and started again. She told Anjali that this was the day of the cricket match.

"I was planning to go, too," Anjali said. "Let's just drive over together."

Amina nodded, because this made an unavoidable kind of sense. Prakash was Anjali's brother; of course she would want to go. But as Amina showered, scrubbing at her body with exfoliating apricot gel, she felt indignant. How had she gotten into this? What would Prakash think—that she and his sister were becoming best friends at just the time when she was dumping him?

30.

WHEN THEY GOT TO the field, Anjali trotted right up to Prakash with Amina trailing behind. Prakash looked between them, a puzzled expression on his face.

"Amina was helping me with some work last night, till really late," Anjali explained, with tact and a less-than-reverent attitude toward the truth. "So I just stayed the night at her place."

He accepted this and welcomed Amina with a surreptitious kiss on the cheek, which Amina returned with a squeeze of his hand. Anjali said nothing.

Omar and Marcy were late. Amina waited until match time, and then went onto the field to ask Prakash if he had heard from them. He said no. She called Marcy's cell phone and there was no answer.

The match began, the miniature players taking the field all in white for this mock tournament, Prakash's team in blue armbands. There was still no sign of Omar. She saw Anjali down at the field, holding hands with Rafael, the consideration of which helped a few more minutes pass. She watched as one of the Patel girls was the first to pitch for Omar's team.

Finally Amina saw them arriving, Omar sullen and Marcy

with a flustered air. He was not wearing cricket whites. Amina went down to meet Marcy at the bottom of the bleachers.

"What happened?" she asked. "You're really late."

Marcy looked at her. "We had some issues at home." She didn't look like she was going to elaborate.

"Do you want to come and sit with me?" Amina asked, confused. It seemed that Marcy was still angry at her after all.

"I'm going to get a soda, and I have to make just one call. And then I'll be up."

Amina felt a little like Omar must feel all the time: put off, shut out, and left in the dark. She noticed that Omar was on the bench; no doubt he would not be allowed to play as he hadn't come in uniform.

Amina sat alone near the top. Marcy came back once for a few minutes, until she got another call, and she didn't volunteer any more information then. Though it was hot, Amina's skin felt cool, as though she were sitting in her own temperature zone. Her hair flipped around in the warm breeze, and she felt her skin tightening in the sun, but she didn't feel the heat. Maybe she had finally adjusted to the DC climate, or maybe she had simply ceased to feel any connection to reality. Or maybe she just had a hangover.

The cricket match was uneven; the other team had played in a league, and they were crushing Prakash's beginners. Still, there were some good moments. The older Patel girl had a half-century, and Hari proved to be a great fielder, and the pitching by the son of an Australian embassy staff member provided one crucial out.

Amina considered going to talk to Omar to see what was wrong. He sat on the sidelines with his head down, wearing long basketball shorts and a black-and-white rugby shirt, one of his sneakers untied. Staring at him, knowing he wasn't hers to fix or console, that he was not her child but Marcy's and Mo's, made her ache. It felt, against all logic, wrong.

By late afternoon, Marcy was back at her side.

"I'm sorry, Amina," she said. "What a day." Her hair was pulled back into a bun, which made her face look tiny and narrow. Her eyes looked tired.

"What's going on with Omar?" Amina asked again.

"Amina," Marcy said, "don't take this the wrong way, but it's none of your business."

Amina breathed in and out three times.

"But maybe you'll tell me anyway," she said, looking out at the game and not at Marcy, "to be polite."

Marcy shook her head. "Not now, okay? I've got enough on my plate dealing with your brother and my son. I don't have time to catch you up on the nephew you every once in a while pay attention to."

"Every once in a while!" Amina said, her voice rising with every word. She noticed people looking over at her, and lowered it. "How can you say that? You know I love Omar. You know I do."

Marcy blew air out her mouth. "I'm on my own and I expected that you would be around to help. Instead we've seen even less of you, and now you're moving out of the country? You can't even be bothered to drive Omar to cricket anymore."

"I thought it would be good for you and Mo to be involved in something Omar loves," Amina said. "That's all." And she didn't say, *I've been avoiding you because I have a heart full of broken glass and guilt. I've been avoiding you because I don't want to hurt Omar. I've been avoiding you because I need to distance myself, to help Omar get used to my absence, to make it easier for him to understand that if he and I are going to get by in this world it is not going to be together.*

"You did, did you?" Marcy said. "You thought it would be good for me to be involved with Omar? Well, let me tell you something, I am involved with Omar. I cook his breakfast and make his lunch and we eat dinner alone together every single goddamned night. I drive him to Mo's for the weekend, I drive him to his doctor's appointments, I go to his parent-teacher meetings. I do it alone, because your brother is worthless." She was ignoring the tears that streaked down her angry face as she said this, and Amina handed her a tissue in silence.

"You're right, Marcy." She felt terrible.

"Amina," Marcy said. "I'm taking Omar and we're moving back to Charlotte to be near my sister. I have cousins there, and they have kids. Omar can have the family he wants." She put a hand up as Amina opened her mouth. "It's already decided. It's done."

They both sat in silence for a few minutes. Stunned, Amina didn't know what to say. *Stay and I'll stay, too?* What did she have to offer?

Suddenly Marcy stood and looked out toward the field, and Amina did the same. Omar and Hari were caught in some sort of tussle at the bench; they seemed to be engaged in a tug of war over something. Then Prakash stepped in and blocked their view. Marcy and Amina trotted side by side down the bleacher steps and onto the field. Omar took off just as they got there, toward the maze of parked cars.

"I'll get him," Amina told Marcy, and broke into a run after her nephew. "Omar," she called, "Omar, stop."

She caught up to him as he reached Marcy's green Saab. His hand was bleeding.

"What happened?" she asked, pulling some more tissue out of her bag and pressing it into his hand. He was breathing hard.

"Hari and I had a fight," he said, tears falling from the corners of his eyes.

"Why?" Amina asked. She checked to see that the cut on his palm had stopped bleeding; it had, and it didn't look deep.

"I'm moving," Omar said, breathing hard. "Mom said we have to move to North Carolina. I have to go to a new school. I can't live with my Dad; she won't let me."

"I did hear," Amina said, "and I'm sorry. I really am."

"Can I live with you?" His eyes were huge and brilliant with tears, like black holes of need that pulled her in.

"You can't, Omar," she said. "It doesn't work like that." She put a hand on top of his hot, dark head and tried not to break into tears herself. "You can visit me, though." She did not specify where.

He nodded and looked up briefly, snot running from his nose and down his chin. He no longer looked like Bambi, she realized; he looked like any other kid who had been disappointed by the world.

31.

BACK HOME, AMINA PUT on some music, the Chet Baker record that Prakash also owned, and lay on her couch. It was fair, she knew, that Marcy take Omar and leave. She had no right to complain, but she hurt for Omar and she hurt for her brother.

She had met members of Marcy's family at various times, had known her parents well when Marcy and Mo were first dating. Marcy's father had died when Omar was a baby, and her mother had moved back to North Carolina where Marcy's grandmother and sister and other relatives lived. The families had met for a couple of Christmases, although with little in common—Amina's dad the abstract professor and her mom the perky housewife, while Marcy's dad had been a construction foreman and her mother a nurse. They tended to partition the holidays, with Omar spending Christmas at Marcy's parents' and New Year's at the Abduls'.

The Benoits were nice people. They were a little old fashioned, there was alcoholism in the family, and one of Marcy's brothers had killed himself. There were lots of them, however, which was, as Marcy said, very much to the point. If Omar wanted family, and the Abduls wouldn't provide it, then he could have the Benoits. Amina knew what it would be like for him—the only brown kid, the cousin with the funny name—and yet maybe, just maybe, it would be enough to see him through.

She turned on the TV; there was something silly in black and white on Turner Classics, and she settled in to watch it. And then there was a knock at the door.

She straightened her shorts and put a sweatshirt on over her tank top because she wasn't wearing a bra. She peered through the peephole to see who it was and then she stopped breathing for a second because it was Prakash. She ran her fingers through her hair to smooth it and opened the door.

"Amina," he said. He looked upset.

She opened the door wider and stepped aside. "Prakash?"

"I really need to talk to you," he said. "I'm sorry I didn't call first."

She let him in. *This is it*, she told herself. She had to tell him now. She poured them some wine and they sat on the couch. But then he took something wrapped in a handkerchief out of his pocket and tossed it onto the coffee table where it fell with a thud. Amina put her glass down.

"This is what Hari and Omar were fighting about," he said.

Amina turned back the handkerchief to reveal the silver knife. She closed her eyes for a moment, sick.

"I assume it's the same one Omar had before," Prakash said.

"I thought the police took it," she said.

"Hari borrowed it from Omar, and he said he was returning it at the cricket match because he didn't want to bring it to school. Omar was mad that he'd taken so long to return it. End of story. I didn't want to tell Marcy because of what happened before, but I should have. I should have put both the boys off the team for fighting with a weapon."

She nodded.

"Maybe," Prakash said, "Marcy is right. Maybe Omar does need to see someone."

"A shrink, you mean," Amina said.

He shrugged. "Recurring incidents like this are not good, Amina."

"It's gotten more complicated," she said, hesitating. It seemed absurd to tell him about Marcy's move before she announced her own.

"So has everything, it seems." He looked angry and exhausted. "I just wanted you to know. I couldn't think what else to do with the knife."

"Prakash," she said, reaching to take his hand. "You're a good man. Thank you."

"Omar needs you," he said. "You're good for him."

"Me?" she said. Her head ached a little and she heard her own voice as if from a distance. She had to tell him. She had to.

He leaned toward her, rubbed one of her hands with both of his. "You."

"Well," she said. "I'm not terribly reliable, you know. I'm cranky and I don't like people and I have a terrible track record with commitment. And I might be moving to India."

He froze and then looked her full in the face.

"India?"

She looked down. Fuck, she wanted a cigarette. It was not polite to drink the entire bottle of wine herself, and she needed something.

"It's a possibility," she managed to say, and her voice shook.

"Do you want more wine?" he asked.

This made her want to cry, but instead she nodded, and he poured out the rest of the bottle between them.

She said, "I applied for this thing, this job, and it just happens to be in India, and I didn't tell you because when I applied for it I didn't know you. I mean, I knew you but not the way I know you now. And then I couldn't make up my mind about whether to go and so I never found the right way to tell you." She paused. "And now I have been reduced to a blithering idiot." She swallowed some more wine.

He was looking away from her, out toward the living room, and she actually felt that she missed his eyes.

"Prakash?" she said. "I haven't really made up my mind." It was a lie, but it felt like the truth.

He looked back toward her, his expression even, and spoke in a composed voice. "Do let me know when you have."

32.

WHEN AMINA RETURNED TO work that week, she did it half-heartedly. Anjali's dilemma weighed on her mind; she had half a mind to tell Chris to go fuck himself, but what would be the point? Chris continued as if nothing happened, and no one mentioned Anjali. Finally, near the end of the week, a memo went around that she was on a medical leave and that one of the other grad students would be taking over her work. Chris himself rewrote the report and corrected the errors he had accused Anjali of making. And then Anjali called Amina one morning while she was sitting blankly at her computer in her office.

"How are you?" Amina asked. "You're missed around here."

She sounded calm and professional, even a little cool. "I wanted to thank you for your help, and to ask you another favor."

"Anything," Amina said.

"Well, it's two things. One is, I didn't really tell my brother the whole truth about what happened. I told him I screwed up some information in a report and that I didn't understand why

Chris was being so harsh. Can you just not tell him about the other stuff?"

"What's the other favor?"

Anjali's voice shook a little. "Can you ask Chris to take me back?"

Amina hesitated. "I don't think I could get him to do anything he doesn't want to."

Anjali paused and then began again with a stronger voice. "Then would you support me if I filed an appeal with the university?"

"What would that appeal say?" Amina said.

"An unjust punishment for a small mistake."

"I can do that," Amina said. "I'd be happy to do that. I'll write a letter. But Anjali, I think you'd better talk to Chris. You need to figure out if you'll be comfortable coming back."

"Do you think I should just drop out, then?"

"No, of course not. But also," Amina said, "I should tell you that I'll be leaving the lab. I have a new job in India."

"I heard," Anjali said. "My brother is devastated, you know."

"I didn't think he'd tell you."

She could practically hear Anjali shrug over the phone. "Prakash is one person with no need to keep secrets."

A couple of days later Anjali sent Amina an email with the information about where to send an appeal letter. However, she said, she had taken Amina's advice and talked to Chris, and they had decided it would be better if she did not come back. Her appeal would be for a leave of absence. All Amina needed to do was write in support of her character.

That, Amina thought, *is ironic*. She would rather write attacking Chris's. Then she thought, *why not?* And she composed a careful letter to the dean of sciences, saying that she was leaving her postdoc early after a difficult year, and that she was concerned that Chris discriminated against women and was sleeping with a graduate student whose career was in jeopardy. She licked the envelope with relish.

• • •

AFTER A FEW EMAIL parries, she and Prakash met at a neutral location, an Irish pub not far from his store. She wasn't sure how to greet him, but he gave her a hug and a kiss. He looked as good as ever, severe and sensual and fit-looking in his white work shirt and charcoal slacks. She ordered whiskey.

They sat on opposite sides of a wooden table heavy with graffiti. He sipped at a light beer that came in a tall glass with a lemon wedge, the metal bracelet on his wrist peeking out from his cuff.

"What happened to Anjali?" he asked. "Why is she leaving the department?"

She didn't want to lie to him anymore. "I think she should tell you."

"Well, I think," he said, "you should tell me that and any other things you've been keeping from me." His voice was even, but there was no doubt about his anger.

"I did mislead you," she said. "And I'm sorry."

"You didn't really, Amina," he said. "I knew what type of person you were."

"Wow," she said. "That's a little harsh."

"I don't mean it to be," he said. "I enjoyed spending time with you. But I was vain enough to think that I could change you, and that is never a good basis for a relationship."

"This sounds very final," she said. The words lay between them for a few seconds, as after-work groups chatted around them and Sinéad O'Connor wailed a bit of Irish ballad over the sound system.

Prakash frowned. "What shall I say? That I'll come skipping through the mustard fields to visit you every summer? You are moving far away. I'll continue to know Omar, I hope, and I look forward to finding out how you are doing from him."

"Prakash, I hurt you," she said, reaching to touch his hand. The words felt soft in her mouth, like mush instead of the real things, the distinct words, she had to say.

"No more than you have hurt yourself," he said, and she took her hand away.

They finished their drinks with some awkward chat about the Thakkur Institute and the weather in the Himalayas. She offered to drop him home. Once they were there, they both continued to sit in the car as if unsure what to do next.

"You won't explain about my sister?" he asked again.

"I want to," she said. "I think you can probably guess."

"Why would I be able to?"

"Have you looked at your sister lately?" Amina said. "Can you imagine the effect of someone that beautiful in a lab full of repressed scientists?"

He looked at her, long and hard.

"Did you try to protect her?" he said.

Amina shook her head. "It was a miscalculation. I didn't think she needed my help. I've written a letter of complaint, but I know that it's too little, too late."

"A miscalculation." He thought about that. "I should have seen what was happening."

"I am far more to blame," Amina said. They sat for another minute in silence.

"There's a parking space," he said, pointing down the block. "I have some books for you, if you want to come in and get them."

She agreed and parked the car. They walked up the street in silence. A breeze carried the scent of flowers, and Amina had a sense of déjà vu, as though she had been here before, as though sometime in the past she had said goodbye exactly like this.

Inside his first-floor apartment, he handed her three hardcovers from the last book fair: two new Indian novels and a biography of Walter Sweadner, the first scientist to document a hybrid zone, the scientist who had discovered the field site she had worked at as graduate student studying wild silk moths.

"Prakash," she said, "you are . . ." Kind, she wanted to say. Thoughtful. Fuckable, brilliant, decent, and good.

They stared at each other for a moment and then he lifted

her up off the ground and into his arms, her legs were wrapped around his hips, and they were kissing. The books dropped to the floor. By the time they had fallen onto his couch, she had a brief return to reason. Breathless, she pulled her mouth from his and they looked at each other.

"This isn't rational," she said.

"That's okay with me," he returned.

33.

IT HAD BEEN ALMOST a year since she had moved to Washington, DC. It was not a generous city nor a beautiful one, but it had things to appreciate: free museums, the cherry blossoms on the Mall, the Library of Congress, restaurants from every region of the world, markets with Shah Rukh Kahn and palak paratha, multicultural cricket teams for confused young nephews. Amina's life had taken a step up when she moved here.

And so it was hard to think of leaving, and she kept putting off buying her plane tickets to India. She had until August to really decide, she told herself; she could still change her mind, find another job, dig in and stay.

She decided to have Mo over to celebrate their birthdays. He resisted at first, saying there was no need for any celebrations, but when she said she'd like to do it on her own birthday, he had a hard time getting out of it.

She was cooking him Indian food. This time she skipped the biryani—it would be too hot to have the oven on—and prepared instead a lamb curry that she had seen Prakash make. She finished it and left it on the stovetop by five p.m., fairly certain that it was a success. To go with it she prepared a simple lettuce-and-tomato salad, working on a tiny plastic cutting board that was meant for slicing nothing larger than a lemon wedge. She considered attempting a cake, but reason prevailed and instead she went back to the spice market near her house and bought carrot halwa and naan, and then stopped again for wine and a packet of birthday candles.

In her mailbox at home, she found a package from Prakash. Inside was a necklace, a silver chain with a pendant made of milky-white stone. It glowed like pearl but was set flat into a necklace in the shape of a slivered moon. She read the accompanying birthday card and put it on. The card said that Prakash loved her, that he would love her wherever she was, even India.

The late-afternoon sun drifted through her living room windows. She played Thelonious Monk, and dressed in a loose aqua tunic over shorts; she'd told Mo to come casual too. The day was in the high eighties but she kept the AC off and the windows open, and a breeze came through every once in a while. Her parents were back from their cruise. Though Amina's mother said that her dad still had some sort of lung irritation, Omar would soon be flying out alone to stay with them for three weeks. Marcy was speaking to real estate agents about the house and crying nearly all the time.

When Mo arrived, he sniffed the air and looked at her quizzically. "Did you *cook* something, Amina?"

He was carrying her birthday present unwrapped, a book on Indian flora and fauna, and she took it from with thanks—and not a little surprise at his thoughtfulness—and offered him a root beer. She had decided to skip serving the wine.

They sat in the kitchen and sipped from their bottles together. She noticed that he finally had his hair cut back to its usual shortness. "Your apartment is pleasant," he said. "You'll miss it, I'd guess."

She shrugged with one shoulder. "I haven't lived here long enough to be nostalgic."

He nodded. "Marcy wants to sell our house."

"And do you want her to?"

He set his soda down. "Of course not."

"What do you mean, of course not?"

"I thought I would always live there."

"Mo," she said, "I don't think Marcy wants to sell it either." He didn't say anything, or drink his beer, or move. He looked exhausted, she thought. He was turning thirty-six and he looked fifty.

"Ask her if you can go home," Amina said, her voice very soft.

He shook his head, and she wondered if he was fighting off tears. She remembered what Prakash had said to her, the morning after they slept together again. He told her that he loved her but that he wanted a house and kids and his faith and his business, all together in one cohesive life. He told her that she didn't feel like home.

She knew that Marcy felt like home to Mo, and she now understood how much pain he must be in.

"Let's eat," she said. She brought out the rice and lamb and salad, and they sat down at her small round table. Mo seemed to recover himself, and he was amiable throughout the meal. He told her about his job, how he had been promoted and how he hoped that would mean less, not more, work because he would be supervising rather than producing numbers, and he would be more able to set his own hours.

She told him about the research station in India, about the ecological zone created by the conjunction of a river, the mountains, and a stretch of dry plain. She told him the history of the site, how the original researchers had seen family groups displaying phenotypic characteristics of more than one species, and had posited a kind of hybrid zone long before the DNA work had been done. There were all kinds of groups, it seemed, some with only purebreds, some with only hybrid males or only hybrid females, some with more hybrids and some with fewer, and Chinese researchers in the nineties had seen strong behavioral differences in both mating and foraging behavior in the groups with many hybrid individuals.

She rose and cleared their plates, and he followed her with the serving bowls.

"Do you think," he said, setting the dishes on the counter, "that Omar will always have difficulties?"

"Fitting in?"

"Exactly."

She leaned against the refrigerator. "I don't know," she said. "But I think he can be happy."

Mo nodded.

"You have to stop drinking," she said.

"I will," he said. "I am."

They went to sit in the living room, and she gave him his present: a book of poetry by Li Young Li, a recommendation from Prakash. She watched Mo closely as he opened it.

"Poetry," he said, turning it over in his hands.

"I saw you had some on your kitchen table, that night . . ." She stopped.

He nodded once. "I was rereading. I wooed Marcy with those poems."

She couldn't help but smile. "Does Dad know?"

Mo gave a sharp laugh and leaned back. "I never would have told him. But I read a lot of poetry then. I even wrote some for Marcy."

Amina put a hand on his, moved. Her brother, a poet? She hadn't known.

"I have something else for you," she said.

"I hope it's wrapped better than what I brought," he said.

She looked at him. He had picked out an appropriate present, he had helped her clean up, and he had made a joke. Maybe there was hope for him after all. She went into one of the kitchen drawers and pulled the knife out, still wrapped in Prakash's handkerchief, from its resting place among cigarettes, twine, tin foil, and sandwich bags.

He unrolled the knife onto his hand and then let out a long breath, leaning against the counter, his eyes looking at the ceiling.

"Omar got it back, somehow, and Prakash found him with it at the cricket match. He took it from him and left it with me."

"I can't give this back to him," Mo said.

"Don't," Amina said. "It's yours. I gave it to you. It belongs to you."

A look passed over his face, then, like shadows and light over land on a bright day with quickly passing clouds. He swallowed.

"I don't know how to be a parent," he said.

"Just try," Amina said.

She went and put some more music on, Cole Porter, and turned the volume up. She went back into the kitchen, where Mo still leaned against her faux-marble counter holding the knife. He looked at her and nodded.

"Go sit," she said. He picked up the knife and went to the living room. She pulled out slices of carrot halwa and sank a candle in each and lit them with a cigarette lighter.

"I won't sing," she called out as she carried the plates in. In school, growing up, it had been Mo who sang in the choir. Amina had quit after being asked to only mouth the words.

"Ah," he said as she set his portion down in front of him. "Thank you, Amina."

"Thank Manuhanif's Halal Grocery."

"Together?" he suggested, and she nodded.

For a single second they each shut their eyes to make their separate wishes. Amina pressed her lids down hard on her eyes and thought of Omar; *let Omar be all right*, she prayed. She opened her eyes and looked at Mo, her brother, Omar's father, and together they blew their candles out.

IV. THE HORSEHEAD NEBULA

34.

ONE THING WAS CERTAIN: this was going to be the worst summer of Omar's entire life. His parents were getting divorced, and he was being forced to go back and forth between their two homes. In one, his mother was usually depressed, and in the other, his father was depressed and drunk. There was no family vacation planned, just this trip alone to his grandparents' house in Ohio, which usually he got to do in addition to a real vacation to Disney World or the beach. And he had overheard that his aunt Amina, whom he had begun to feel like he could count on, was moving away to India.

In retaliation for all of this, Omar decided to change his name. It was too hard to take away the Abdul part, but his first name was his, and if things continued the way they were headed, the name Omar would have to go. This was especially true because his mother was making them move to North Carolina. He didn't want to move away, and he knew he had the wrong name to live there.

His cousins always teased him, calling him "Oh-my-you-are-stupid" and "Oh-man-you-are-ugly" and then sometimes they asked him why his skin was so brown and why he didn't look like his mother and why his father was so quiet. Once, his cousin Freddy asked if his dad was a terrorist. Everyone laughed but Omar, even though he could see it was a joke. He would go to a new school for the third time in just a year, and he was certain everyone would tease him there, too, and he hated his mother and he hated his father but he didn't know what to do but make the best of it, like everyone said.

He was going to adapt, like one of his aunt's moths. He was going to be flexible and adventurous and hopeful; he would be all the things his mother told him to be when they discussed the move. He was thinking of the name Chris, which was the name of the lead scientist in his aunt's lab; he liked the long name Christopher, but he thought it sounded too flashy to choose a name with so many letters. He would announce his final choice to his mother when he got back from visiting his grandparents.

IN LATE JUNE OMAR was allowed to fly alone to Cleveland for the first time. His grandparents' house was enormous, like a mansion. It had two floors and four bedrooms and a basement that held an enormous TV set and a bar with its own refrigerator. The lawn was vast and green, and there was a two-car garage to park their cars in, and just a couple of blocks over there was a golf course even though neither of his grandparents played golf. Inside, his grandmother kept everything almost frighteningly clean, but he had learned over the years where he could spread his things out and where to go if he wanted to play and which rooms to avoid altogether.

He once heard his aunt refer to it as "suburban hell," but he liked the neighborhood, the way each house sat on its own perfect square of green, each the same approximate size and shape, everything newly painted and crisp looking, like a drawing or a movie. It was the opposite of his own house, the one his parents wanted to sell, which was narrow and a little crumbly in places and had hardly any yard at all and was the smallest one for blocks. He loved that house, too, though. He didn't want them to sell it.

He had been coming to his grandparents' house all his life,

and in a way, he always thought of it as another home. But now, this year, after so much had happened—being expelled, the knife, learning cricket, his parents' looming divorce, the fight with Hari, the start and end of his project—he felt almost like a stranger.

This was also because his grandfather was sick. He had something wrong with his lungs—"the wrong kind of air," he told Omar—and so he didn't spend as much time with Omar as he had promised to. Instead Omar was mostly relegated to spending long stints at malls and garden stores and beauty salons with his grandmother, who was nice to be with but who didn't like to do the same things as he did and who never talked to him about books or about India the way his grandpa did.

On top of that, there was no more Indian food. His grandmother said it was too spicy for his grandfather to eat while he was ill, and his grandfather said she was trying to kill him by denying him the very sustenance he needed most. Omar missed the chapatti, though he liked his grandmother's spaghetti just as much as anything. Plus there was ice cream instead of rice pudding, which was better for the summer, so after he got over his initial disappointment, it wasn't so bad.

His grandmother was extra nice to him, and at first Omar felt like he was the one who was ill, not his grandfather. She gave him his favorite fruit, blueberries, at every lunch and let him pick out the movies at the video store and said, "Isn't he handsome? Isn't he gorgeous?" to all her friends when they ran into them in stores. She also asked him more questions about school than usual, and she asked him if he would like to take some music or dance lessons (he wouldn't), and she even announced one morning that she was taking him shopping for school clothes.

"Mom always buys those." He was used to getting unlikeable, useless outfits from his grandmother, things he only wore if there was a special occasion, or when they all got together for holidays.

"This year I am helping your mother with these things," she said.

"Why does she need help?" he asked.

His grandmother looked at him sharply over tiny glasses. "Because now that your father is living separately," she said carefully, "your mother can't do all of the things for you that she did before."

This seemed backward to him. If they were alone, didn't that mean that his mother had to do everything? That, at least, is what she had told him. It hadn't occurred to him that his mother was now less capable. In fact, he thought of it as kind of the opposite: it seemed like suddenly she had all the power in his life while his father, away in his tower apartment, had almost none. He thought maybe this was why his father had to get drunk now, because he was left alone, but now his grandmother was saying that it was his mother who was alone and needed help, and he felt, for the thousandth time, like he didn't understand what grown-ups were talking about at all.

It had been better when he had the project, his Abdul family history. He'd imagined so many times giving his dad the book, showing him all that he had learned, reading together about Hyderabad, the City of Pearls.

He had loved that idea, of a city named after the white gems his mother wore. But now that he thought about it more, he realized what pearls really were: the grit, the dirt and unwanted trash, gathered up in the shell in all its glitter and glory, only later to be spit out, ejected from their home and taken away to benefit someone else.

35.

EVEN THOUGH HIS GRANDFATHER was "slowed down," as his grandmother put it, he still managed to find some time to spend with Omar alone.

Once, they went to an old Indian movie together at what his grandfather called an "art house" movie theater, although it turned out to have very fast and faint subtitles. Omar missed much of the plot and there weren't any songs and dances like he expected. Grandma scolded them both for wasting money on an old film that, as she put it, "was not interesting for a young boy," but Omar liked looking at the land and the cities and all the brown people who looked like him, even if he didn't always understand what was happening.

Another day, he helped his grandfather sort through the books in his study for volumes to give to a charity sale his grandma was organizing.

"Why do you have to get rid of these books?" Omar asked, as his grandfather handed him yet another hardcover tome for the donation pile.

"Because your grandmother insists."

"But why do you let her insist?" Omar pressed.

His grandfather snorted, and then waited a minute for his breath to regulate itself.

"Because she is right," he said. "Because I am too old to need so many material things. Because the time for books is passing for me."

This, to Omar, seemed like far too strange an answer. He thought it would have something to do with space, because his grandmother always complained that his grandfather's study was too crowded and dirty. It was the one place his grandfather didn't let her apply what she called her "decorative touch."

Omar waited a little while, studying the latest volume his grandfather had handed over: a history of Scotland.

"Don't you care about Scotland anymore?" he asked.

His grandfather looked at him, puzzled. Omar held up the book.

"I am caring about Scotland as much as ever, Omar," he said. "I care too much, in Grandmama's opinion, about too many things. But I no longer need that book. What I need, I have here." He tapped his skull with a spotted hand. "The things I care about travel with me."

Omar nodded. "Like when you've studied really well, and you don't need your notes."

"Yes, like that." His grandfather held out a couple of books to Omar. "Here. Perhaps you would like to take these?"

One was a history book, the other a novel, and both seemed to be about India, by writers with long and confusing names. Omar was worried for a second that they would be in the wrong language, like the movie, but when he opened them, they were in English.

"Okay," he said. "But you do know that my project is over?" He was worried that his mother would be told he had been given the books, but he didn't want to flat-out ask his grandpa not to tell.

His grandfather moved his head from side to side, suddenly looking sad. He went back to the books on his wide shelves, his hands moving over the volumes like he was reading them with his fingertips.

"Omar," he said, and Omar looked up from the novel in his hands. "What you have learned will travel. You have taken very good notes."

36.

OMAR HAD BEEN IN Ohio for a week and a half when his grandfather became really sick. Omar found him out in the backyard, slumped on a chaise lounge, his eyes closed and his breath coming in huge, ragged gasps.

"Grandpa?"

Grandpa's eyes flickered but didn't open.

Omar ran back into the house, to where his grandmother sat in a maroon track suit watching a talk show in her immaculate chenille sitting room.

"Grandpa isn't breathing right," Omar said, fighting back tears.

His grandmother rose at once. She touched Omar's shoulder and then walked out back with a cordless phone in her hand, dialing 911 even before she reached her husband. Omar watched from inside the house as she bent and shook him, talking into the phone as she listened at his mouth and stroked his forehead.

Just as Omar heard the sirens approaching, his grandfather seemed to wake up. He half rose, until his wife pushed him back, and then they seemed to be arguing. Omar was relieved. They always argued, always in small ways, and so he must be all right.

Omar and his grandmother followed the ambulance to the hospital in her car. She asked him first if he would like a soda or a cookie, and when he said no, she asked if maybe he wanted to call his mother or father. He shook his head as hard as he could.

She drove to the hospital in downtown Cleveland. He watched her out of the corner of his eyes, trying to see if she was upset. If it had been his mother sitting next to him, he knew she would have been sobbing, screaming at traffic, talking on her cell phone, patting Omar's knee, and cursing her husband for making her worry so much. That was what his mother was like. Whereas his grandma was always collected and kind, like a peppermint candy, in alternating bright stripes of clarity and sweet. He watched her all the way to the hospital and never saw a tear.

At the hospital, they had to walk through corridor upon corridor, like in a maze. Omar felt lost before they started, because everything seemed bigger here. The beds were tall, and the nurses wore bright bulky outfits, and the elevators were big enough to hold a pale man on a stretcher and three nurses and a lady doctor with a stethoscope and him and his grandmother all at once.

Finally they got to where his grandfather was, and the nurses told them they couldn't see him yet. His grandmother left him in the corner of a blue-carpeted armchair, his legs stuck out in front of him, and went downstairs to the gift shop to buy him a comic and a candy bar.

"I stepped outside and made a telephone call to your father, Omar," she said when she returned. "He will try to take some time off to be with us here."

"He won't be able to," Omar said.

His grandmother looked at him over her eyeglasses. He knew he was being a brat, but he couldn't help it. He wanted his grandma to know that his dad wasn't really able to help anymore now that everything was so messed up.

"I think he will." She sipped at a paper cup of tea, the label swinging from a string. "I think we can depend on him," she said, and then she opened her *Living* magazine and left him to his comic.

THE VERY NEXT DAY, to Omar's surprise, his father did fly up. He rented a car at the airport and came to the house around lunchtime.

Omar and his grandmother had already visited his grandfather that morning. He looked better than he had the day before, except that he was hooked up to a lot of machines and he was grumpy. But Omar felt cheered, looking at him, at least until the doctor came and spoke to his grandma and he thought he overheard something about an operation. Then he felt bad, because he knew his grandpa wouldn't like an operation at all.

When Omar's father came in the door, he did something he never did, which was to hug Omar's grandmother a long time. Omar watched them from the kitchen door and then went back to his lunch. They stayed in the entry hall, talking in whispers, while Omar sat at the kitchen table with his sandwich in front of him, his appetite gone, somehow, now that his father was here.

His father had apologized for the time he was drunk and Aunt Amina had to come and get him, but Omar still felt a little nervous around him, like there was always this secret, this hiding, between them. He didn't know if his grandma knew about his father getting drunk. Maybe she did and that's why she wanted to help his mom.

When they came into the kitchen together, Omar half rose, unsure if his dad wanted to hug him too, but Mo just ruffled his hair and asked how he was.

"Fine," Omar said. He looked at his sandwich.

"I'll make you some lunch, too, dear," his grandma said, and then she busied herself making his dad a roast beef sandwich with cheese, which she gave him with a large glass of icy Coke. To Omar she gave another glass of milk, with a significant look at his uneaten cheese-and-butter sandwich. He picked it up and took another bite.

The adults talked about things he didn't care about, like his dad's work and his apartment and whether or not grandpa's "affairs" were in order, whatever those were—Omar didn't think they meant love affairs—and what kind of money was on hand to pay the bills while grandpa was in the hospital. Omar tuned it out, turning over in his mind a list of possible names for his new life, mostly ones from comic books: Peter or Clark or Bruce, regular names that might be interpreted as a cover for his real, super self.

He started paying attention again when they started to talk about his aunt Amina.

"But isn't there someone special?" his grandmother asked, looking at Omar to see if he could decode this language. He tried to look dumb and took a huge bite of cheese sandwich.

"Marcy said it seemed serious. So perhaps she will reevaluate this absurd idea to move to India." His grandmother said the word *India* like it was a curse.

Mo shrugged and finished a bite of sandwich. "With Amina, it's hard to tell. Even if this is serious, who's to say she'll stick with this relationship more than she did the last?"

His grandmother sighed and sipped at her herbal tea. "I don't see how she can be happy living this way. How can she move alone to a country she knows nothing about? It's ridiculous, at her age."

"She lives the way she wants," Mo said. "I think she thinks she's free."

Omar's grandmother set down her cup. "Isolation is not freedom. She needs a family of her own."

Omar decided to risk another bite, moving his hands slowly so they wouldn't notice him and stop talking. But his dad put an end to the conversation anyway.

"That doesn't turn out to solve all problems, either, does it?" he said.

Omar's grandmother pursed her lips, looked at Omar, and rose to clear the dishes.

OMAR WAS WORRIED THAT his dad had come to stay for the rest of Omar's scheduled visit and that he would have to share his vacation with him. But after a couple of days, once his grandpa was home from the hospital and set up in his bedroom at home with a nurse to sit with him at night, Mo told Omar they were going home. He thought about arguing, because he had been promised three weeks in Ohio and he did not want to go back to Washington, DC, at all. But when he thought about the smell of sickness in the house and his grandpa hardly being allowed to talk to him, he agreed without a fuss.

His grandmother told him not to worry, and his grandpa said the same, although Omar thought he could detect a note of insincerity in both. Aunt Amina would arrive the next day, at least, and Omar was glad because he knew he could count on her to tell the truth and so maybe then he would find out what was really going on.

On the plane, his dad drank a beer even though it wasn't nighttime, but to Omar's relief he only had the one, which he knew wasn't enough to make his father very drunk. From the airport, his dad drove him back to the old house, and for a brief moment Omar thought *at last, at last, something good is going to happen, my dad has moved back in and they saved it for a surprise.* But instead his dad left his bag in the car and didn't kiss his mother when she met them at the door. Things were the same as they had been.

37.

THE DAY HIS DAD had moved out, Omar had watched from the porch, kicking at the wooden floor with his feet, as his dad and some strange workmen carried his boxes out of the house. His mom stayed in her room. Mo took hardly any furniture, just his desk from his study and some bookshelves. Later, Omar found out that his dad got to buy all new stuff for his apartment. That made him excited to see it, but he was disappointed when he did, because something was wrong with what his dad had picked out, and the apartment didn't look right at all.

Omar had missed a cricket practice that day, and one while he was gone in Ohio and one a few weeks before, when his mom had decided to take him with her to see some friends in Virginia. And really, he hadn't felt good about cricket or Prakash or anything to do with the team ever since he had begun to suspect his aunt was in love with his coach. And since he had begun fighting with Hari. His aunt told him that it was best to make up with his friend, and that was something that Omar both did and didn't want to do. Regardless of these feelings, all the adults in his life seemed to agree that cricket was something that was good for him, and this was almost the only thing they did agree about, and so he soon found himself saying he wanted to return to practice.

His mom called Amina to ask about the cricket.

"Well, why not?" His mom didn't say it very nicely.

There was another pause, and then she said, "That's just like you, Amina." Omar could hear the sound of his aunt's voice over the line then, though he couldn't make out the words. He studied his mother's face; she looked pissed.

"I should have known better than to rely on an Abdul," his mother finally said. Omar gulped a little, like she'd pinched him, and he felt tears come to his eyes.

DURING THE WEEKDAYS HE had to go with his mom to the day-care center, where he spent the long mornings reading and playing video games while around him younger children shrieked and grabbed. By three o'clock, his mother was usually free to go, but then they would just go home, and she would immediately go up to her room on the top floor, telling him she was tired.

She didn't cook much anymore, and at first that was good because they had a lot of pizza, but now he missed her in the kitchen, the way he had been able to find her there in the evening, taking things in and out of the fridge, telling him to set the table or to find the colander or to rinse the lettuce for the salad he never ate. Now they sat together in front of the TV and ate thawed frozen dinners or food that was cooked in stores and that she bought cold and then microwaved.

He considered asking Amina if she wanted to cook with him again, but then he kept hearing everyone say she was really busy.

Last year, he'd overheard his mother tell a friend on the phone that she felt bad that he was bored but that it was his own fault for not making friends who would invite him over to their houses. This made him feel extra terrible and alone, but he didn't want to say anything to her about it because he was afraid she'd set up something herself, like she had with Davy Madsen.

And every time he called to talk to his grandfather, it was his grandma who picked up the phone, and she almost never let him talk to him. She would say he was resting, or if she did let Omar talk, she'd say just for a minute, and then when his grandfather got on the phone Omar felt constrained and awkward, unsure why he'd called and worried his grandmother would get on the phone at any second and cut them off.

THE MOVE, HIS GRANDFATHER'S health, his dad's drinking, his aunt maybe moving to India: all loomed like thunderclouds on the horizon. He wanted to run away from it, but instead it all only got closer. No one bothered to try to organize cricket for him again. He started spending all his weekends at his dad's apartment. Together they watched movies, mostly science fiction, and ate Chinese takeout or sometimes just sandwiches, and once or twice they played catch in the park even though neither of them owned a glove and they had to use a dirty old Wiffle ball instead of a proper baseball like the other fathers and sons seemed to have. The nights always ended up with his dad asleep in front of the TV, a beer still in his hand, the recycling bin in his kitchen filled with bottles and cans.

Omar wondered which he would choose if he had to, his mother or his father. He leaned toward his mother, because he wanted to live in the same house and keep his bedroom, but she was always tired now and never spent any time with him at all. He hated his father's apartment, but his dad didn't pretend he wasn't there, even though he didn't know exactly what to do with Omar.

Omar sometimes daydreamed about living with his aunt. He thought that maybe his grandmother was right, that Amina needed a family, and sometimes he thought it would make her happier if he could live with her.

He imagined surprising her, showing up one Saturday

with his duffel full of CDs and movies and books. *Isolation isn't freedom,* he would say to her, and she would say, *Omar, you're right,* and they would spend evenings cooking together and then gazing at the stars. Or maybe she would take him with her on a vacation to India, and there no one would ask him if he was Indian or American or anything. They would just say *Nice to meet you, Omar,* like his name was the most natural name in the world, like he belonged.

HIS MOM WAS STARTING to pack up their things, which Omar hated, so it was a relief when Amina finally called and asked if he'd like to go to a movie.

"What do you want to see?" she asked.

He wanted to give her an answer that impressed her, an answer that showed his sophistication, when really what he wanted most of all was to see the new *Transformers* movie, which was maybe one she wouldn't like.

"Omar," she said after a minute, and then she suggested that very movie.

He tried not to sound too excited and then he hung up the phone and went to tell his mom.

"Aunt Amina said she'd take me to the movies this weekend," he said, after he found her in her room, lying in bed in a room filled with half empty boxes, even though it was nearly six and time to start thinking about their dinner.

She turned her head to look at him and wrinkled her nose. "Oh, she did, did she?"

Omar was confused. Was she still mad at Amina about not driving to cricket practice?

"Yes," he said, and then stopped to see what else she would say.

"Fine," his mother finally said, rolling over so she was facing away from him. "I don't feel like cooking tonight. How about ordering a pizza?"

"Are you sick?"

"You can order plain cheese if that's what you want."

He waited a minute to see if she would say anything else, but she seemed to have fallen asleep. He went downstairs and called Domino's.

WHEN AMINA PICKED HIM up, she brought two books. One was all pictures of trees, and the other was some kind of fairy-tale book about a kid named Haroun that looked weird.

"Sushil, Prakash's writer friend, said you might like that," Amina said, watching him study the second. "And the other one I picked out myself."

"It's not my birthday."

"I know." She said it very gently. He guessed she probably felt sorry for him, the way that his mom's friends did now.

"Mom's in her room," he said.

"I'll just go up and say hi," Amina said.

He waited for her in the living room. The plant book was just page after page of old drawings of plants. Why did she think that he would like this? And then he started to read a little, and it was about how to put plants in families, and it talked about how looking at the plants used to help people figure out where they belonged. It was about science. He missed having a project to research. Now he mostly thought about astronomy. Sometimes when he looked at the stars he felt like an explorer, like he was traveling to a strange place. He was making a chart just of the stars he could see from the backyard. But somehow he didn't feel like a scientist when he did his star work; he didn't have a telescope to do any real research.

He heard his aunt coming down the stairs. She was frowning, but she gave a brief smile as she walked into the living room.

"Ready?" she said. He nodded and got up.

AFTER THE MOVIE, WHICH was good but made him feel a little sad, he had his chance to ask about his grandfather. They went to an ice cream place where she had vanilla in a cup and he had strawberry and chocolate-caramel-swirl all together on a cone.

"Why is Grandpa having an operation?"

Amina paused with a cup of coffee in her hand and looked at him over the top of it.

"Because he's sick," she said.

"What is he sick with?"

"His lungs are sick."

"With what?" Omar insisted. "What is it called?"

"Emphysema," Amina said. "It makes it hard for him to breathe."

"Will he die?" Omar asked.

"I hope not," Amina said, putting her coffee down, and he suddenly remembered that Grandpa was her father.

He licked at his cone, but he was no longer hungry for the ice cream. Amina watched him for a minute and then got up and retrieved a cup for him to upend his cone into. He let go of it with relief.

"No one will tell me if Grandpa is going to die," Omar said, feeling that he had to explain. "I just wish people would tell me the truth. I'm twelve now."

She nodded. "The truth is, Omar, nobody knows."

He would hate it if his dad was dying; it was hard enough to have him move away. Was that how bad Amina felt? It had never occurred to him before. Maybe that was why she looked sad sometimes lately, when she thought he wasn't looking.

38.

FINALLY, IT WAS TIME for his grandfather's operation. His grandmother tried to reassure Omar, telling him that everything would be back to normal soon and then he could come and finish his visit before the summer was over. His mother spent that day with her hand on her cell phone, waiting for the call from Omar's grandmother.

When the call came through, she sounded relieved but then sad. Omar came and stood by her, waiting to be updated.

"He's okay," she told him when she hung up. "Your grandpa's fine."

"When is he going home?" Omar asked.

"I don't know, sweetie," she said. "We'll find out soon. But the operation went well, so let's just count our blessings."

There was something evasive in this, but he couldn't think what else to ask. Later that night, when he finished watching a TV show and went to say good night, his mom was talking on the phone.

"He's dying," she said, her voice low and somehow bitter-sounding to Omar's ears. "All the more reason to move close to my mom, to Missy and her kids."

When she said this, Omar felt a strange feeling, like he too was leaving his body, like hearing what he had suspected all along was a kind of release. His grandpa was going to leave Omar alone, and there would be no one left in the world who loved him like that ever again.

THAT NIGHT HE WAS invited to dinner with Aunt Amina and Prakash. He had heard that they didn't want to be boyfriend and girlfriend anymore, but now he had seen them together again a couple of times, so maybe they had changed their minds. Amina picked him up on her way home from work and brought him to her apartment. Prakash wasn't there yet, so he helped her clean up the kitchen. Then his aunt put him in front of the TV while she went into her bedroom to change. He glimpsed boxes inside, half-filled, just like at his house, and he felt like someone had punched him in the stomach.

When Prakash arrived, shopping bags in hand, Omar's mouth literally fell open. Prakash had stopped wearing his turban. He still had his beard, but his hair was short. He looked like a different person.

"You . . . ," he started, and then stopped.

Prakash laughed. "My turban is gone. Yes. What do you think?"

"I didn't recognize you."

Prakash began unloading groceries. He was going to teach Omar to make samosas, and he had brought other snacks: spiced nuts, cucumbers and cherry tomatoes, and papadam to fry.

"Why did you do it?" Omar asked.

"It was time," Prakash answered. He set out flour and a large bowl, started searching for something in Aunt Amina's bare cabinets.

"How did you know it was time?" Omar persisted.

"Because I didn't know anymore why I was wearing it. Because when people asked me, I didn't like my own answers."

Omar waited for more.

Prakash tried again. "Wearing a turban was about expressing the beliefs of my father, and his father, about their culture and their past. I respect those things, and I wanted to honor those traditions, but I didn't have my own reasons."

"Plus people probably thought you were a terrorist," Omar offered.

"Yes," Prakash said, not pausing in his kneading. "Probably some did."

"That sucks," Omar said.

"Language," Prakash admonished.

"They keep thinking that I am."

"I don't think that's quite true."

"Yes," Omar said. "My classmates. It keeps happening. Moving's not going to change anything. It'll just be different kids. But I don't care anymore."

"Your parents are making the best choices they can, Omar."

Prakash stopped kneading and covered the bowl with a dish towel before turning to wash his hands. Omar was proud that Prakash was talking to him about these things, and so he went ahead with another question. "Have you ever seen the Al-Qaeda websites?"

"What?" Prakash turned quickly to look at him.

"Have you ever watched their videos? Like on YouTube or anything?"

"No," Prakash said. "And I don't wish to. Have you?"

"I didn't like it," Omar said, trying to reassure him. "But they said some things . . . They say that they want to make the world better for people like us."

Prakash looked shocked. "Omar, the world they want would not be better for you, or for me, or for anyone that we know. The world they want is unjust and violent. Please tell me you won't watch those videos again."

"But why do I get in trouble just for asking about it? Just for watching what they say? What's wrong with doing research on them?" Omar's voice, against his will, sounded babyish.

Prakash did not let him off the hook. "I think you know, Omar: those men are our enemies, and if you choose to listen to their words, then our government will not like it. And now that you have had one problem, you cannot do it again. You cannot. Is that clear?"

Omar cast his eyes at the table.

"Omar? Is that clear?"

"I heard you." Omar slumped in his chair.

Amina appeared and looked between them. Omar felt a moment of panic, and sat up, thinking that Prakash was going to report him.

"I am letting the dough rest," Prakash said, after a brief hesitation.

Omar could remember 9/11. Ms. Woo was his teacher, and he still remembered the way she had sheltered the class against one wall of the classroom, and the smoke he had seen out the window.

He could remember his parents talking long into the night, and the look of terror on his mother's face when she picked him up kept flickering back into his own mind as he tried to sleep. "It's a new world," he'd heard his father say.

He understood now that there was some sort of connection between that day and the wars that were happening now, the ones that were making people in other countries hate Americans.

When he was younger, he would play 9/11 with friends, pretending to crash planes into buildings. Then one day, at the playground near home, another parent came and took his son by the hand, pulling him away from Omar.

"That's wrong," he heard the father say. "It's not right to pretend to hurt Americans. Not unless you are the enemy." And the father had looked back at Omar, his knees in the sand, his favorite stealth model plane frozen aloft in the air. For the first time, but not the last, Omar wondered if he was somehow the enemy.

39.

HERE ARE SOME OF the things Omar thought about as the summer settled around him, while he sat in the day-care center and waited for his mother's workday to be finished, or waited in his room for his dinner to be thawed, or sat on the front porch in Georgetown.

He thought about Indian movies, and the actor Shah Rukh Kahn, who was in the one that his aunt had bought him at the spice store. He had watched that movie maybe ten times, even though it truly was very long, and the actors wore silly clothes and talked too much about love, and he had trouble with the subtitles. Mixed up with his feelings about the movie were his feelings about the spice store, which was not the kind of place other kids liked to go to but which he longed for the way others longed for Disney World. He kept hoping his aunt would take him back.

He thought about beautiful Anjali, and wondered when he would be old enough to date her or at least go somewhere alone with her, to a movie or back to that park alone without Rafael or Greg or Prakash, where maybe he would kiss her as she smiled at him wearing her gleaming slippers, her radiant pearl earrings.

He thought about the stars. He'd taken a book about astronomy from his grandpa's study, and at the top of his Christmas list, which he kept in a drawer on his nightstand, he had placed "telescope" above "iPod." Sometimes in bed at night he read the names of planets to himself, his lips forming around the words *elliptical galaxy* and *planetary system* and *globular star cluster*. He was fascinated by the strange, shifting beauty of nebulas and the sinister darkness of black holes, and he had tried a couple more times to find the constellations in the night sky from his backyard, but there were never enough stars to see. Amina said it was because of pollution and refraction, which made a kind of sense but then didn't because how could you be kept from seeing the lights in the night sky? What kind of pollution was that?

He thought about Hari and about being Indian. Some days he imagined himself maturely sticking out his hand and saying he was sorry and that they should let their disagreement fall into the past. Sometimes he could imagine Hari shaking his hand and smiling and inviting him over to his house, and other times he knew, absolutely and all the way through his gut, that Hari hated him. Sometimes he worried that this was because his name was Omar Abdul and Hari's mother thought he was a Muslim. He was still confused about the difference between being Muslim and Indian, and he didn't know what he would say if Hari's mother asked him if he was really from India; he felt like she would find him out, would tell him that he couldn't be.

He thought about the headlines in the newspaper, too, because he had once overheard Prakash telling Amina that reading the newspaper was the duty of every citizen and that there was no excuse for ignorance. His aunt read a lot, and she always had newspapers and magazines at her house. He respected his coach, even if he was having a secret love affair with his aunt, maybe even the serious one his grandma had talked about. But the headlines were serious in a very different way: serious and awful; sometimes there were articles about India and Pakistan, which again raised his questions about being both Indian and Muslim, but mostly the articles were about Iraq and Afghanistan and the War on Terror, which was also a war about Muslims.

Every once in a while, Omar wondered why people said he was a Muslim, even though his father wasn't, even though his mother wasn't, even though he had never read that book or been to a mosque, even though he wasn't from Arabia and he didn't speak any other language but American. Yet it seemed that in some way he and his father, his father named Mohammed, were Muslims and that his grandparents in their big golf-course house were, too, and as far as he could tell, this mostly had to do with the fact that their name was Abdul.

And so most of all he thought about changing his name. He no longer liked Chris, and a new favorite had yet to emerge. He went through the names from his mother's side of the family, but none of them seemed right. He wished sometimes that he had kept all the notes from his project instead of burning them, because there were a lot of names in there that he had liked, but choosing one of those wouldn't solve his problem. Indeed the problem seemed to be that there was no name that was appropriate; he couldn't take one of his mother's, because people would laugh and ask why did he have brown skin and black hair, and he couldn't take a name from his father's side because people would still think he was a Muslim.

He worried and worried over these thoughts, sometimes thinking that he had found the right name—once Alexander, another time Boris, and once, for three days altogether, Byron, after the poet his grandfather liked—but mostly feeling that he would never find a new name in time, before the summer had ended and his exile would begin.

40.

His MOTHER WENT AHEAD to Charlotte to look for a house to buy. He wanted to stop her, as if doing so would also stop his grandfather from dying and his aunt from moving. His mom dropped him off at his dad's on the way to the airport, and his parents had a fight. His dad told her she was stupid to try to buy a new house before she had sold the old one, and she said she wasn't going to let him sell the house before they had a place to move to, and he called her irrational and she called him a stingy bastard.

Mo drove Omar to his apartment in silence and that night instead of going to the video store they watched *The Abyss* for the third time while his dad sucked down one beer after another. The pretty lady in the movie reminded him of his aunt: tough and practical but also caring, someone you could depend on.

When his dad fell asleep on the couch, Omar got out his list of names. If his mom was successful this weekend, then time was running out. He added two Greek names from mythology that he had previously dismissed as too flowery, and then he opened his book of astronomy to see if there were any scientists with good names that he could add.

The best thing about the book was the pictures. He found

it hard to believe that space could be that colorful, that full of design and beauty, because when you looked at it from Earth everything was black and white, just darkness with white spots. He remembered learning in school about Kalpana Chawla, the Indian astronaut, and he wondered if maybe he should be an astronaut too. She was a woman, so he couldn't take her name, and the rest of the names of the book were just regular: more Roberts and Josephs and Pauls and then Russian and Chinese names that he couldn't pronounce.

His favorite thing in the book was the Horsehead Nebula. There was one picture in particular he could stare at for hours. There was a red background, the glow of hydrogen gas, and the nebula itself reared up into a majestic head, like a storming stallion, with young stars twinkling like white pearls at the base as they were born. It was more beautiful than anything could be, so beautiful he couldn't believe it was real, and yet the pictures were from NASA, so they had to be. The book said that it took over 1500 years for light from the Horsehead Nebula to reach the Earth, which Omar knew meant that the picture was of the nebula that long ago; he wondered what it looked like right now, at this exact moment, and he wondered if people would ever be able to travel that far.

The Horsehead Nebula was in Orion. He knew that he would need a telescope to see the nebula itself, but Orion was something you could see just in the regular sky. It was one of the constellations in his grandfather's book of charts. He decided to look for it the next time he had a chance.

THE NEXT DAY HIS dad had to go in to work, even though it was the weekend, and he took Omar with him. He worked on the Mall, but when you were in his office, there were hardly any windows and the offices were a little dreary, with coarse holes cut out of the walls to make space for air conditioners and an army of black and beige filing cabinets lined up as far as Omar could see in every direction.

There were only a couple of other people working that day. His dad introduced him to one lady.

"Omar—what a nice name," she said, but her eyes narrowed a little as she looked at him, and her voice wasn't very kind.

Omar had never been the kind of child strangers patted on the head and cooed over. There was always that hesitation. At least when he was with his dad, people didn't ask if he was adopted.

He spent the morning reading and studying his star chart in a chair just outside his father's office. Around noon his dad came out and said they could get some lunch. Omar put his stuff back into his bag with relief. They walked outside; his dad bought him a hot dog and a Coke, and they sat on the grass in the middle of the Mall.

"Later can we go to the Air and Space Museum?" Omar asked hopefully. He thought he would find some help about Orion there. A few weeks before, his dad had suggested it, but he seemed to have forgotten since.

"It's a bit crowded today, Omar. Maybe on a Sunday morning sometime."

"When everyone's at church," Omar said, trying to show he understood. "That's why it's quieter."

His dad nodded.

"Why don't we go to church?" Omar ventured.

His dad looked at him with his eyebrows drawn together. "We've never gone to church."

"But why?" Sometimes he had to really push to get his dad to explain something.

His dad pulled up some grass and rolled it between his hands. "Because my parents didn't go to church."

"But Mom's do."

"Yes," his father said, drawing out the syllable. "But your mom and I agree that we don't want to go to church."

"Because you don't believe in God," Omar said.

"Because I don't believe in God," Mo agreed.

"Not even in Allah?" Omar asked.

Mo looked at him again. "Allah and God are the same."

"Then why does everyone fight over them? Like in the Middle East?"

"You've been reading the papers again?" his dad asked.

Omar nodded.

"Okay," his dad continued, "it's a matter of opinion. Some people think they are different, some the same. I, personally, do not care."

Omar thought, watching his father tear up more grass. He decided to risk one more question.

"Does Grandpa believe in God?"

His father sighed and crunched a hunk of grass in his left fist. "His parents did."

"And Grandpa too?"

"In India. But now your grandfather does not believe, even though—" Omar's father stopped, and looked at the crumpled grass in his palm, and didn't say anything else.

Even though Grandpa is about to die, Omar thought. *Even though he's afraid.*

41.

WHEN THEY GOT HOME there was a message from his mom, saying she wanted to stay in Charlotte an extra couple of days, and could Mo watch Omar until Tuesday? Omar watched his dad's face screw up in something that wasn't quite anger, or hate, but was something that seemed more like sadness even though it scared Omar.

Later that evening, after placing their standard order of fried rice, spring rolls, and Hunan beef, his dad called Amina.

"Listen," he said, "Marcy's staying in Charlotte for a couple more days. Do you think you could watch Omar from Sunday night? Maybe work at home?"

Omar studied his book and listened, trying to track the course of the conversation from the tone of his dad's voice.

"How about just Monday? Amina, come on. I have a project at work. But if I say no, she'll say I'm unreliable." He lowered his voice. "I don't want her to start keeping Omar from me. Just help me out."

That was more than his dad usually said at one time, and it seemed to do the trick.

"I'll need some more clothes," Omar said, after Mo hung up the phone.

"Amina will pick you up tomorrow and she can take you by the house for more stuff."

Omar didn't like it. That one time, his mom got mad that Amina was taking care of him instead of his dad. It seemed like grown-ups never learned from their mistakes.

He asked if he could call Grandpa.

"It's a little late," his dad said, looking dubious.

"But Grandma said I could call anytime," Omar insisted.

His dad told Omar to go and talk on the bedroom phone, where it was more private.

His grandma sounded doubtful, too, when she answered the phone, but she said Grandpa was awake and had only just now taken his nighttime medication and so she went to put him on the phone in his room.

"How is my grandson?" There was a wheeze in his voice, like he was speaking through a tube filled with water. "My favorite boy."

Omar felt embarrassed. His grandpa didn't usually talk like this.

"I'm okay," he said. "I'm fine."

"When you go to India," his grandpa said, speaking very slowly and connecting his words so that it was hard for Omar to understand, "you won't feel so bad anymore. They won't tease you, they won't hit your brother anymore. Mo will be safe."

"I'm not going to India," Omar said.

"I remember," his grandpa said. "You watched but you couldn't help him."

"Grandpa? It's Omar."

There was a long pause.

"Omar." His grandpa gave a long watery sigh.

"Dad," Omar called, removing the phone from his ear. "Dad!" he yelled, louder. His dad came into the bedroom with his beer.

"What happened?" he asked.

He handed his dad the receiver.

"Dad? It's Mohammed." He waved at Omar to leave the

room. "Yes, that was Omar," he continued, and Omar breathed a sigh of relief that his grandpa was still talking. But when he went to lie down on the couch in the living room, he was all twisted and shuddery inside. What had his grandfather been talking about? It was awful that he couldn't remember Omar, even if it had just been for a minute. It was awful to hear that sound in his voice, like having death talk into his ear.

He missed his grandpa and he didn't know who to turn to. Maybe his mom was right and everything would be better—new and different and nicer—once they moved. But it felt like all the time he just got farther and farther from the things he loved, no matter how hard he tried to keep them close.

42.

WHEN AMINA PICKED OMAR up from his dad's apartment
the next afternoon, she didn't look happy. Omar's dad had
already drunk a beer or two with lunch, and Amina picked up
one of the cans and held it up between two pointed fingers, her
eyebrows raised in reproach. But she didn't say anything and
neither did his dad, and she and Omar left almost right away.

She smiled at him, driving back to the house in Georgetown,
and asked about the weekend, but he could tell that she didn't
want to be in charge of him. Probably she wanted to be with
Prakash or Anjali, with grownups like her, talking about science
and rated-R movies and the wars all over the world, instead
of being stuck with a useless kid. He was tired of feeling that
he was a burden to everyone, an unwanted package to pass
around and argue over, to be transported from house to house,
to be resented.

When they arrived at his home, he turned away from the
bare-walled living room and the boxes lining the walls, and
went up the stairs to his room and lay on the bed instead of
getting clean clothes from his dresser like he was supposed to.
After he had been lying there feeling sorry for himself for a few

minutes, he heard Amina walking up the stairs. She came in without knocking.

"Are you feeling okay?" she asked.

He nodded.

"You must miss your room." She sat down on his desk chair. "When you stay with your dad, I mean."

"It doesn't matter," he answered, and it didn't because soon it wouldn't be his anymore; soon he would have a new room in Charlotte. His mom promised that it would be bigger than this one, that she would look for a house with a dogwood tree, one that wasn't sick, but he knew that he wouldn't like it as much. But it didn't matter.

"Why don't we stay here tonight?" Amina suggested.

He felt tears of gratitude come into his eyes and then he felt stupid that such a small thing could make him want to cry. But he did want to stay in his room; he wanted to stay home and never leave it, only he wanted it to be the home of last year or the year before or the year before that, the home he had before the knife incident, before, he felt with a twinge of guilt, before his aunt had come.

LATER THAT NIGHT, HE settled in to watch a movie on TV with his astronomy book on his lap to leaf through during commercials. Amina had made one of her strange stir-fries for dinner, and now he was eating an apple for dessert because there was nothing else sweet in the house, not even Oreos hiding in the high cupboards.

Amina finished washing the dishes and came into the den.

"I'm thinking I might get a little work done tonight after you go to bed. Would you be all right if I drove over to my apartment real quick to get my computer? I'll just be gone a few minutes."

"Sure," he said. His mom said he was too young to be home alone, but he didn't see what difference it made whether she was there or not. "I'm just watching a movie."

"When I get back, maybe we can watch that Bollywood thing together?"

He'd never told her that he'd gone ahead and watched it without her, after she made so many excuses not to see it in the past. She always said that it was too long, even though sometimes they stayed up late together to watch other kinds of movies. He thought she probably wouldn't like it anyway, because it wasn't very scientific and there really was a lot of dancing.

At the next commercial, his book fell open to the Horsehead Nebula. It was a clear night, and he wondered if he would be able to see Orion. He knew how to pick it out by the stars that formed the belt, if only there would be enough stars visible in the sky from the backyard. He had tried before without any luck. What, he wondered, would it be like from the roof?

It wouldn't hurt to look, he thought. He could wait for Amina, but maybe it would be better to find the constellation first. Then he could bring her up and show her as a surprise. Maybe then she would be happy to be with him.

He climbed to the top floor. The entrance to the attic was through his parents' room, which was messy with boxes and clothes lying in piles everywhere and his mom's makeup littering the top of the dresser and piles of paperback books still on top of both nightstands. The way to the attic was a ladder in the walk-in closet. He pushed open the trap door at the top and reached blindly for the cord to turn on the light.

When the bulb flicked on, he blinked for a moment, waiting for his eyes to adjust. When he was younger, he had been scared of the attic. But two summers ago, he helped his mom organize everything in it, so the mystery and the fear had gone out of the trunks and boxes and old furniture. He knew which boxes had his dad's papers and which was the trunk with his mother's white wedding dress, and he knew which corner held the plastic bins with all his baby clothes and blankets and the stuffed animals he had outgrown. He wasn't really supposed to come up here, and he especially wasn't supposed to go out on the roof, but how could he be punished more than having to move away?

The way onto the roof was through a dormer window whose frame came almost down to the floor. He unlocked it with some effort and then pushed the window open, propping it on a stick.

When he stepped out, he was on a slightly sloping lower portion of the roof, three stories up. All around him were lights—the lights of other houses, of stores and cars and, in the distance, bigger buildings farther downtown. There was a kind of hum, a low roar that seemed to come from the city itself, like it was an animal crouching in wait down around the slow, thick river. But after he paused for a moment, the lights and noise seemed to fade, and he felt how alone he was up on the bit of shingled roof.

He looked up, scrutinizing the sky, evaluating his chances for seeing the stars he desired. Somewhere up there, strangely, impossibly, was the Dumbell Nebula, and the Crab Nebula, planetary systems just like theirs, clusters of dead stars and ominous black holes, spinning comets and asteroids trapped in orbits.

But he still couldn't make out more than twenty individual stars. He had read in the astronomy book more about light refraction, how in cities the lights were reflected off the atmosphere and then back down and that was how the view of the stars got obstructed. He considered going back inside to turn off the attic light, but then he didn't know how he would find his way back to the stairs. Instead he stepped farther out onto the roof.

He had his head turned skyward as he did so, his eyes searching for Orion's Belt. He wanted to see the neighborhood where the nebula lived, to imagine the Horsehead rising there, with galaxies forming all around him, fifteen hundred years ago and now all at the same time.

He took a step farther and his left foot slipped a little. He kept his eyes on the stars, thinking that he had just spotted Orion, but then his foot slid a little more and then he felt a bit of panic, like his heart had stopped and he couldn't find his breath. He closed his eyes and imagined what it would feel like to fall, and for a moment it felt like the world shut down as he imagined himself turning, over and over, his mind like a thousand bursting stars, spinning toward the edge.

And then he opened his eyes and there were flashing lights and sirens and Omar, dazed, stepped back through the window to see what had come for him this time.

V. WHERE THE MIND IS WITHOUT FEAR

43.

WHEN NO ONE WAS watching, as Amina later pieced together, Omar's internet studies had taken a turn. He studied Hyderabad, and he studied stars; he looked up ancient Egypt and watched videos of cats and dogs; he googled *divorce* and *cricket* and *Britney Spears* and played online video games.

And, several times over the last six months, he had watched jihadist videos calling extremists to join a war against the West.

When the police, arriving that day at the house in Georgetown, found the door answered by a pudgy twelve-year-old boy, they were armed, and they were looking for the owner of the internet account, Mohammed Abdul. They were there to arrest him on suspicion of intending to engage in terrorism. Omar, terrified, did them the favor of calling his father, who arrived at the house just after Amina did and surrendered. Mo spent the night in jail.

The next morning Amina went to the jail and waited as a guard went to retrieve her brother. When Mo came through the metal door into the waiting area, he hugged Amina for the first time since his wedding. In the car he cried, looking out the window, pale and shaking, but when they got back to his apartment, he was dry-eyed and silent.

She followed him inside without invitation, and he disappeared into his bedroom. She made coffee and toast, which she placed on the table on two plates. After a quarter of an hour, Mo came out of his room. He sat at first in silence, as did she, but then, after a bite of toast, he began speaking.

"The fuckers," he said. "The fuckers. Without knowing anything about me or my life or my family, they just assume I am a fucking terrorist. From what happened on a computer at my house? What kind of standard is that?"

"Mo," she said, "it will just take a little time."

"You don't know that. Fuck, Amina. Fuck: what if they had disappeared me? I have done nothing, but what if they hadn't let me out?"

"Mo," she said again, "it was a misunderstanding. It was Omar."

He was very quiet then, though his eyes did not leave hers, gauging her honesty. "*What* was Omar?"

"He looked up jihadist websites. He found videos. He watched them, and he didn't tell anyone."

"Were we bugged? How the fuck do they know this about Omar?"

"I think the sites are watched. Or maybe they aren't even real; maybe they're set up to entrap people. I don't know. But what matters is he told them. He told them he looked at the videos, and I think they believed him."

"What are they going to do to him?"

"I don't know. Nothing, maybe. Maybe counseling. They will definitely ask him more questions; I think he's going to be interviewed with Marcy today."

"My son is not a terrorist."

"I know," Amina said. "Neither is my brother. I know. But they found evidence on your computer, and they will need to question you both more."

• • •

IF SHE COULD REEL it all back, Amina wondered, what would she take out and what would she leave in? Why hadn't she given her nephew guidance on Islam and terror, and search engines and entrapment, on the smart ways to act as a young Muslim boy in America? Why had he been ignorant enough to look at those videos?

She called later that afternoon and asked Marcy if she could see Omar, and Marcy said no. She asked if she could talk to him on the phone, and Marcy hesitated.

"Please."

"Okay, but just for a minute. He's pretty upset."

Amina waited for what seemed an eternity, her eyes closed, searching for the right words to say. Finally she heard a rustling and Omar said hello. She sighed with relief when she heard his voice.

"Hi," she said. "How did it go? Are you okay?"

"Yeah," he said.

"Did they seem to understand? That you were just curious? That you were doing research?" She knew she was talking too much; she should let Omar talk, she should listen.

"Yeah," he said. "I guess so."

"What did they ask you?"

"Just what I was doing, why I looked. I don't know."

"Omar, I'm so sorry."

"Yeah," he said again.

"This is just crazy."

Was he mad at her? There was a long silence, and she could hear the sound of him breathing, a sound faint and whispering, like a moth flapping its wings.

He broke the silence. "What did they do to Dad?"

"Your dad is fine."

"That's what Mom said. But what did they do to him? Did they hurt him?"

"No, of course not," Amina said. Why *of course not*, she wasn't sure. There was Guantanamo, and extraordinary rendition, and the Patriot Act. It was all too clear to her that her family was skirting a dangerous and unforgiving line.

"What did he say?"

"He said they just asked him questions. He's upset, but he's fine. He's worried about you, Omar."

"Mom says I can't see him."

"I'm sure that's temporary. He loves you, Omar. He doesn't blame you."

"He should," said Omar. "I did it. Anyway, I have to go. We have to see a counselor."

"I'll see you soon, okay?"

"Right," Omar said. "Bye."

THE POLICE WERE UNDERSTANDING, up to a point. There was no program for rehabilitating preteens who had watched things they shouldn't have. The authorities made noises about a pattern of behavior, after they found out about his expulsion and the knife, but, legally, they had nothing to allege. Omar was a boy whose parents had not put the proper parental restrictions on his internet use, a boy who had been left alone too much, a boy who was both curious and alienated, and who had investigated a mystery, Islam, into the realm where it became a nightmare.

Marcy reacted by immediately filing for a legal separation from Mo. Amina could hardly blame her: she hadn't signed up for anything like this. How was she to know, when she married her high school sweetheart, how the world would change? They thought they would have a child who belonged only to them. They never dreamed how much the world around them could circumscribe that child's thoughts and hopes and fears.

For now, Mo was letting her have what she wanted. Amina knew that wasn't quite right; she suspected that he would regret it. But for all her sleepless nights, for all her brains and love and hope, she could not figure out how to fix the mess they were in.

And then her mother called her: her father was in the hospital again. She said she would come the next day.

44.

TRAVELING TO BE WITH her father while he died, Amina was restless. It was an evening flight, and she stayed alert as they left the city behind, as the land turned to a quilt of patterned squares and then to forest and then back to farm. They flew into the remains of a flamboyant sunset, and she stared down at the illuminated towns, each a collection of small lights, each a building or a car or even a person. The individual spots revealed elegant designs, the consequence of city planning: circles and squares and linked avenues, red brake lights trailing in straight lines, larger malls and office buildings glowing with self-importance.

Looking down from the dark and humming plane, she saw how beautiful, how structurally ingenious and yet organic, the things humans made could be. The world of lights pulsated, an ecosystem of color and refraction, as lovely as anything living, as beautiful as biology.

The outlines of her own life were becoming confused. Her job in India would start in September, her tickets were booked, and she had started to pack up her apartment. Her father was dying. Mo was drunk all the time and resented her interference.

Her nephew grew more sullen each time she saw him and no longer peppered her with questions or asked to come to her house. Marcy had offered only perfunctory communication ever since Mo's arrest and filing for separation. And Amina was letting Prakash continue to believe that they maybe had a future together.

Yet her time was almost up. Dilpa was expecting her. She shifted in her seat. It hurt, literally hurt, to want all these things at once: to want to love Prakash and to take the job in India; to protect Omar and to prepare him; to help Mo and Marcy and Anjali and to learn to love and yet to want so badly to be free.

45.

AT THE AIRPORT, HER mother was waiting for her, looking pressed and purposeful. She gave Amina her father's car to drive, an old Mercedes, and Amina slipped back into her parents' house almost as though she had never left. Her room, though officially a guest room, was one she had stayed in now for many years, and out the window was a familiar view of oaks and sky, with plenty of stars at night.

And it was weirdly satisfying to be with her dad. At the hospital, Amina didn't hold his hand, didn't touch him, just sat with him, day after day. He couldn't talk much, his effort concentrated on taking each labored breath, but he stared at her constantly with eyes like daggers, eyes that saw through her. Once, she thought she heard him mumble Omar's name, and she leaned in closer.

"Did you say something, Dad?"

". . . needs you," she thought she heard.

Who? Omar? Her father himself? Mo? The list of those she had let down felt infinite.

DINNERS WITH HER MOTHER were the most difficult part of her day. The first couple of nights, they ate at home: salads and crackers and other diet foods that her mother subsisted on. But they each failed to fill up the space left by Amina's absent father, and the third night they agreed to go to a restaurant, where there was noise and movement to break up their awkward tête-à-tête.

After her mother placed an order for a side salad and a gin martini, Amina ordered a burger and fries and a glass of cabernet with satisfaction. She was tempted to order a milkshake, or jalapeño poppers, or extra bacon: something to really shake her mother up.

"You are blessed, Amina, to be able to eat like that and remain slender," her mom said. Her mother had never *not* been on a diet, as far as Amina knew. "And you're really going to go through with this move to India?"

Amina nodded and took a deep breath. "It's a great job."

Maya sighed. "Always, your career. What about this man I've heard about?"

"I don't want to talk about him," Amina said, her voice flecked with warning.

"Amina," her mother said after a minute. "Thank you for coming."

"Sure," Amina said.

"You surprised me."

"I did?"

"Yes. I didn't expect you to be the one to offer support."

"Thanks, Mom," Amina said, not bothering to hide her sarcasm.

"I only mean because you are . . . not as interested in family as Mo. Not as close to us."

"True." Amina sipped her drink, uncomfortable.

"And I'm sorry for that. I'm your mother and I love you and I'm glad you're here with Dad. It means the world to him."

"I want to be here."

"I expected . . ." Her mother stopped, then tried again. "I assumed that Marcy and Mo would be available to help. But it looks as though they are going to continue on this ridiculous path."

"It's not ridiculous," Amina said reflexively.

"What else is it, to fight over nothing and divorce when you have a young child and a home together?"

"I doubt it feels like nothing," Amina said, "to them. I think they are really unhappy."

"But they should think of the child. Omar should come first."

"There are lots of ways to give happiness, Mom."

"I knew you would say that." Her mother sat up straighter and put a hand to the opal necklace at her throat. "You are all so unconventional. So ready to dispense with the usual ways of adulthood."

"I would not call Mo unconventional," Amina said.

"He is to me. He is not happy; he has never been happy. And neither are you."

"Mom."

"It's true!" Her mother's voice rose a little. "My children are unhappy. And I have no idea how this happened."

"I'm happy enough. And Mo and Marcy will figure it out."

Her mother nodded, but her composed face looked a bit blurred around the edges, as though the world was moving too quickly for her to keep up. She seemed to hesitate, and then she said in a near whisper: "I am so shocked about Omar."

Amina sat back, hating her mother's dramatic stance. "Your being shocked doesn't seem relevant."

"It *is* shocking!" Now her mother's voice rose. "To watch those movies from terrorists! Mo and Marcy should be ashamed, letting him remain so unguided."

Amina had rarely seen her mother so riled up.

"No young man should have an interest in those things! Not unless he is troubled. Not unless his parents are acting irresponsibly. Why don't they see that this is the consequence of their selfishness? How can they get divorced when my grandson is so obviously needing them?"

To Amina's surprise, her mother seemed to have tears in her eyes.

"Omar didn't know what he was doing. He's just a kid."

"And my son, going to jail!" her mom continued. "My son! Who is always dependable, a family man, my son who has never broken a law. The kind of boy you trust with your life!"

Here, Amina was silent. Because she did believe that Omar would make it through, but on the subject of Mo, she was not so sure.

46.

ON THE FOURTH DAY, her father died. Amina was packing up books in his study, preparing them for storage. She was tired of packing. Her mother called with the news and Amina sat down hard on the floor, a book of Blake's poems and engravings in her hand. *Songs of Innocence and of Experience.*

"Could you call Mo and Marcy for me? They have so much paperwork here." Amina's mother sounded purposeful, like she was organizing a PTA meeting or a country club fundraiser.

Amina called Mo and left him a message and then called Marcy, who promised to continue to try to reach Mo. Marcy was cordial and said that she would fly out with Mo and Omar the next day.

"We'll come together," Marcy said. "For Maya."

Death was not something Amina had a lot of experience with. She knew, when she wasn't on her high horse about one of her many pet peeves about people and the world in general, that she was lucky. Her parents had given her a sound home, had paid for a good education. She had chosen her own career and made all her own decisions, and never once had she suffered great fear or hunger or despair. Her only real enemy was herself.

She told this to Prakash when she called him next. "It doesn't seem right, does it, that I haven't done more with what I've been given? My dad was happy. What right do I have to be unhappy? Why couldn't I just love my parents? That's all they wanted from me."

"Not all," Prakash said. "It's never so simple."

"You love your parents. That seems simple for you."

"I love my parents, I disappoint my parents, I resent my parents—all of those things. I'm not exactly what they want, and they are not exactly what I want."

"But you're perfect," Amina said, with only a little sarcasm.

"Ha. I am a bookstore owner. A failed writer. A kids' cricket coach. I'm not a doctor or an engineer. I'm unmarried. No kids. Pretty bleak." He tried to make it sound funny, but Amina felt the sting.

"Are those things you still want?" She wasn't asking about being a doctor.

There was a long silence.

"Your father just died," Prakash said slowly. "I don't want to place any further burdens on you."

"The truth is not a burden," she said.

"Maybe," he said. "Amina, I . . ."

There was a long pause. She felt as though all the words she was frightened of were floating around her, buoyed by his silence: *I adore you, I love you, I want to marry you, I want to live with you.* All the words she would not let herself say.

"I want to be there with you," Prakash said at last. "Please let me come to the funeral. I can fly out tomorrow. Just tell your mother that I'm a friend."

"No," Amina said, "I'll tell her who you really are. Thank you. I think I need you here."

"Then that's where I'll be."

AMINA'S MOTHER INSISTED ON a large reception at her country club after the memorial instead of the quiet open house that Amina had recommended. Maya spent the rest of the day making phone calls. Amina listened for a while, then decided she needed a good stiff drink, and she went to the small wet bar in the family room to help herself.

She sipped a shot glass full of gin and studied the family photos on the wall. They were lies, she realized, or hopes: they showed the family her parents wanted to have. Her mother wanted to be proud of her children, and she was no doubt baffled at how she had ended up with these two: a son about to be divorced and a daughter who failed to follow the conventions she valued so much, ones that she had crossed an ocean to embrace.

Amina felt her father's absence; she would have liked to talk to him now. What would he have said to her about Prakash? And she had never really talked with him about moving to India; what would he have said? Probably he would have told her to stay, to love.

The problem was that the choice wasn't just about Prakash. In truth, it was a career choice above all. Even a few months ago, that choice had seemed much less fraught. Then, September had seemed far away, and she'd told herself the transition would be easy. She'd give notice, and spend the summer packing and studying up on her new field site while she waited for the project start date. Now, deep into the messiness of Mo and Omar, with her father gone and her mother alone, and with those extra weeks of phone calls and dinners and lovely, liquid sex, it felt impossible.

She paused in front of a picture of her father playing golf, in gray slacks and a matching cardigan, his earnest focus on the ball. Her father had lived a real life. He had a career and a family and hobbies, he had raised two well-educated and presentable children, he had tangible social status, and he was loved and admired. She couldn't imagine how she would ever build a life like his.

47.

WHEN AMINA PICKED THEM up at the airport the next morning, Marcy, Mo, and Omar walked into the baggage claim area like a family, herded into closeness by economy class and the narrow exit corridor. Marcy was very thin and very pretty in a red dress, while Mo looked scruffy with mismatched socks and a shirt that had a stain on it. Omar seemed once again to have aged years overnight. He was wearing a T-shirt that said something on it in Arabic.

"It says 'I am not a terrorist,'" Marcy explained on behalf of her son, and Amina got the feeling she had been explaining the entire trip. "Mo seemed to think it was funny."

At home, there was some confusion over where to put everybody—there was a room that usually belonged to Mo and Marcy, but now they needed separate bedrooms, and everyone felt uncomfortable at the bald truth contained in that fact. Mo solved it by offering to sleep in the workshop over the garage, which was minimally finished but warm enough at this time of year. And Omar took Amina's room, because she was going to stay at a hotel with Prakash, who was arriving later that day, en route from a book fair in San Francisco.

Her mother had accepted the news of his coming with

admirable calm, saying that it was nice and thoughtful of him and that she would be delighted to meet him. Amina felt that her mother's respect for her—her regard for her possibilities in life—had suddenly been bumped up a notch by the actual, solid reality that a man would make an effort to be with her at this time.

After lunch, Amina went back to her hotel to meet Prakash. She was nervous, she realized. It felt momentous that he was here, and she was a little embarrassed at this girlish response. But lately, she hadn't been able to tell: was blushing at the thought of being with your lover silly, or was it evidence of something right, and true, and healthy?

She checked in, left her bag in the closet, and then waited in the lobby and watched as he walked in and asked at the desk for her room number. Then she followed him to the elevator, hopped in after him, and kissed him before he could finish exclaiming her name.

"You are pretty," he said.

"You are pretty, too."

They looked at each other for a long moment, until the bell chimed and the doors opened.

Without his turban, he looked extremely handsome, not beautiful and dreamy but prosperous and polished. On seeing him like this for the first time, Amina had felt betrayed, for reasons she could not figure out: what, to her, in her utterly westernized form, could be her argument with his decision?

She also felt guilty because more and more she felt that she should leave, that it was time for her to go. The field site in India was calling to her: it could be a new beginning, the right beginning. And she could visit Omar, and her mother might come, and who knows, maybe Mo could be convinced to at last see the land of his ancestors. That just left Prakash, whom she knew was under the impression that she would not be quitting her job, who believed she was in love with him—which she was—and who expected her to act accordingly.

It was not nice to feel that she was once again in the dilemma she had been in with Matt; it was not nice to feel that one possibility would be to break Prakash's heart, to be the bad guy again, to look like a runner.

But it was also not, after all, very nice to think about staying in DC, to think of the year's lab work that lay ahead, to face the drudgery of grant writing and research design in that cold, hostile laboratory. She had always known she wanted something different. How could she possibly let herself be derailed now?

THAT EVENING, INTRODUCING HIM to her mother, she felt proud of Prakash, and a little chagrin at her pride. She had always been so defiant about her boyfriends with her mother, insisting they weren't essential, keeping them at a distance from her father. Now she felt a pang of regret that her father had never met Prakash.

Her mother went all out to charm him. She insisted on taking him on a tour of the house to show him old photographs. With each photograph came a story, and Amina heard the traces of each, along with laughter and exclamations, as she settled into a chair in the den with a glass of wine.

After a minute, Mo wandered in from his habitat above the garage, his beard long, dark circles under his eyes.

"Amina," he said. "I didn't know you were here."

"We're here," she said. "Prakash is upstairs with Mom."

He nodded and went to the bar to pour himself a highball glass of vodka.

"Did you hear on the news," he said as he sat down heavily in the armchair next to hers, "about that woman fighting to get her husband out of our government's rendition program?"

"Yes," Amina said. "It's terrifying."

"I'm sure you have nothing to worry about."

She studied him. "That's not what I meant. I'm sure you have nothing to worry about either."

"I think the point is that I do."

"Whose point?" she asked him.

"Mine," he said, with a heavy sigh. He took a long drink. "Mine, I guess. I think I have no future in this country."

"Mo," she said. "That's ridiculous."

"The FBI know my name. They're watching me."

"I doubt that," she said. "They know what happened was just a kid fooling around. They believed you."

He shook his head slowly. "I feel . . ." He stopped. "I feel as though everyone has turned against me."

She leaned forward and touched his hand. "Mo, that's not true. Lots of people are on your side."

He shook his head, faster this time, then stood up abruptly. "I'm sorry, Amina. I don't know what I'm talking about. I'll go get dressed for dinner."

She let him walk away, her head spinning. She heard her mother and Prakash coming down the stairs, and she picked up her own glass and gulped it before wiping the tears from her eyes.

48.

LATE THAT NIGHT, AFTER they had all struggled through a dinner of Chinese takeout while ignoring the number of martinis that Mo poured from his father's collection of gin, Amina and Prakash returned to the hotel in near silence. They lay in bed together, legs entwined, arms across each other's bodies, their noses touching each other's cheeks, that close. *This is love*, Amina thought. *This is love*. And it was hard not to be in love with being in love. So what was wrong with her? Why was she still thinking of leaving?

"I'm worried about Omar," Prakash said. "He doesn't want to move, and I don't think he should have to."

Amina pushed away from his body so she could look him in the face. "I don't think Mo can handle him on his own, and Marcy is definitely on her way out."

"What if we helped? What if he lived with us part of the time?"

Amina stopped breathing, and moved her face farther from his, so she could look in his eyes.

"But we don't even live together," she stalled, stupidly, knowing full well what he was saying.

He kissed just her upper lip, without pressure. "I think we

should. Live together. I think we should get married. I think you should forget this stupid idea of going to India and you should stay. You should be with me."

She felt time stop then. Her vision blurred and the secret in the pit of her stomach threatened to come up. She couldn't see because there were tears in her eyes, and then he touched her face with his fingertips, and she started to breathe again.

"Prakash," she said, feeling disembodied, numb. "I don't want to refuse the job offer in India. I think it's the right opportunity for me. You know I'm not happy in the lab. Sometimes I feel it would kill me to stay." Her voice was neutral, but it shook at the last sentence.

His hand flew away from her face, and she felt his whole body tense. "I thought this was still up for discussion. Have you decided already?"

She brushed away tears. "I have. I did. I told them I would start this fall." Her voice gave a little as she said the last words.

Prakash pushed away from her and sat up. "What a cold person you are, Amina Abdul." He got up and began to dress.

"Prakash," she said, rising too. "Wait."

"Oh no," he said, "that's exactly what I have been doing, and now I am done. With you and all the Abduls. You have the same sickness, all of you, and I am a fucking idiot for getting involved."

"Stop it," she said. "You knew this was a possibility. You knew."

He paused with only his pants on and looked at her.

"You're right," he said. "I knew exactly what you were. You never said you loved me. I'm the fool here."

"That's not what I meant," she said. Her tongue seemed to catch in her mouth before she could say *I do love you*.

"But it's true." He finished dressing and picked up the room keycard. "I'm going downstairs to get a drink. I'll stay for the memorial. And then I think we're done."

49.

THE MEMORIAL FOR PROFESSOR Abdul Mohammed Abdul, known to friends and colleagues as Alan, was at her parents' country club: there was to be a service in the hall followed by a reception in the club restaurant.

Amina and Prakash sat in a front row, Omar between them and Marcy and Mo on the far side of their mother. Amina's dress, a new black sheath from a department store, itched. She had either forgotten to remove a tag or the itch was part of a diabolical plan to keep her looking appropriately perturbed. There were two speakers from the university, and then it was Omar's turn to read a poem that Amina's mother had picked out: a sonnet from Keats, of course.

Omar at the podium looked grown; he had changed so much in the year Amina had been in DC with him. He was taller and heavier, his eyes seemed more dull than sad, and he was quieter. Up on the stage he seemed substantial, in ways both comforting and threatening; he was growing up, but what was he growing into?

Amina had worried he would be too nervous to speak, but now he started with no hesitation in his voice.

"My grandpa," he said, "loved poetry. He always told me

that if I lived life with a poet's heart I would be happy. I don't write poetry or even really understand it," he continued, to a ripple of amusement, "but I loved my grandfather, and I liked to hear him read poems. This summer I asked him to tell me what his favorite poem was, and this is it."

Amina looked over at her mother, wondering if this was the one she had picked out, but her mother's eyes were on her grandson.

"It is by Rabindranath Tagore, who is the most famous writer in India. He won the Nobel Prize, which is the most important writing prize in the world." Omar's voice was strong, and Amina realized she had never seen him so confident.

He read the poem, about striving for truth while freed from constraint and tradition, ending with a plea for his countrymen to find this place of logic and praxis. After he finished, Omar paused, and it looked for a moment like he would cry. But as Amina held her breath, he recovered.

"My grandpa had two countries," he said. "But I think this place in the poem is the place where he lived."

AT THE RECEPTION, AMINA stood in a line beside her mother and brother, Omar and Marcy, greeting guests, while Prakash sat alone at an outside table. Amina thought her mother looked tired, too, the burden of the last weeks finally showing on her coddled face. Marcy and Mo stood stiffly next to each other. Why they had chosen to participate in the charade of still being a couple, Amina did not know. Maybe it was to please her mother; maybe it was just habit. They were, as always, handsome together; Mo had cleaned up well in a suit that looked brand new.

Omar dropped out of the receiving line quickly, filled his plate from the buffet, and went to sit with Prakash. Eventually she was able to join them, exhausted from the choreography of condolences and appreciation, the call and response that passed for honoring the dead and his family. She put her hand on Prakash's knee when she sat, and he gave her a sad smile back.

"What a beautiful poem," she said to Omar. "What a great choice you made."

Omar shrugged. The light that had seemed to fill him at the service, that glimpse of the passion that had once seemed to define him, was gone. He looked chubby, withdrawn, and vacant in equal measure. Her heart broke a little.

Amina sipped at her wine while Prakash picked up the slack, chatting with Omar about the recent cricket adventures of the Indian national team, ignoring Omar's cursory responses and continuing as though he had an interested audience. She liked that Prakash could do this; she liked that he could talk to anyone and make them comfortable, that he didn't need to feel he was doing a great job or that the other person liked him. It was exactly what she needed, she realized. It was the exact opposite of how she felt and acted most of the time, and it was only lately that she had started to feel this as a character flaw, a weakness. She was always so proud of how independent she was, but her life in the last year had made her feel the limits of that autonomy. She did not have the freedom to love and be loved, she recognized now; she had not allowed that for herself. And so not everything was going to be possible.

As the last guests began to trickle out, Mo came over and said their mother wanted the family to go back to the house together. Amina had been looking forward to going straight back to the hotel, to saying something to Prakash that could atone for her behavior. She had led him on, been callous and uncommunicative to someone who was tender and open, and she felt like a terrible cad. But when she started to say it was time for them to go, Prakash squeezed her hand and murmured that they should go and have one more drink. Maybe he didn't want to be alone with her, she thought, and so she agreed.

She was tired, no longer drunk and not quite hungover; she felt done. She had talked to more people in one day than she usually did in a week, she had helped them to praise her father and fielded their inquiries into her private life, she had survived the beauty scrutiny of her mother's friends, and she had not hidden or cried or embarrassed herself. But she agreed: it would be polite to have a nightcap and to say a private goodbye to her mother. They would be leaving early the next morning.

50.

BACK AT THE HOUSE, Omar was told to shower and go to bed. Amina followed him to the bottom of the stairs.

"When we get home," she said, "I was hoping we could go out to dinner one night. I want to talk to you."

Omar stepped close, looking her in the eye. "Take me with you," he said, looking for a brief moment like the kid she had fallen so hard for. "I don't want to go to North Carolina. I want to go to India. I want to go with you. Please, Aunt Amina."

She shook her head. "Omar, I can't."

"Yes, you can. You can. Ask Dad. Please. Just ask him."

"You belong with your parents," she said, and then caught her mistake. "It's up to them," she amended. "It's not my choice."

He turned toward the stairs and began to climb them.

"I hate you," he said, in a voice drained of feeling. "I hate all of you."

"Omar," she said. She wanted to tell him that nothing in the world would make her happier than to take him to India with her, except she knew that was a lie, and Prakash was right: she was a cold person, and she would have the life to match.

• • •

THE ADULTS WENT OUTSIDE on the patio, where Mo poured whiskey and water. They sat for a time in silence. Amina sat next to Prakash, full of the sense that this was all a charade: all of them here together, Marcy and Mo together, Amina and Prakash together. Everything was a lie, and no amount of whiskey could hide it.

"I just don't get it," Marcy suddenly said. "Your dad had such a great life. He didn't feel the need to think about India all the time. I don't understand why Omar wants these things that his parents don't care about, that his grandparents never even cared about."

"Marcy," Mo began.

"No," she said. "I'm serious. I don't understand this obsession he has. If this life was good enough for your dad, then why are we acting like my son has been deprived of something essential?"

"Marcy, he doesn't exactly have a choice," Amina said. "Other people ask him all the time about being Indian, and what is he supposed to say?"

"I don't know," Marcy answered. "I just don't remember that being an issue with you and Mo."

"Then you remember incorrectly," Mo interjected. "It was an issue. We just didn't dwell on it. We didn't talk about it."

"The times were different," Prakash offered. He had been silent up until now, as if already edging himself away from the Abduls. "We forget how much the culture wars in the nineties changed things. Now we don't hide or pretend or assimilate. We embrace our roots."

"But these are Omar's roots," Marcy insisted. "My family is Omar's roots. Why does this have to be so one-sided?"

"Look around you," Mo said. "Look at the world we live in now. How can he not think about these things? What choice does he have?"

"The same as everyone else," Marcy said, an edge to her voice. "And let's face it: he was looking at those crazy fucking jihadist websites because he's unhappy and confused and angry at us, not because he wants to feel Indian. I don't know which of you pointed him there," she said, looking between Amina and Mo, "but I know that one of you must have. How else could he have known about those videos? In our world? In my world?"

"It was me," Prakash said. He said it with such a low voice that at first Amina's mind skipped over it as she fought back anger at Marcy. But then it hit.

"What?" she said. Everyone's eyes were now on Prakash.

"It was me," Prakash said. "He asked about them, and I told him about how bad people posted them and made people scared of people like us. And then later he told me that he had seen them."

"He told you?" Marcy said, her voice like ice. "He told you he watched Al-Qaeda videos and you didn't think to tell his parents?"

Prakash looked at her with steady eyes. "I promised him I wouldn't say anything, and he promised not to do it again. How was I to know the FBI would find out?"

"Fuck," Amina said. "Prakash. I can't believe you knew."

"I'm sorry," he said, "if I made the wrong choice."

Mo set down his glass and fixed his eyes on Prakash. "Go," he said. "Now." Then Mo stood up very fast, knocking his chair over. "Get the fuck out!" His words were slurred, but no less frightening for it. "You too, Amina. Just go. You're leaving anyway. Go!"

"Mo, calm down." Amina stood up to put herself between her brother and Prakash. She touched Mo's elbow, hoping to calm him. He pulled out of her grasp with a quick and violent motion of his arm, and his elbow struck her on the head. She sat down and blinked.

Marcy started toward Mo. When he started to push her away, Marcy slapped him, and then Mo turned and ran. He disappeared around the side of the house.

Amina heard the screech of his tires as he pulled away in the black rental car, and it was only when Prakash bent down to check on her that she began to feel how much she hurt.

Prakash drove them back to the hotel. She opened a window and let the night rush through the car. She knew she was breathing, but still the oxygen seemed to bypass her, a river just out of reach. Something irreversible had happened: for Mo, for her and Mo, for her and Prakash. The world had switched, and all she could think was *I'm leaving, I'm leaving, I'm leaving.*

Once they were back inside the hotel room, they both stood and finally looked at each other. Prakash looked heavy, all quickness gone. Amina's hand went to her mouth as she struggled not cry.

"I'm sorry," Prakash finally said. "I should have told you."

Amina's hand moved to her side and she met his eyes. "Everything was already completely screwed up. I'm sorry about Mo."

"This is not—" Prakash started to say, but he stopped when the phone rang. They looked at each other and then Amina went to pick it up. Her parents' home number.

"There's been an accident," her mother said, in the strangest voice: businesslike, robotic, but scraped somehow, as though her vocal cords had been dragged on a road. "It's Mo."

"What's Mo?" Amina said.

"Marcy and I are at the hospital. We left Omar alone at the house. You have to go there."

"Go where? What?" Amina felt cross-eyed, in shock.

"Please go to Omar. Someone needs to be with him."

PRAKASH AGREED TO GO to the hospital after dropping Amina at her mother's house. She kissed him goodbye, without thinking, a long kiss, his beard stubble stinging her face.

As she walked up the path, she stopped and bent over, feeling for a moment that she could not keep going, that she could not do what she was about to do.

Omar came out of the house and walked toward her, his eyes huge.

"Aunt Amina?"

She unfurled herself and looked up at him.

"What happened? Where's Dad?"

"I think he crashed his car," she said. "I think he's been hurt."

Omar took several breaths, and with each, he seemed to fill with anger.

"He's dead, isn't he?" he said.

"Omar, I don't know anything yet," she began.

"He's dead," Omar said again, and then he turned and started to walk back toward the house. Halfway there, he turned, and Amina could see that tears were trickling down his face, over the slope of his cheeks, and dripping onto the front of his T-shirt. "It's your fault! I hate you! It's all your fault!"

He turned and began to run.

"Omar!" Amina called, but he did not turn around again. "I love you, Omar," she said, into the night. Her ears rang with silence and she covered them with her hands, her eyes closed.

AMINA WOULD NEVER FORGET the night she first discovered moths. She had always known they existed, of course, but, like most people, she had ignored them. As a girl, she was given butterfly things she didn't care for: taffeta wings and silk-screened T-shirts and coloring books with pages of the creatures.

One day Mo came home from school with a science project: he was to hang a sheet in the night and attract moths to it, then document what he found. Amina was his assistant, as she so often had been when they were younger. She helped him rig the sheet in the backyard, between two silver birches, and after dinner they were given permission to stay out until ten p.m. to conduct their experiment. They carried out flashlights and a camping lantern Mo had asked for as a birthday present, though they as a family had never gone camping.

The stars were endless that night; it was early spring, so they wore sweatshirts and boots and lay on a flannel blanket while they waited for the moths to come. Mo read to her from his textbook with a flashlight, but Amina was impatient.

"Are you sure?" Amina asked her brother. "This is all we have to do?"

And then they started to arrive. Soon there were so many that Mo was having trouble counting them. They were all shapes and sizes, some tiny and fluttering, others large and languid. Several of them beat themselves against the brightest section of sheet in a monotonous rhythm while others flew away and back, over and over. They crawled over each other, indifferent to anything but the incandescence that was just outside their reach.

Amina stood and watched from a distance at first, but was drawn in closer and closer. She gave up trying to count and instead put her arms out, her fingertips just centimeters from the sheet. They started to land on her and buzz her ears; one got tangled in her hair. She discovered, to her surprise, that she wasn't scared, that she didn't mind. One landed on her hand and she held it up close to her face to admire its stripes and spots, its dark-outlined wings and tiny antennae, its intelligent face.

"Mo!" she said. "I want to keep this one. Can I get a jar and keep it?"

Mo looked up from his clipboard in surprise. He was just fifteen, and already very serious and hard to ruffle. Amina was sure he'd say yes, and her mind had already turned to how she would convince her mother to let her keep moths in her room, when he responded at last.

"No," he said. "Let's not keep them. Let them be free."

A moth is not the same as a butterfly. Moths are the forgotten cousins of their fanciful others. Though they too hatch from a cocoon, unfurl their wings, and transform into a creature of air, the moths are creatures of the night. They crave light and seek it. Their varieties are infinite, their patterns as unique as snowflakes. But it is butterflies that are beloved, butterflies that are cherished and protected. Through eons, they have been collected and preserved, drawn by children and traced into happy dreams.

Yet it was in the moth that Amina found her way. They were overlooked, but still they filled the earth.

51.

PRAKASH CALLED AND SAID that Mo was in surgery and they should come to the hospital; he said it didn't look good. He picked them up and they drove in silence, Omar staring blankly out the window. Inside, they found the waiting room, where Marcy sat in a chair, studying her phone with tears streaming down her cheeks. After a moment she looked up and jumped to her feet, hugging all three of them at once and then taking Omar by the hand and bringing him to sit with her.

Amina stood at the large windows that framed the room, staring with a blank mind at the streets three floors below. She forced herself to think about Mo, to connect her numb mind to what had happened. She did not cry.

She remembered how protective of her he had been when she had started kindergarten, the way he looked for her at each lunchtime and recess. She remembered how he'd grown his hair long at thirteen, and how their father had bullied him into cutting it. She remembered how he blossomed when he met Marcy, how she took him to parties and dances and sat next to him at school assemblies and made him seem complete: a real and successful teenager. She remembered how she had envied him, all that he had: his normalcy and his conventionality, the way he met everyone's expectations.

Except his own, she thought. He never met his own. He was everyone else's regular guy, but he had never become himself.

"My mother?" she asked Marcy. Her lips felt like they were sticking together, resisting her voice.

"She's getting us coffee."

Omar sat down in a red leather chair, a blank expression on his face. Amina sat next to him.

"Omar," she said.

He said nothing.

"Are you all right?" she asked.

He looked at her, then, with begging and anger competing in his eyes. "I'm not all right. I'll never be all right."

"You will be," she said. "I know it doesn't seem like it, but you will."

He shook his head and mumbled something.

"What was that?"

"You could help me but you won't. You don't really care."

"Of course I care!" she said. "Omar, I'll do anything I can."

"Then stay," he said. "Don't leave me."

She shut her mouth, taken aback, and then realized that her mother had returned, without coffee and with a very somber-looking surgeon.

She took a long, deep breath, and caught Omar's eyes and held them. To her surprise, she felt tears gather and roll down her face.

"I'm sorry," she said.

"I'll never speak to you again," Omar said. "I swear it."

"I love you," Amina said. "I love all of you. But I have to go."

She stood up and walked toward her mother, preparing herself to hear what she already knew.

VI. NO MATTER WHAT OCCURS, I WILL FIND YOU

52.

EVERYONE FLEW HOME TO bury Dad in DC, and somehow his grandma was mad about that and that made Omar mad. At the burial, he stood with his aunt instead of his mom, but he regretted it when he saw his mom's face from across the casket. She was wearing her pearls, but she didn't look pretty. She looked sadder than he'd ever seen her.

The night after the funeral, Omar stayed up all night. He didn't tell anyone; he went to bed when his mom told him to, after all the guests had left. He saw his mother and Amina and his grandma all settle into the couches in the living room, each with a drink in hand, each looking exhausted. He took the stairs two at a time and closed and locked the door behind him. But he didn't get into pajamas and he didn't go to his bed. Instead, he sat on the floor near his closet and thought.

He thought about the service, about the people from his dad's work who all looked so shocked, and about the friends of his mother who crowded around her like birds at a feeder, chirping away with their words of consolation, their arm squeezes and sad smiles. He thought about his grandma, and how she had cried and cried in silence after they returned from the hospital with the news that his dad was dead, and how unfair it was that she had lost Grandpa and his dad at the same time. He thought about his aunt, and how much he hated her for leaving him now; he was sure he was doing the right thing by not talking to her.

He thought about his dad, too. He went over in his mind the words of the Unitarian minister who had performed the service, though he had never known Mo, and the careful, measured tributes of his father's colleagues and a friend from college Omar had only met once before. Everyone said the same things: that he died too soon, that he was a devoted father, that he worked hard and was dependable.

No one said the things that Omar thought now. He thought about how small his father's life had been. There were no awards or honors to speak of. His years as a husband had been erased by the divorce. No one talked about how fun his dad had been, or told stories about how he had helped them through a diffi-cult time, or raised laughter with a tale of skydiving or a fishing adventure or some silly quirk.

Omar felt torn between two thoughts: his father's life was not the life he wanted to live, and he wanted, with a keenness he had never felt before, to honor the man his father was.

It was after midnight when he began to write. He wrote more than twenty pages, more than he had ever written before, about his family, the Abduls, and their history, using all the things he had learned long ago when he wanted to be Indian. By dawn, he was starting to tell his father's story, the story of Mohammed Salman Abdul, and he fell asleep, pad of paper on his chest, just at the point where his parents met in college, just at the point where he began.

HIS MOTHER CRIED A lot at first. She cried on the airplane home; she cried at the memorial; she cried at home in the mornings after that and in the evening when she got home from work. After Omar's grandmother left, his mother talked on the phone with Amina a lot, which he thought was strange, and sometimes on the weekends Amina would come over and sit with his mom, drinking diet soda and talking about things they'd shut up about when he walked in.

They were supposed to move before September, but first they were delayed by his grandpa getting sick, and then after his dad died, his mom kept telling him there was too much to do, so they stayed. He would have to go back to school in DC, maybe for a month or more.

He and his mom spent a lot of time packing. He helped first with the kitchen and dining room, encasing china and glassware in little safety packages of cardboard and bubble wrap. He packed up most of the DVDs in the den, and all the CDs—most of which had been his dad's.

His mother left her room for last. Omar knew this was because it was full of boxes of his father's clothes and shoes and ties and belts and toiletries; he knew because he had checked. Some of these were boxes that had never left, even when his father had, and others were boxes that had returned home from his father's apartment, including boxes of books and pictures.

His mother had told Omar once that he could take anything he wanted, and one afternoon he pawed through some of the clothing. He found crisp shirts and shiny ties, his father's well-polished loafers; and he found sweatpants and sweatshirts that were stained and full of holes, T-shirts that were worn thin and stained socks and a battered raincoat that had a tiny, empty bottle of brandy in the pocket. None of these were things that felt like his father; none of these were things he could use.

He did find the knife, Amina's knife, which was the one thing he was not supposed to have. This he did take, promising himself to keep it hidden. He also took a photo of himself with his parents, in front of the house on Mother's Day, from when he was eight. It was this he showed to his mother and asked to keep, and she said yes, of course, in the new, sad way that she had, the way that suggested everything was already lost.

He wrote about the knife in the book he was writing about his father, telling the story of his father giving it to him, and he wrote about the day the photograph was taken. He wrote about how his dad always looked so sharp when he was dressed for work, leaving out the dirty T-shirts from the end. He wrote about the time his dad practiced cricket with him and threw the ball into the bed of a pickup truck. He wrote about how his dad cooked eggs and toast for him on the mornings when Omar stayed at his apartment, and how his dad never forgot to pick him up from school, not once. He wrote about how his dad had trained to be a pilot and how he had built a copy of the Red Fort when he was a boy and about how he was able to recite whole poems at dinner parties when he was a kid. And he wished he had spoken at the memorial service, wished that he had stood up in front of all those almost-friends and said that Mo was a great dad, that he loved him and would never forget him. He wished that he had made it clear that he was his father's son.

He had a copy of *Devdas* that Amina had given to him, and he watched that a lot; Dev was an alcoholic with a broken heart, too, and sometimes there was a turn of Shah Rukh Khan's mouth that reminded him of his dad. Probably Amina hadn't known this when she bought the movie, and Omar didn't tell her.

He watched reruns of *Friends* and *Seinfeld* and some nights his mother let him watch the programs he chose, like *Lost* and *Alias*, shows with storylines far more confusing than his own. He became interested in *Star Trek* and watched its different versions with interest. Now, when he felt disassociated from the world around him, he told himself there was a break in the space-time continuum; he spent hours wondering if the Prime Directive was the best policy. If you could save another civilization and make it better, shouldn't you?

53.

WHEN OMAR RETURNED TO school, everything felt unreal. The halls echoed like caves, and the mass of kids around him in classrooms and the lunchroom and outside the building at the end of the day was as abstract to him as a flock of starlings, swirling in unknowable patterns, diving for treasures he couldn't see. He stood apart, not really there, not one of them. Because he was marked now, because his dad was dead.

Omar tried repeating this to himself over and over, chanting it in a whisper in cars and at school and while watching TV: *My dad is dead.* He said it to himself when he went to bed at night and again when he woke up in the morning. He thought it while sitting at the dinner table with his mother, and while working his way through math formulas, and while watching *Star Trek. My dad is dead.* And still it did not seem possible.

All his teachers had been told what had happened. Some of them asked him if he needed anything, and some of them steered clear of him like he was a freak, and the only person Omar felt should know, Hari, didn't talk to him at all and passed him in the halls like they were strangers.

Still, the word got out, and he felt a sheepish satisfaction to be viewed as a person with a terrible tragedy, rather than as the nobody he had been before. There was a girl at school who asked him about it nearly every day: "Are you thinking about your dad?" He got her phone number one day, and sometimes he would call her and tell her things about his dad. Her name was Sabrina, and she thought it was funny his dad was called Mo and cool that he'd worked at the Smithsonian and sad that he had, as Omar told it, died of a broken heart.

Of course, Omar had been there that night, and he knew better: that his dad had been drinking, that he drove away in a rage when he shouldn't have been driving, that he went too fast and hit a stop sign. He overheard, from his window, parts of the argument that night, bits and pieces of his mother talking about him, with a complaint he didn't fully understand, of his father's raised voice and his mother yelling and pleading. He heard the car and, to his horror now, in that moment he felt relief: *thank god he's gone.* Had his father somehow heard him? Had he wished his father away too strongly, with a magical thinking that he didn't know he had?

He looked online at school, so he wouldn't worry his mother or the FBI—the idea of thoughts becoming action, of willing the world to change through telepathy and astral projection and other fantasies—but he soon lost interest in the possibility. Everyone told him that it had been an accident, that his dad had been drunk and made a mistake, that he never would have wanted to die and leave Omar behind.

Except that didn't always make sense either, since he and his mom had already been planning to leave, and his dad hadn't seemed to enjoy his life very much. Omar thought it was because his mother was planning to divorce him, and that's why it seemed to him that his father had died of a broken heart. Would he have gotten drunk and driven away if they were still a family, if none of the events of the last year had happened? Omar did not think so.

He was allowed to take the bus home from school on his own now. His mother bought him a silver phone to use in emergencies and cautioned him to do his homework. He had little choice. There was never much food in the house now, and his mother had canceled their cable TV, and he was scared to use the internet. He drew sometimes, pictures of planets and moons and comets mostly; once, he tried to make a picture of his grandfather, but he threw it away after the paper tore from so much erasing.

One afternoon after school he watched *The Last of the Mohicans.* That started a new obsession, one he fed with a battered DVD he found at a local garage sale. He watched parts of it almost every day. He liked when Daniel Day Lewis leaped through the waterfall and the terrible scene when the little sister jumped off the cliff. And that's what he felt like: Omar, last of the Abduls.

There had been Abdul Mohammed Abdul, his grandfather, also known as Double Abdul to his family and Alan to his colleagues; his father, Mohammed, always known as Mo; and now just him, Omar. His name felt small, too small to reduce further in a nickname; it was as though the first names in the family had been diluted over time. For a long time he had wanted a new name, but now all he wanted was more of the family one.

He told Sabrina this, over the phone, and she said she understood. One day, she took the bus home with him and watched part of *Devdas* sitting next to him on the couch. He could not believe his luck, and yet he was also paralyzed: should he kiss her or hold her hand or touch her hair or tell her she was pretty—and she was, very very pretty, with long golden hair—or should he keep his distance, like a gentleman? What did she expect? She did not let on, so he sat an awkward six inches apart from her and chattered without cease through the movie, explaining each scene's backstory, each character's dreams and foils.

OVER LABOR DAY WEEKEND, his mother invited Aunt Amina invited over for a farewell dinner before she moved. He had hardly talked to her since his dad died. In a way it was like she was already gone.

Omar placed the pizza order before Amina arrived, adding on spicy chicken wings and a liter of diet soda. He took out paper plates and placed them on the counter, along with paper towels and the remaining plastic cups.

Amina arrived at the same time as the pizza, looking thin, looking, if Omar were honest, a bit as she had when she had first arrived: uncomfortable, blunt, and out of place. Then, he never would have expected that he would know her so well, or share so much with her. Nor would he have expected that they would say goodbye so soon, or that she would be moving to India. When he first met her, he realized, he had been obsessed with India, and now she was the one who would have it.

Amina and his mom hugged for a long time when she arrived. Omar nodded at her as he opened up the pizza boxes and the wings and poured Diet Coke for everyone. Then his mom and Amina sat on the living room floor, in front of the glass-fronted gas fireplace.

"I think this was my one truly favorite thing about this house," his mom said. "The fireplace. I always felt comfortable in here."

"Really?" his aunt said. "You seemed so into the decorating."

His mom shrugged. "That was like playacting. At least it seems like it now. I don't know what I was thinking."

"Tell me about your new place," Amina said.

Omar had seen pictures. It was a small cottage under large trees, in the same neighborhood as his grandma's. His room had a window seat, and the living room had a bay window, and there was a bar between the kitchen and dining room with two stools, one for him and one for his mom. It was old, nearly a hundred years old, and much smaller than this house, with no attic or basement. The outside was painted in goldenrod and green, and the oaks outside held a tire swing, which he was too old for, and a makeshift tree house, which he was not.

"It's beautiful," his mother said, and Omar thought it was true.

Amina smiled at that. "I'm happy for you."

Omar resented her wishing them well and helping them and trying so hard. "I'm going to eat in my room," he said.

Both women were quiet for a moment, then his mother nodded her okay. He left and went upstairs, setting his plate of pizza on the windowsill, but their voices echoed in the empty house and he spent some time at the top of the staircase, listening to the two women talk.

"I do know what you were asking," Amina said. "I'm sorry if I didn't make that clear at the time."

"No, it's fine—" his mother started to say.

"No, I've been wanting to say this, Marcy. I mean really wanting to say this. I think it's important that we acknowledge that there are in fact negative consequences for Omar if he chooses to identify as an Indian and Muslim man, in whatever way that—"

"But of course that's fine, that's not what I meant."

Omar took a tentative step down the stairs in the ensuing pause, not wanting to miss what was coming next.

Amina started again. "But when you asked, why does he need this, why does he have to have this part of himself?"

"I remember saying something like that. Not that exactly."

"Well, I have thought about that a lot. And the answer, I think, is this: he doesn't have a choice."

There was another long pause.

"I know," his mother said, and for some reason this surprised Omar. "I feel silly, actually. Maybe I was just saying I hate that this is the world we live in. And that I'm not ready for this, because Mo didn't show me how."

"Marcy," Amina began.

"No, I'm serious. He really never let me know that any of this mattered to him, and I was naive enough to think it didn't. But now I know it does, and I am terrified for Omar. I don't know how to save him."

"It's not about saving him. He just needs the time and space to find himself."

"Like you are? By going to India?"

"Oh," Amina said. "I hadn't thought of it quite like that."

"How do you think of it?"

"I guess," his aunt said, "more like running away."

His mother made a sound like a snort. "You are the most accomplished woman I know, Amina. I don't really see this fabulous job as some kind of escape."

"I'm not yet sure what it is," Amina said. "But I'm sorry I won't be closer. I didn't know . . ."

"No," Marcy said. "We didn't know."

Omar got up and went to his room. Would Amina have stayed if his dad had died sooner? He sat on his bed, moving aside a stack of books on Native American history that he'd checked out from the school library. More Indians who weren't from India.

There was a knock on his door, and then it opened and his aunt stuck her head in.

"Omar," she said, "I'm leaving."

He said nothing.

She stepped farther into the room.

"So," he said, in a tone that had a hint of triumphalism.

She looked taken aback.

"I miss you," she said. "I'll really miss you in India."

He tried to focus on the book in front of him.

"Omar," she said again, this time in a firmer tone. He looked up with reluctance.

"Omar, do you blame me?" she asked him. "For what happened to your dad?"

It felt like a tornado inside his chest at that moment, and he closed his eyes and shook his head.

"Then why won't you speak to me?"

He shook his head again.

"Are you mad I'm moving? Is that it?"

He opened his eyes and gave her a level gaze. Something shifted inside and his emotions quieted.

"I heard you fighting with my dad. You were mean to him. And you were always lying to me. You and Prakash. And you never really cared about me. That's why you're leaving."

He could see her flinch as he spoke, and felt a stab of guilt. To his surprise, she sat down on the floor and was quiet. He waited for her to speak, unable now to look at his book and feign indifference.

"Before you," she finally said, "I never really knew any kids. You were my first . . . well, you are like my first child, if that makes sense. I mean, it does to me, because I love you like you are my own child." She paused but he didn't speak. "But you're not. And sometimes I didn't do the right things, with you or with Mo or with your mom, and I didn't say the right things, and I didn't help in the right ways. But that's not because I didn't want to."

"But you're leaving!" He hated that this burst out of him.

"Yes," she said. "I am leaving DC. But I'm not leaving you."

"I don't ever want to see you again. I don't want to know about India. You should leave my mom alone, too. We're going to forget about you."

His aunt's eyes filled with tears. He took the knife out of his book bag and threw it to the ground near her feet.

"Take this and go." He felt a pang of guilt at the shocked expression on her face, but then he thought of her on the airplane, flying so far away, and he finished the job. "Just go!"

And she did.

54.

ONE WEEKEND WHEN OMAR'S father had been living in his awful apartment, he'd taken Omar at last to the Air and Space Museum. Mo surprised Omar by talking with great expertise about all the planes, about their model types and features and capabilities.

"How do you know all this?" Omar asked, a little annoyed at the stream of information coming from his usually quiet father.

"I trained to be a pilot. Or, I started the training," Mo amended. "I took some lessons."

Omar found this amazing. "You did?"

"It was a lifelong dream of mine to be a pilot. Not a commercial pilot. But private jets, that kind of thing."

"So why didn't you?" It was still confounding to Omar that grown-ups seemed so rarely to do the things they said they wanted to do.

His dad paused. "I took lessons off and on for a few years. But I didn't have much free time after you were born, and then it became impossible."

"Impossible why?" Omar insisted.

Mo looked up at the sky for a few moments, studying it as if he expected to see the answer there.

"September eleventh happened," he finally said. "I had only a few lessons left to get my certification, but after that, I knew I would never get it."

Omar felt sick. "Because of your name?"

His dad wagged his head from side to side, in slow motion. "Because a guy with a Muslim name and background with no particular reason to fly was going to be under suspicion. So I quit."

"You shouldn't have! You should have finished and learned to fly so they would know there's nothing wrong with you."

"Maybe," his dad said. "Maybe so. But I didn't. I decided that was one dream that would never come true."

And this was what Omar wondered now, after everything that had happened: Which dreams were the ones he was supposed to give up on? And which were the ones he was supposed to fight for?

FINALLY, IN EARLY OCTOBER, they were ready to move. It was his last night in his bedroom. His belongings were already gone; maybe even now they were at his new home, waiting for him. But to his surprise, it still felt like his room. The blue-green walls and light gray carpet felt familiar and comforting. He could see marks on the paint where his bedframe had met the wall, where the door handle hit when he swung it open with too much force. In the space where his bookshelf had been, the paint was brighter than in the rest of the room, as though that stretch of wall were wide awake while the rest was sleepy.

This room was all he would miss. This is where Omar had become Omar. It didn't matter what Amina said or what his mother thought. This was where he had practiced Hindi and studied the Horseshoe Nebula; this was where he had sat while calling Sabrina or wrestling with Hari; this room, unlike his parents or any actual person, had witnessed all of him, everything he tried to be and everything he had tried to hide.

And then he remembered: he pried up the side of the heater vent and reached his hand in, recoiling a little bit and then trying again, searching with his fingers until he found what he was looking for. He pulled out the roll of paper and blew the dust off. Unrolling it, he had to squint to see the faded pencil marks.

Omar Sheik Abdul lived here, it said, in a fake cursive. *Prince of Pearls, Savior of the World.*

Ha, he thought. It seemed so long ago now that he had written and drawn those stories about the Royal Abduls. So far away.

IN *THE LAST OF the Mohicans,* lots of the characters die: minor characters and important characters, most of them violently. One girl commits suicide; another character, a bad guy, fights ferociously and then accepts the moment of his death in total stillness. Nathaniel lives: but he is the one who doesn't belong, the one who isn't truly Indian. In the movie, he rescues the woman he loves, but he cannot save his own family. They are lost, one by one, until only Uncas remains. And even though Nathaniel is alive and with him, they both know, without anyone really saying it, that the family line is dead.

What if the same were true in his family? Maybe his father had been the last of the Abduls. Because Omar was only half Indian and he didn't really understand anything about his family.

But then he thought, no: it was different from that. He was like a variation, a mutation, the new version, Abdul 2.0. He didn't have to answer the questions his mother and Aunt Amina were asking. He wasn't the last. He was the first.

WHEN THEY WALKED OUT of the house in Georgetown for the last time, Omar felt a shift, like he had stepped into an alternate dimension. There was the boy, Omar, who had grown up here, with a mom and dad and home like anyone else, whose parents worked important jobs, and who played cricket and spent time with his aunt and dreamed about traveling to Lahore or visiting outer space. And then there was this new self, this new Omar, who would live just with his mother, his quieter and sad mother, in a sweet cottage in the South. This Omar wouldn't have a father, or an aunt, or a girlfriend named Sabrina. This Omar would be something else, a person who had left things behind, a person who had experienced loss. And this, he suddenly realized, might be what it meant to grow up.

His mother started the car.

"I'm glad we're going," he said to her, and she gave him a smile that made him, against all odds, smile back.

The car began to move forward and he and his mom both gave the house one last look.

"Wave," she said as she turned to face the road, and he did, looking over his shoulder as the house receded into the distance, watching it grow smaller, shrinking from a home to the model of one, from a place to a place in his memory.

"Goodbye," he said under his breath. And then he rolled down his window and stuck his head out. "Goodbye!" he yelled back at the house, his voice loud and true. Then he turned back around, grinned at his mother, and stared down the road ahead.

VII. THE HYBRID ZONE

55.

NEARLY TWO YEARS AFTER the death of her father and brother, Amina Abdul received a letter.

When she first arrived at the field site on top of a hill near the base of the Himalayas, there was already correspondence: notes from her mother, forwarded bills and junk mail from her old address, alumni news from California. Now, however, mail was scarce. Email was taking over in the US, and here in India the reliability of electricity and ethernet were gradually improving. And, she acknowledged, enough time had passed that her absence was no longer remarkable. She was, possibly, being forgotten.

TRAVELING ON THE TRAIN to Chandigarh, where the Thakkurs picked her up, she felt like a stranger all over again, newly born incognito. She reserved a first-class seat, only to discover that it was not air-conditioned. Second class, air-con, was actually better. So she sat in a compartment with just a few weary-looking passengers, people proud enough to ask for first class but not quite rich enough to buy the better ticket.

The heat put her into a trance. She forgot the few words of Hindi she knew and she sank into herself, into thoughts of

Prakash and Omar and Marcy and Mo. Of Mo. On the train her thoughts returned to him over and over. She thought of all the things she could have done to make the outcome different, all the things she might have said. She had let her brother down. And that was when the idea formed in her mind, for the first time clearly: that her punishment for her many failures was to be alone, to always be alone. That no one could be allowed to interfere.

She was completing the first stage of the hybrid zone project. It had turned out to be more complex than she'd anticipated, but the operation was running more smoothly this second year. The zone was narrower than she'd expected, but the accumulated data was beginning to pay off. Soon, it would be time to write up the work, to take it out into the world to present it, to declare what they had.

That was the part she dreaded. In two years, she had not left the field site except to go to the nearest town. Occasionally she went to the Thakkurs', and once she had gone shopping with Dilpa. In the small village store off a fly-ridden street, they were offered low stools and a local cola, semi-warm and lacking fizz. The shopkeeper unfurled an array of dazzling fabrics, one after another, and Amina felt dizzy. She looked about her in dismay, and her eyes went to a simple white salwar kameez. When she pointed, Dilpa protested.

"Those are widow's whites," Dilpa said.

"Not correct for you, madam," the shop owner agreed.

Amina insisted. Maybe in those clothes, her mind would calm. She sought silence, not the soaking beauty of the gold-threaded saris Dilpa favored, not the clamor of color.

IN THE US, EVERYTHING had been neatly tied up at her departure: Marcy and Omar would be fine once they settled in Charlotte, and Amina's mother, in a conciliatory mood, said she would fly every few months to see Omar. Prakash opened a new branch of his bookstore, and Anjali asked for a recommendation letter so that she could continue her studies. Life went on, and the bit of space and breath that had been occupied by Amina's detached, broken brother was now taken up by new life.

It was a time of the year when the field site emptied out, abandoned by its staff in pursuit of cooler climes. Amina stayed, cooking for herself. Sometimes she was accompanied by a particularly intrepid graduate student, eager to impress the American professor. They always left disappointed.

"She hates me," Amina overheard one tell another at the end of her first year. She'd been surprised, because she felt nothing at all for the student.

This summer, Dilpa and her husband were in and out; they were renovating a house in the nearby town, an old colonial mansion with an attached harem, which they were connecting with colonnades in place of the musty dark hallways. The harem would be his study, and an herb garden would fill the courtyard in between. It was going to be beautiful.

Amina chose to live with the other workers in a barracks at the site. Dilpa had insisted that she take a large room of her own, and in this Dilpa had installed a soft twin bed, block-printed muslin curtains, a blood-red Persian rug, and a ceiling fan. To this Amina added her few clothes—mostly the boots and shorts and flannels of her California years—and some books. Of the books, she had carefully not included anything given to her by Prakash, anything on Mughal history, or on the subject of the planets. They were mostly science texts and a few mysteries, nothing she was very attached to.

India, in summer or winter, proved to be just the right temperature for her. There were all the constraints of tradition and caste for her to pile about her like fence posts, keeping the curious at bay. She was, alternately, the Muslim professor or the American professor or the lady professor, and her predilection for isolation and her uncanny quiet draped an air of foreboding about each title. In short, she was left alone.

Dilpa was the closest thing she had to a friend. She put herself in charge of Amina's bank accounts and mail and the arrangements for her food, and let Amina order the supplies for the lab, distribute tasks, and schedule observational research and the implementation of new branches of the genetics projects. These things Amina could do, easily, with a clarity that almost frightened her. She saw exactly how things should be done, the staff and students and scientists like pieces of an elementary machine, the goal—the establishment and naming of the hybrid zone—always present in her mind, pushed to the front and kept there in desperate necessity.

She had worked this way, concentrated and isolated, for two years before the letter arrived. It was from Prakash. She turned it over in her hands first, looking at the address, which was still Capitol Hill. That in and of itself seemed impossible, that he could be in the same space, a place where she had eaten fragrant foods and drunk wine and made love. She had the strange urge to smell it, as though it had come from some exotic, spice-scented land. She no longer drank or smoked. She ate spare vegetarian meals served by the Thakkur Institute's recalcitrant cook or cooked plain rice for herself or skipped meals altogether.

She opened the letter and read its message, and it turned to concrete in her hands: a bad omen, a harbinger of difficult things to come. Prakash had written that he and Anjali would be in India at the end of the month and they'd like to visit the field site. *Tripping through the mustard fields, indeed*, he had written. He assumed that she remembered things like that, the details of that brief life, details that she spent almost all of her time forgetting.

What could Prakash and Anjali want with her now?

56.

THE NEXT AFTERNOON, DILPA came to the site, accompanied by her niece Kamala, an intelligent and serious girl of sixteen who wore questions like a string of tiny Christmas lights all about her person. She had done an internship at the lab the year before, during her summer break from a private school near Shimla. Amina had assigned her to a colleague, who let her do some basic organizational work with samples in the lab.

This year, Kamala had asked through Dilpa if she could do some field observation with Amina, but Amina had said no. Dilpa instead apprenticed her to a colleague in the small town that lay in a valley below the field site, for computer studies that she convinced the girl would help her with future scientific work.

"Come to dinner tonight, Amina," Dilpa said. "We've finally finished the dining room, and the fountain's working in the courtyard. We want to celebrate."

Amina shook her head. "There's so much to do here."

"Foo," Dilpa said. "I'm the boss. You must come."

She said this with a smile, while her niece stared at Amina intently. Amina did want to see the house.

"Okay," she said. "Just this once."

"Fantastic," Dilpa said, turning to go. As she swept out with her arm around her niece, she turned back briefly. "But I don't accept your terms."

Amina decided to shower and wash her hair. She now kept it cropped close to her head, razor short over her ears. The local barber hated cutting it for her. Each time she went, he begged her to leave it.

"Such a pretty lady," he would say, "should have beautiful hairs to adorn her." Each time she insisted that he apply the blades.

Back in her room, she dug out a decent pair of khakis and slid a midnight blue linen kurta over her head, obscuring her figure. She didn't look well, but at least she wouldn't embarrass herself. Her eyes caught on the knife, and she felt a twist in her stomach. She missed Omar. She missed him. Sometimes she forgot that fact amid the more dominant feelings of guilt and self-recrimination, the muddle of grief over her brother and the unshakable sense of her culpability in his death.

THE THAKKURS SENT A car to fetch her that night, one of the old beige Hindu Ambassadors that had dominated India's streets until the tech boom. The driver was a politician with betel-stained teeth who wanted to discuss evolution.

"Is it okay if I roll down the window?" Amina asked.

He moved his head from side to side, watching her in the rearview mirror with greedy eyes. When she had her window down, he resumed his diatribe.

"What I am asking, madam," he said in a severe and professorial tone of voice, "is that those who are scientists also take into point of view the ideas of men of god. The great books of Hinduism are telling us many things about how we have come to be on this earth, things which the schooling of today simply ignores."

He went on for a while longer and then there was a pause. Amina realized he had probably asked her a question.

"Have you heard of Kansas?" she asked him. In Kansas, she had read, there were laws being passed to forbid the study of evolution, news that had filled her with outrage.

"Kansas? Is this a philosopher?"

"Never mind," she said.

He changed the subject to the Congress Party and their foreign-born leader and upcoming local elections. She let him ramble on while she watched out the window as they came down the hill and into the outskirts of town.

The front of the Thakkurs' house was covered in scaffolding. Dev had shown Amina old engravings of what it looked like in the nineteenth century, which was impressive indeed. It had been built by an English governor and his Indian wife and had been owned by their offspring up until independence. Nominally supervised by the government since, it had been left to rot and ruin; Dev had not had too much trouble in acquiring it with his promises of reviving an architectural landmark in a town with little to offer outsiders. The structure tended toward the imposing, meant as it was to be an official residence, and no doubt both façade and interior would benefit from Dilpa's warm and humanizing touch.

The dust and bird-shit covered scaffolding was not promising, but inside the rooms that were open looked neat and tidy. Dev himself greeted her at the door. He was in his sixties and very self-assured in a striped shirt and sweater vest, open sandals on his pedicured feet. He showed her around, describing the progress of various carving and painting and gilding aspects of the renovation. He complained genially about modern craftsmanship, and spoke with enthusiasm about the contribution of a new Dutch-trained architect.

At last Dilpa showed up, in a charcoal-colored sari set off by the unexpected bright gold of her bangles and the brighter silver of her hair. Kamala trailed behind. Her parents were in Paris, but she preferred to be here. This, Amina had to admit, was admirable.

THE ROYAL ABDULS   285

The Thakkurs had a cook, though Dilpa herself was accomplished in the art, and they were vegetarians. The food was varied and multitudinous: dish after dish was spread across the table and spooned onto blue-and-white china. No one ate with their hands, though Amina thought she could see Dev's fingers twitching a little bit as they hovered over the plate on their way to pick up a fork or spoon.

In spite of this constraint, the atmosphere was far from formal. The dining room had doors that opened out to the courtyard, and there were fans swishing the air in and out so that it stayed cool. The tinkle of water in a large marble basin at the center was soothing. Amina had never equated wealth with anything quite so subdued and pleasant, but this, in a nutshell, was the Thakkurs.

Kamala was wearing western clothes: navy crop pants with a kelly-green polo shirt. Make that Polo shirt. She glowed, even though she wasn't pretty, even though she rarely smiled or said a word. It was the glow of possibility, Amina decided.

Amina told them about the driver's political rant coming down the hill, and everyone laughed. Then the Thakkurs went on at length about the seriousness of educational limitations in India. Dilpa wanted to start the equivalent of a community college for local adult students, someplace where people could study for free, taking language and computer and history courses. Kamala watched her aunt talk, the whites around her eyes luminescent, her lips pursing before taking each small bite of food.

"But in the US, at least, even educated people choose not to believe in evolution," Amina said.

"And here, too, with many similar things," Dev said. "It is this fundamentalism: Islamic, Hindu, Christian—everywhere this is the problem."

There was a general silence of agreement around the table. Though India had recently escaped the throttlehold of a Hindu nationalist government, the ghosts of fascism still blew through the country. Amina could sometimes feel such fingers touch her in the lab, where occasional looks and whispers told her that her name said something she personally did not.

After they had washed their fingers in small bowls, they awaited tea and dessert. Dev wanted to discuss current newspaper headlines. He asked Amina where she thought the Americans intended to go after Iraq, and she threw out the standard suggestions. She read the paper here maybe once a week; he knew much more than she did about contemporary events.

"But I am asking," he said, "what you believe, Amina. You have lived in Washington itself, after all."

She accepted a cup of chai, already sweet with sugar and thick with whole milk. "I wasn't paying as much attention as I should have been," she said.

"What about this Barack Obama?" Dilpa asked. "Do you think he really can be elected? Such a man?"

"I can't really believe he will," Amina said carefully. "Maybe a black man, but not a man with a Muslim name. Not that."

Heads nodded around the table.

"That's too bad," Kamala said.

AFTER DINNER, DILPA INSISTED on driving Amina back to the field site herself in the Maruti. She drove like it was made of eggshell.

"We never have a chance to talk, you and I," she said when Amina protested.

Starting off, they covered the standard subjects: the lab, the newest employees, Dilpa's hopes for Kamala's future.

"I was hoping you would go to the genetics conference with me this year," Dilpa said, as she turned the car up into the hills. There was no other traffic, just the headlight beams of the Maruti glancing off the trees ahead.

Amina cringed inside. She had been hoping Dilpa would not ask. The meetings were to be in Atlanta, close enough to Charlotte that she would not be able to avoid visiting Marcy and Omar.

"Dilpa, I'm not sure," she said, then stopped. What could she say?

"Not sure about the meetings, or not sure about returning to America?"

Amina swallowed. "Both. People I know will be at the meetings."

"And so what?" Dilpa asked, her voice softening.

"And so," Amina said, "I have been avoiding seeing people I knew."

"Two years is a long time. Whatever you have done, Amina, you will find that no one blames you as you blame yourself."

"I'm not worried about blame," Amina said.

"Then what?"

Amina shook her head, unsure how to express herself. "I want—" she started, and then stopped. "My intention was to leave that life behind. Permanently."

"But this is impossible," Dilpa said. "You cannot leave your own life behind."

"My life in DC," Amina said, turning to look at Dilpa's smooth face, "was such a short time. In scientific terms, it was an anomalous period, an irrelevancy. It was only a year that I was there."

"A year is not so long, granted." She glanced over as if to check Amina's composure. "You can't measure emotions like so much liquid or gas. An important thing of a moment, a hurtful thing, weighs more than twenty years of happiness."

Amina shrugged, looking away again. This was not a productive way to think of it. It was better to be patient, to wait for her memories to fade.

"The man who writes you letters," Dilpa said, "I think he was there?" Amina gave a slight nod. "And your nephew, I think you love him, no?"

"I do," Amina said.

"Seeing them again might feel good," Dilpa said. "Better than this."

Amina didn't have to ask what she meant. She sighed. "Do you need me to go? I mean, are you asking as my boss or as my friend?"

They were approaching the top of the hill and the field site, dark except for one bare bulb above the main barracks door.

"I ask, as both, for you to think about it," Dilpa said. "To really think about it."

57.

AMINA WENT BACK TO work the next day, trying not to think about the conversation or the letter from Prakash. She needed to review two year-end reports and decide which direction to take from this point. What she was tempted to do was something risky: to suggest a new taxonomy, a way of categorizing that accounted for hybrid individuals and groups as long-term realities.

This approach addressed the fundamental conundrum presented by a hybrid zone, which related to the concept of naming. If two species, defined by their inability to reproduce, begin to reproduce, what to call the result? In the past, common wisdom said that two separate species simply did not mate; if they did, as in the case of the horse and donkey, the result—the mule—was infertile and thus deemed a biological failure.

But the discovery of hybrid zones, first in the work of pioneers such as Sweadner, and later in the more detailed genetic study that Amina had participated in, required a new framework. If, in certain "natural laboratories," separate species intermingled, producing hybrid offspring that themselves continued to mate both with other hybrids and with "purer" specimens, what to call the resulting population?

And if that population perpetuated itself for years on end, as Amina was trying to demonstrate in her current project, creating a stable zone of fluctuating but persistent hybridity, what did that suggest about the categorization of beings into species? If species could simply ignore the categories that humans placed them into, did humans then need to rethink those categories? Were such definitions, with their implied immutability, things of the past?

SEPTEMBER CONTINUED AND THE heat crept farther up the hill, making it difficult to sleep at night. Lying in bed, fan swirling above her, she conducted imaginary conversations with her nephew. *Omar,* she wanted to say, *India is nothing like you imagined it. The mountains where I live are far from Hyderabad. This India is nothing like the jeweled kingdoms you wanted as your own, unrecognizable next to the great cities and palaces and forts you dreamed of.*

India is hot, she would tell him. *India is ugly. It is overpopulated, crowded, and filthy. Men spit red betel juice on roads and sidewalks and walls, and goats die swallowing the plastic bags that litter the streets. Everywhere you go, hand-painted café signs are replaced by Coca-Cola umbrellas, Japanese cars brush the rumps of wandering cows, boys wear MTV T-shirts and sunglasses, and everywhere, all around you, are the beggars.*

And sometimes, too, she would think, *Omar, you would like this. You would like the way the eagles sometimes visit, swooping in the sky above the roofs of the lab, the way the butterflies hover over the flowers like lovers. You would like drinking masala Cokes and eating samosas fried in a huge vat by a vendor on the sidewalk. You would like the power outages that come every night, halting the ceiling fans and forcing you out into the night to sit and soak up the cool breath of darkness. You would like Dilpa's silk saris and Dev's elegant pajama suits and the embroidered shawl they gave me for my birthday last year. You would like Kamala; you would understand her, and she, you.*

Some nights, in her room, Amina fingered the latest letter from Prakash. She had kept every one that he sent, against her better judgment, in a box at the back of her closet. She read them, too, gulping them down and then filing them away, so that she wasn't entirely ignorant of events back in the States.

She knew, for example, that Anjali was married. She had married the Rafael Amina had met at the picnic, and together they had moved to California, where Anjali had reenrolled in her studies at a state university near the one Amina had attended. Prakash had even hinted that she might focus her dissertation on the wild silk moth, just as Amina had. The university forced Chris to put a recommendation permanently on file for her, one vetted carefully by the dean and recommending Anjali with no reservation about her capability, her training, or her intelligence.

She knew that Prakash still worked at his store, that the rest of his family was well, that the cricket team had finally won its first match.

When she added this to news from her mother, about Marcy's new job at a local university's early-education center, about her mother's plans for redecorating her living room and turning the backyard into a rock garden, about Omar's star turn on the debate team, she had a clear picture in her mind of what others called "her home."

The curious thing about Prakash's letter, she noticed now, was that it simply announced his intentions. If she wanted to stop him from coming, she would have to write to him herself.

58.

AMINA SLACKED OFF ON her work as they waited for the monsoon and the temperature seemed to increase daily. She spent more time at the Thakkurs', where she loved to go and sit in the shade near the fountain, listening to its cooling trickle. She spent a day in the herb garden, planting borders of sage with the help while Dev and Dilpa looked on, amused at her dirt-encrusted hands. She went for long walks around the field site with a compass and an ancient British map of the region to guide her. There were ruins scattered around the hills, remnants of past glories and battles. Most everything had been left to crumple back into the earth, attacked by weather and animals and favored only by amateur historians and lovers looking for privacy.

On her walks she thought about the two decisions to be made: she needed to write to Prakash, or call, or email, anything to stop him from coming. She would email soon, she told herself. And meanwhile, she needed to decide whether she would go to Atlanta with Dilpa.

But both decisions took on an air of unreality as the days passed. It seemed impossible that anything could disturb the cocoon Amina had placed herself in, impossible that she could be found, or that she could escape. And so she did nothing. In the back of her mind, she knew that Prakash had given a date, one that was very near. But she never let the thought push to the front of her mind. If she did, she would have to figure out whether she wanted to see him again, and that was against the rules she had set for herself. Not knowing, not caring, was her prescription.

Instead, she thought around it. She wondered, was this the conclusion of the story of her life? Could this quiet, this work and isolation and detachment, be the end, the long finale that she would live out from this moment forward?

For two years she had said *yes, yes,* with every cell in her body. *Yes: let this be it.* Let there be no more loves and friendships and worries about her family. Let there be no more attempts to carve a place in the world. She would simply cling to the surface of things, live in her study only. She would make the work count, make it stand in for all the rest.

Because what else could she do? Even on days when she missed Mo the most, when rational thought told her that feelings of guilt were pointless, even when she knew that Omar would forgive her in time, even on those days, she still wanted to be alone. She used the institute as a shell to hide in, the mask that claimed an engagement she did not own.

The fact that she was in India as opposed to anywhere else seemed almost irrelevant. When she had landed at the airport in New Delhi, still in a stupor of shock, there had been a brief moment of recognition: the smell, the heat, the press of people. Those were the most vivid impressions of her visit years before, for Tara's wedding.

KAMALA'S COMPUTER APPRENTICESHIP DREW to a close, and she began to spend more time at the lab. With the absence of the holidaying staff, Amina grudgingly gave her a few minor tasks to perform. At first she was irritated with Dilpa for bringing the girl with her, but Kamala was useful and organized, and the lab felt a little less empty with someone else in it.

They were working together on a spreadsheet one day when there was the unusual sound of an unexpected car pulling up. Hearing it, and then the sound of doors opening and feet crunching on the gravel walkway, Amina knew it was not Dilpa or one of the staff. She took a deep breath and touched the sides of her face, suddenly hot. She wished she had hair to hide behind. Kamala looked at her, puzzled and unsmiling, as she rose from her seat.

At the door, Amina had to lean a little against the frame after she opened it and saw that it really was them heading toward her, like a mirage of past and future bound together: Prakash and Anjali and Rafael behind them, wearing a light blue pajama suit and lifting a bag out of the car.

"Amina," Prakash said, raising a hand and smiling.

"Amina, hi!" Anjali called out.

"My god," Amina said, all grace and wit gone, "I didn't really think you would come."

Prakash looked the same, but older, slivers of silver in his still-short hair. He seemed as formal as before, perhaps stiffer than he had been. Anjali was looking demure in a long dress with shoulder-length hair, and she held a baby in her arms.

It was their first child, only four months old, tiny and blinking and helpless. When they reached the doorway, and Anjali came close to give Amina a kiss, the baby stared at Amina and then grabbed her finger. She froze and then extracted it with care. Prakash was watching her. He offered his hand only, and she shook his and then Rafael's, and then she invited them all to come inside.

She showed them around the facilities: the shining abandoned labs and the compound where she slept. She explained the progress of the last two years, and the direction she planned to steer the project for the next. Through it all, it was as though she wasn't really there, as if she were standing next to herself as she spoke to them, listening in as the public Amina she had buried acquitted herself in social duty.

They met Kamala, and then Dilpa came in, looking more than

pleased to see that Amina had visitors, and invited everyone to dinner. The visitors were staying in town, but Dilpa took care of that, too, insisting that the whole group stay overnight at the house, "if they didn't care about the mess." Amina thought this was a little disingenuous, as she was inviting them to stay in what was virtually a palace.

"Amina, you'll stay the night too," Dilpa said. "It's silly to keep sending for you back and forth."

"Do you mind?" Prakash asked Amina.

She felt trapped. Everyone was looking at her. "You've come all this way," she said, and left it at that.

"Amina," Anjali said, coming forward and putting her hand on her arm, "we really looked forward to seeing you again. I wanted so much for you to meet my son."

Amina took a deep breath, trying to calm her racing mind. Why? Why had they come? Prakash seemed to see that she was upset.

"We'll get our things from the hotel," he said. "And see you at dinner."

"I'll drive with you," Dilpa said, giving Amina a hard look. It was clear she wasn't going to let these visitors, these phantoms from Amina's past, slip away. "I can show you the way to the house."

Amina and Prakash sat across from each other at dinner. There were seven of them at the long table. The baby was upstairs with Dilpa's housemaid, sleeping in a room graced with nineteenth-century murals of war. Rafael and Dev discussed politics—nuclear weapons, Korea, upcoming elections in Iraq and India—while Dilpa cooed over Anjali and Kamala studied them all in her customary silence.

Despite the short notice, the meal was luscious, extravagant, and copious. Rafael could not contain his praises about the food, the beauty of the house, the generosity of the hosts. He was doing a PhD in art history, and Dev promised to show him their archives on the history of the building, its English founder, and his native wife. Amina avoided Prakash's eyes, asked Anjali about her study, ate more than she wanted to. The meal seemed to last for hours.

After the tea and pastry, Prakash stood to help clear the table, but Dilpa stopped him with a hand on his arm. "The courtyard is lovely this time of night," she said.

She came over to Amina and gave her a small push. "Talk," she said. "You are old friends, and must have much to speak to each other about. I'll help the young people get settled with the baby upstairs."

Amina and Prakash went outside dutifully and sat on a stone bench. All around, the herbs were flowering, giving off scents savory and sweet, and the water flowed in light music through the fountain. Turquoise tiles lay in complicated patterns, tracing pathways through the open square, while around them the house loomed like a fortress wall. Up above, the sky was black and moonless, and it seemed there were thousands of stars.

"Amina," Prakash said. "I have never stopped thinking of you."

She shook her head a little. "Thank you for all of your letters," she said, trying to set a tone. "I appreciated them."

He nodded and took her hand. "I didn't want you to think you were alone," he said.

Amina felt the echo of Mo's voice in her head then, saying *I think everyone has turned against me.* Was that how she seemed, she wondered? Did she seem like someone who needed to be saved?

The stars shone overhead, reaching down to brush the tips of the mountain range high on one horizon. She stood to go, and when she looked back, she could see his face as clear as if it were midday, as if at that moment they were not already deep into the night.

59.

AMINA WOKE AT DAWN, in a bed of unfamiliar breadth, her body cooled by a breeze coming through the large windows of the extravagant bedroom Dilpa had put her in. She slid her legs around in the silky sheets and stretched, savoring the unaccustomed luxury of the beautiful room and the soft light and the fresh air that carried the scent of sandalwood and mango.

But then she remembered that the night before, she had promised to write regularly to Prakash. She'd told him that she might be in Atlanta later in the year. What had she been thinking?

She got up and went downstairs. The charwoman, Dilpa's maid, had lit incense and candles at a small altar in the hall, and she could hear the sounds of pots being stirred in the kitchen. She hesitated, and then went out the front door and walked down the long gravel driveway toward the Greek-columned gateway.

As she walked, her feet kicking up dust, the light began to fill the sky, erasing the damp traces of the night. The day would be hot, hotter than the one before. She began to walk back. Halfway there she stopped and turned to study the Himalayas, and then she heard the sound of the heavy front door opening and the ping of footsteps rearranging the gravel and dirt. She looked, her eyes shaded by her hand, and saw that it was Anjali.

Her beauty was quieter, deeper than it used to be, her body softened by the child, her face leaner and more solemn. She stood next to Amina, who gave a curt greeting, and took her arm, ignoring the way that Amina's body stiffened, the way that she almost involuntarily tried to pull it away.

Anjali looked at her, her mouth half open, for a few moments. "I have thought of you so often, and of your brother," she finally said, in the voice of a mother and the young woman Amina had first met all at once.

Amina nodded, trying to extricate her arm and succeeding.

"I've been in California, at Sweadner's field site, you know," Anjali continued.

"I heard." Amina's voice was hoarse and she cleared her throat.

"Everyone there remembers you. They complain that you were such a workaholic when you were there and that they hardly knew you, but the work you did is still used. I'm basing my dissertation on it. I didn't have to do much fieldwork—I mean I couldn't, because of the baby—but I've been working with your samples."

Why is she telling me this? Amina wondered.

"It's hard," Anjali said, "being a woman. You told me once that the way people perceive you is as important as the way you perceive yourself—do you remember that?"

Amina shook her head, wondering if she had really believed that. "Not really."

"Well, I think that's true."

There was a silence, and Amina could feel the heat beginning to rise from the building and the gravel around them. She felt like she had to say something. "I'm glad you stayed," she said. "In science, I mean. It's good that you're finishing your degree."

Anjali nodded. "It's easier there, in California. And Rafael helps. But it's hard, still. It's hard becoming an adult and having all these people rely on you, expecting things of you just because you're a woman. It's hard to love Rafael and the baby and do my work and deal with the people in the lab and feel guilty I'm not near my parents and worry about Prakash being alone."

Amina said, "I left things like that behind."

"No, you didn't," Anjali said. "You only tried."

"Oh, Anjali," Amina said. "I will never stop trying." She wanted to say more, to say it was hopeless to console her, but as she looked at Anjali's face she saw something that made her stop. It was a look like grief, but also eagerness and hope were there, mixed up with the sorrow.

Amina surprised herself by taking Anjali's arm in turn. She guided them away from the gate and walked Anjali back to the house, where her husband and child and brother waited. Above them the sun rose higher in the hazy morning.

Inside, in the dining room, Rafael greeted them with a smile, and as if by prearrangement, slid his child into Amina's arms while he hugged a good morning to his wife. The baby was asleep, and stayed that way when Amina bent to kiss him, inhaling deeply the scent of his new and fragile skin.

The four visitors left later that morning after a gargantuan breakfast prepared by Dilpa herself. Anjali's baby obligingly smiled for a group photo orchestrated by Dev, and then they all piled into their small Japanese car. Prakash got behind the steering wheel and started the engine. For a moment he did not do anything else, and did not take his eyes from Amina, his aged face looking as sad as she had ever seen it. Then finally he shifted into gear and the car rolled forward, its windows filled by the waves of its occupants. As they drove away, Amina felt a tug inside, a surprising twinge of regret; she felt like she would like to go with them.

60.

AT FIRST THINGS WENT on as before. Amina worked and slept and walked in the hills with the great mountains framing the horizon. At night, she avoided the sight of the stars in the sky and read in her bare room.

The staff returned from holiday and filled the lab with voices and the smell of their tiffin lunches, eaten hot at midday under a banyan tree behind the main building. Kamala returned to her parents before the resumption of boarding school, saying she might be an architect instead of a biologist.

Dilpa pressed Amina about Atlanta: would she go to the meetings? She finally said yes, but only if Dilpa was going too; if she didn't have to give a presentation or poster; if she could take an extra week to visit her mother and then her nephew, Omar. Dilpa looked self-satisfied, and threatened to take her shopping for new clothes.

If. That was a word, an idea, that should be banned, she thought. *If.*

IN NOVEMBER, SHE WATCHED CNN from her room to see the results of the election. Kamala was visiting for the weekend, and she sat with Amina for a while, looking bewildered as pundits talked over images of people streaming to the polls.

"Will they really elect such a dark man?" she asked Amina.

"I hope so," Amina said.

"Here, everyone prefers fair."

"I know. Same there. But sometimes, things change."

Kamala nodded, fidgeting with her braids. "But he's a Muslim," she said. "That's so weird."

Amina looked at her. "You know I come from a Muslim family, right?"

Kamala sat up straight. "Yes, didi, I didn't mean . . . I just meant weird for America, you know?"

Amina smiled a little. Indians were so rigid about religious identity, something she'd had a hard time getting used to. There was no arguing with anyone about Obama's identity any more than her own. It wasn't about practicing religion, but about family, and as sensationally wrong as calling Obama a Muslim might seem in the US because his father was a Muslim, here there seemed to be no other way to talk about him. "It is weird. I never expected to see such a thing in my lifetime, and certainly not now."

"But you know," Kamala said, "he's only half. He's kind of a hybrid. Sort of like your moths!"

Amina laughed. "True. Maybe if he loses, we can invite him to our hybrid zone."

"And if he wins," Kamala said, "then America itself will be a hybrid zone."

Amina thought about that last comment for the rest of the night, long after Kamala had gone to bed, through the long home stretch of the results coming in, the numbers being tallied, the predictions veering right and left. Because of the time difference, it was a day earlier in America, always just starting out.

When the results were finally called, she herself had been up for too many hours. She raised a glass to the TV, tears streaming down her face. *Never in my lifetime,* she thought. *I wish Mo could have seen this.*

And then she thought about how Omar would live in a world with this man as president, which meant that maybe he could be president, that maybe there were no limits, at least not as she and Mo had always perceived them.

And she understood then why people have children, why species fight so hard to persist. Because no matter how Omar's life turned out, no matter whether he came to India to visit her or became a college-town poet like her father, he would be a living part of all of them, a thread that kept unspooling through time, like a reverse memory, like a hope.

She thought about what Dilpa had said to her, about all the things she had tried to leave behind. Her project here was ready to be presented to the world, and she knew it. She had cocooned herself in this remote corner for two years, grieving and working in equal parts. And now it was time to emerge.

SHE CALLED TOO EARLY, and she could hear the surprise in Marcy's voice. Breakfast dishes clattered in the background, and Amina heard the deep voice of a man asking who was on the phone; with a start, she realized it was Omar's voice. *I'm coming,* she told Marcy. *I want to see you. I want to see Omar.* She didn't try to explain more than that.

"Wait," said Marcy, "talk to Omar."

Amina heard rustling noises and her nephew's slightly raised voice, and then there was a pause and he was speaking to her.

"Hello, chachi," he said.

Amina felt her breath stop and her heart expand at the same time and for a moment she couldn't speak.

"Omar," she said, "I've missed you so much."

When she hung up the phone, agitated, she pulled on her shoes and began walking. The sun beat down, merciless and golden. Aimless at first, she thought then of a nearby temple dating from the twelfth century, in ruins and now visited only by local teenagers. She walked the dusty paths until she reached the crumbling structure. She had never before been inside. In its battered interior, beneath a partially collapsed roof, she stepped over bottles and wrappers and plastic bags, the detritus of the modern world.

In a sunlit corner presided a chipped sandstone idol, so worn by time that it could have been an icon of any religion of the world. Shapeless, it had once been covered in silver foil, but now only fragments remained, stained by red powder and dark earth.

Amina bent to her knees before it, her atheist heart humming with feeling, the sun hot on her uncovered head. From her shoulder bag she pulled an offering to lay at the foot of the god, an inarticulate barter for better fortune and wisdom: Omar's silver knife.

ABOUT THE AUTHOR

RAMIZA KOYA HAS AN MFA from Sarah Lawrence College, and her fiction and nonfiction have appeared in publications such as *Columbia Review, Lumina, Washington Square Review,* and *Mutha Magazine.* She has been a fellow at both MacDowell Colony and Blue Mountain Center. Her father was born in Fiji, her mother in Texas, and she was born in California. She lives with her daughter and two cats.

ACKNOWLEDGMENTS

The Royal Abduls is the product of many years of work. Thanks is owed to many for supporting me:

To the extraordinary team at Forest Avenue Press, including superwoman Laura Stanfill, Gigi Little, Joanna Rose, Samm Saxby, and Maya Myers

To Winifred Tate, for being the brilliant, challenging, and thoughtful friend of a lifetime

To Bella Brodzi, first for seeing my potential when I arrived as an undergraduate at Sarah Lawrence College, and then never losing sight of it or allowing me to

To Carolyn Elges, for more than forty years of unconditional friendship

To my family, near and far: the Inwoods, the Koyas, the Cookes, the Barritts, and Milo and Adley Schwartz

To those who offered me writing space and time:

Janet Buskirk and Jim Koudelka
Blue Mountain Center
The MacDowell Colony
Sarah Lawrence College Summer Writing Workshop
Tin House Summer Workshop

To all of my advance readers: Mo Daviau, Susan DeFreitas, Jenny Forrester, Madhushree Ghosh, Joanna Rose, Karen Shephard, Monica Uddin, Mary Wysong-Haeri, Jackie Shannon Hollis, Kim Bissell, Carol Zoref

To Literary Arts, a remarkable organization that has blessed me with a fulfilling, challenging, and meaningful career

For all who have shared in an eventful life, friends and mentors and colleagues, too numerous to name here, but never far from my heart:

Thank you.

THE ROYAL ABDULS

READERS' GUIDE

1. In July 2019, *The New York Times* ran an article titled "16,000 Readers Shared Their Experiences of Being Told to 'Go Back.' Here Are Some of Their Stories." How does *The Royal Abduls* address the immigration experience? The second-generation experience?

2. Consider Amina's relationship with her nephew. How does it change throughout the course of the book? Can you think of any other aunt-nephew novels?

3. Omar only uses his performative Indian accent in certain situations. Why? Have you ever found yourself breathing life into a cultural stereotype? Have you ever felt like you had to perform a stereotype to gain authenticity and/or acceptance? Why or why not?

4. Name some other novels that feature female protagonists like Amina—opinionated, driven, and self-sufficient. Discuss how the word "difficult" is often applied to women with agency to discount or take power away from them.

5. List the similarities and differences between the household Mo and Amina grew up in and the homes they have chosen to set up for themselves. What about Mo's apartment? Amina's quarters in India?

6. Marcy begins bringing home her preferred soda—Diet Coke instead of regular—around the same time Mo's drinking increases. What other fault lines do you see in their marriage? Do you side with one character over the other?

7. What does Omar see in his grandfather's passions and lived experience as an immigrant? How is his view of his grandparents different than his father's? His aunt's?

8. Moths are of special interest to Amina, and we learn near the end of the novel that she has been introduced to them by Mo. How does the metaphor of hybrids dresonate through the novel?

9. Amina arrives in DC, prepared to get to know her nephew better, but her role quickly expands beyond what she imagined. Do you think as a childless woman, she is seen by others as available for caretaking? Do Mo and Marcy take advantage of her? What are some of the things that Amina learns or receives from living nearer to her brother and his wife?

10. A number of U.S.-published novels are set during 9/11 or the aftermath, but *The Royal Abduls* is written by a secular Muslim and Indian American. Why is it important to have #ownvoices novels? Name some other 9/11 novels, if you can. Are any of the authors people of color or Muslims? What authority and insight does Ramiza Shamoun Koya's perspective bring to the literary conversation?

11. In her blurb, Jenny Forrester says of the author's debut: "She's cut to the heart of the devastating effects of colonialism and white supremacy on multi-generational American immigrant families." Name some of these moments in the novel and talk about the impact of each on the characters.

12. What does Amina initially think of Anjali? Is her assessment fair? Are there any similarities between Marcy's initial assumptions about Amina? How does Amina's view of Anjali shift by the end?

13. Who in your life has influenced you the most? Whose influence have you been the most surprised by?